DEADLINE

A JACK McMORROW MYSTERY

Praise for *Deadline*

"The rhythms of the weekly newspaper work a wonderful counterpoint to the building tension of McMorrow's investigation, and the writing is sharp and evocative without being showy."
—*Washington Post Book World*

"A crackerjack debut . . . a genuinely surprising ending."
—*Boston Sunday Globe*

"Boyle deftly transplants a big-city-noir atmosphere to the western Maine mill town of Androscoggin realistic characterizations, diverting subplots, and evocative descriptions of rural Maine a powerful, scary denouement. A fine debut . . . One hopes to see more of McMorrow."
—*Publishers Weekly*

"Boyle lets his suspense build to an excruciating point."
—*Library Journal*

"A great plot, even greater writing. This guy is good."
—Janwillem van de Wetering, author of *Outsider in Amsterdam*

"I can't believe *Deadline* is Gerry Boyle's first novel . . . Terrific."
—Susan Kenney, author of *One Fell Sloop* and *Graves in Academe*

"Part detective, part humorist, part novelist, [Boyle] shows us the real lives of real Mainers with wit, insight, and love."
—James Finney Boylan, author of *Constellations*

DEADLINE

A JACK McMORROW MYSTERY

GERRY BOYLE

ISLANDPORT PRESS

DEADLINE
First Islandport edition / November 2014

Printing History
North Country Press edition published 1993
Berkeley Prime Crime edition / March 1995

ISBN: 978-1-939017-06-2
Library of Congress Control Number: 2014942414

Islandport Press
P.O. Box 10
Yarmouth, Maine 04096
www.islandportpress.com
books@islandportpress.com

Publisher: Dean Lunt
Cover Design: Tom Morgan, Blue Design
Interior Book Design: Teresa Lagrange, Islandport Press
Cover image courtesy of © Tim Martin

Printed in the USA

For my father
and for my mother
and for Vic,
who is always there.

INTRODUCTION

In 1979 I returned to Maine after a stint in New York City, where I had tried my hand at the business of book publishing. For a few weeks I'd sat in a windowless room high in a Midtown skyscraper and read other people's book manuscripts. I was supposed to decide whether they were worth publishing. I performed my task halfheartedly. I realized I didn't care about other people's books. I wanted to write my own.

So by mutual agreement with my employer, I ended my book-publishing career and headed north. Back in Maine, home of my alma mater, Colby College, I scoured the job ads and came across one posted by a weekly newspaper in the western part of the state. The *Rumford Falls Times* wanted a reporter. I'd never been one, but I could read and write, and I liked to talk to people. I drove over to Rumford, which I'd never seen but knew as a paper-mill town on the Androscoggin River. As the car crested the rise on the road into town from the south, I was awestruck.

At the center of the three-street downtown, white clouds of steam rose from towering stacks. Logs were piled nearby, the jumble of tree trunks looking like toothpicks in the distance. Trucks loaded with pulp logs idled in the wood yard, waiting to be unloaded. Gigantic loaders pivoted. Steam billowed high into the sky like a nuclear bomb had detonated. The town, built on an island in the river, was sidled up to the mill, the community clearly existing for one purpose: to make paper.

It was marvelous. Better yet, I was hired. I covered town government, general news, even a little sports. And, more importantly, the police blotter. The seed for this novel, *Deadline*, was planted.

Very early into my six months at the *Rumford Falls Times*, I concluded that the town was shrouded by more than steam clouds from the mill. The townspeople were welcoming and helpful, but I felt there was a deeper layer to the place that I could never quite grasp. People had histories that went back years and generations. These backstories—some illustrious, some dark and grim—were rarely talked about, especially with a newcomer. And the relative isolation of the town and region could, on a bad day, turn it claustrophobic. The result was a place that was intimate but vaguely threatening, beautiful but sometimes scary.

And wonderful fodder for a mystery novel.

I used it as the basis of the fictional town of Androscoggin, and placed it securely in the rugged landscape of western Maine. I peopled it with small-town characters, including the newspaper editor. His name was Jack McMorrow. He had been dispatched by the *New York Times* to write about a far-flung place on the edge of the western Maine mountains. He was so intrigued he stayed on. And, like me, he soon realized that there was much more to this Maine mill town than showed on the surface. In McMorrow's case, the unknown threatened to be his undoing.

After I'd left the weekly newspaper to take a job at the daily *Morning Sentinel* in Waterville, I sent my manuscript to a half-dozen literary agents and publishers, three of each. I got six rejections, mostly positive. There is much to like in your novel, and if you change this, rewrite that . . . I was happy with *Deadline* the way it was, so I ignored their advice and instead printed out one more copy on my dot-matrix printer and sent it to a small publisher called North Country Press in Belfast, Maine. The proprietors and sole employees of the press, Bill and Linn Johnson, said they liked it very much; not only that, they wanted to publish it, and pay me for the privilege.

I remember hanging up the phone and sitting in stunned, dumb-grin silence while the newsroom clattered all around me. I felt like screaming, dancing, sprinting around the room. I didn't do any of that, but I did sign the contract and send it back before they could change their minds. They didn't, and *Deadline* was published in November 1993. It received strong reviews in the *New York Times*, *Washington Post*, and beyond. I was amazed that the wider world was so eager to read the real-life crime story I'd made up, set in small-town Maine.

Deadline, which I'd started writing on a portable Smith Corona electric typewriter, turned out to be the start of the Jack McMorrow series, including the tenth novel, *Once Burned*, to be published in May 2015. I hope you enjoy meeting McMorrow and, like me, are fascinated by this wild part of Maine, which remains to this day a mysterious, magical, and sometimes dangerous place.

Gerry Boyle
October 2014

1

They laid Arthur on a green canvas tarp, so close to the crowd that a few people tried to back away but couldn't because the people at the rear were still pushing forward to see. Nobody could move so we just had to stand there in the cold night and stare down at Arthur and his head that was at a funny angle and his wet hair that was starting to freeze to his forehead and his hands that were gray-blue with darker gray fingernails. We all stood there with our hands in our pockets and nobody said anything except an old guy from mill security who was in uniform but looked like he'd spent a few hours drinking at the Legion.

"Eh, Christ," he said, pronouncing it the French way, *Crist*.

We all stood there and wished something would happen but there was some screw-up with the hearse being blocked by a fireman's pickup so we had to wait, like people gathered around somebody who had collapsed in the street. There was nothing you could say so we stared dumbly at Arthur—at his glasses that were still on his face but perched crooked, at the bare patch of hairy white ankle that showed because his socks had fallen down.

He really didn't look bad, considering.

"Come on, move it back," somebody said behind me, and I turned to see firemen in boots and raincoats with ANDROSCOGGIN FD stenciled on the backs. They were pushing a stretcher through the crowd and behind them was Steve Theriault from the funeral home, bald and chubby and carrying a light green sheet. The four of them pushed through and raised the stretcher to waist height, then stood eyeing Arthur and huffing steamy breath into the night air. Two of the firemen hunched over and picked Arthur up by the legs and the other two, including Theriault, got him by the armpits. One of them grunted.

I guess that's why they call it dead weight.

After they got him up and on, they straightened Arthur on the stretcher and put the sheet over his face, just like on television. His feet still stuck out, also just like on television, but they didn't cover them. They just plowed back into the crowd, which parted and then followed as if the whole thing were some strange public funeral procession, held under the glare of the lights.

I brought up the rear, scanning the crowd as it dissolved among the cars and pickups like fans leaving a football game.

"Come on," I said. "Where's a cop when you need one?"

The cop turned out to be Lieutenant Vigue who, by the time I got to him, was all worked up—not by the tragedy of Arthur's death, but by the traffic snarl it was causing where the mill road met the highway.

Vigue was standing in the road, waving a flashlight and motioning like one of those people who direct jets on the deck of an aircraft carrier. Half the town had stopped to see Arthur pulled from the water, and now their cars and trucks were streaming back onto the highway while Vigue held back the log trucks that waited in a long dieseling line, their air brakes hissing impatiently, drivers commiserating into the mikes of their CBs.

"Hey, Lieutenant," I said. "What's happening?"

"You know what we know," Vigue said.

"What's that?"

Vigue looked at me sideways, tense and irritable in the flashing glare of the strobe lights.

"Not much. It's Arthur. He was in the river. He's dead."

"Who found him?"

He looked at me sideways again.

"You in a hurry or what?"

I shrugged. He pulled the clip mike off his jacket collar and held it up.

"Nine-one, nine-three."

His radio chirped something unintelligible.

"You got the names, times on this one?"

Another chirp.

"Bring it down here, will ya? *New York Times* is here."

Chirp again.

The last of the viewing audience pulled out of the mill road and high above us the trucks began to move through. They roared and rumbled and spouted plumes of exhaust smoke, like huge mechanical dragons. We stood by Vigue's idling cruiser and waited. He lit a cigarette, his face taut and handsome in the flicker of the lighter's flame.

"So what do you think happened?" I said.

"Who the hell knows?" he said.

"Where's the autopsy?"

"Augusta."

"State guys in on it?"

"Only on paper. Unless it turns out to be something."

"Like what?"

"Not suicide. Not accidental. Five bullet holes in the back. Something like that. But don't get your hopes up."

"Even without that it's strange," I said.

Vigue waved a balky truck through.

"That so?"

"Don't you think so? I mean, how'd he get here? Out here in the middle of nowhere. Mill people don't even come down here. He didn't drive. You see him walking all the way down here? In the cold? What's he gonna do? Go for a swim?"

"Wouldn't be a long swim," Vigue said. "Friggin' ice water sucks the life right out of you, Mister Man. Only good thing is they don't smell when you pull 'em out of the water."

"Nothing like a silver lining," I said.

"Yup."

We stood for a minute as the cars wound their way up to the main road above us. A police cruiser came down the access road, driven hard and fast the way cops like to drive. It pulled up and stopped and a patrolman got out, leaving the motor running. Cops like to do that, too.

His name tag said LEMAIRE, J., and Vigue looked at him and then nodded toward me, just barely.

"How's the mild-mannered reporter tonight?" LeMaire, J. asked.

"Just wonderful."

"What can we do you for?"

I asked for names. LeMaire, J. told me a trucker from Quebec, a chip hauler, called it in. There was some confusion because the trucker, one Yves Martin, forty-six, of St. Agathe, called it in *en français*. He'd been flagged down by two kids, boys in their teens, who were wandering through the mill yards, probably looking for something to break or steal, when one saw something in the water where the river cuts through the mill canal.

"That was Arthur?" I said.

"You saw him, didn't you?" Vigue said.

I had my notebook out.

"For the record. Official, you know? You ID'd him as Arthur Bertin."

"Two-thirty-five Carolina, Androscoggin," LeMaire, J. said, reading off a tiny yellow coil-bound pad. "DOB six twenty-six forty-six."

I scribbled. My hands were stiff from the cold.

"Any sign of foul play?"

"Not at the present time," Vigue said, his voice slipping lower, more serious. "No sign of anything except a dead body. You have to wait for the results of the autopsy. So it's under investigation. Pretty much. I can tell you we won't have much to move on until the cause of death is determined."

"But what do you think now?"

"What do I think?" Vigue said.

"Yeah," I said, stuffing my pen hand in my pocket. It was an old trick: The pen goes in the pocket; the source tends to relax.

"What do you think?" I continued. "On the face of it, you know? Preliminary or whatever."

"Hey, preliminary, it looks like a guy drowned. He's in the water and he's dead. But preliminary is preliminary. It isn't the final ruling."

"You mean accidental drowning? Accidental?"

"Under investigation. That's what I mean. When the autopsy comes in we'll know more."

"But Lieutenant, you know how you were saying the cold, how it sucks the life right out of you—"

"That was off the record."

"Okay. Off the record. Between us. If somebody got thrown or pushed in the water, or whatever. You know you wouldn't be able to find a way up that concrete wall. You saw the wall. What I'm saying is, the guy would drown but it wouldn't be an accident. Right?"

Vigue lit another cigarette with the lighter from his breast pocket. The lighter was green plastic. It glowed under his face and then went out and then he looked at me.

"Friggin' A," he said. "I thought this guy was supposed to be a friend of yours. What's the matter? Drowning ain't good enough for you? Ain't front-page? Gotta be a homicide?"

"Doesn't have to be anything. Just has to be true."

"Well, here's what's true: Arthur Bertin is in the water. He's dead. We don't know what happened, but we'll find out. Maybe."

I wrote in my notebook.

"And they say cops are cold bastards," Vigue said.

"We're all cold bastards tonight," I said.

In the glow of the cigarette, I saw him smile.

2

I woke up the next morning with a vague, nagging pain in the back of my head that reminded me I'd had too many beers too fast the night before.

I'd come home straight from the river, pulling into the Food Stop at the bottom of the hill to buy a six-pack of Ballantine Ale in sixteen-ounce cans. The girl behind the counter, a kid with a mane of bleached-out mannequin's hair, had been watching a cop movie on the television and had kept her eye on the screen as she took my five-dollar bill and handed me change. I'd gone out the door in a hail of gunfire, and had driven up Oxford Street to the big yellow house that, with its rotting trim and faded paint, was a last slap at the Victorians who built this town, and on up to my place on the second floor. My parka and notebooks and pens and wallet had gone on the kitchen counter. I'd sunk into the big chair and, with the beer and the cabled-in news of much more dramatic tragedies on the television, did a pretty good job of blotting Arthur and Vigue out of my mind.

But now it was time.

I got out of bed and went to the window in the living room and looked out on a slate-blue sky behind bare brittle oaks. It was clear and cold, the kind of late November day that is neither winter nor fall, but something drier, more pure. Through the trees, above the roofs, I could see the steam plume from the mill, bent sharply to the east like a billowing white pennant on a wizard's castle. The blast of cold air from Canada would keep the wizard's laboratory stench from settling on Androscoggin, sending it downriver instead.

In Androscoggin, the air would be sharp and clean. Fit for a tourist, not that many tourists would breathe it.

They didn't come to Androscoggin, the tourists. They did go by it, pounding down Route 2 as fast as the weather and the pulp trucks would allow. Some were headed west, people from places like Fredericton and Woodstock in New Brunswick, making a dash for the White Mountains, which began cropping up thirty miles outside of town. Since the McDonald's had gone in across from the Route 2 Exxon, there had been no real reason for anyone to turn off the wide two-lane highway. They did slow down, but it was usually only long enough to gawk at the mill, wonder how people could live with "that awful smell," and hope New Hampshire was nothing like this. When tourists did make the loop through downtown, their foreign cars and new Blazers bristling with skis, their Suburbans pulling travel trailers, you knew that it was because of a wrong turn or a leaking water pump or some other mistake or misfortune.

In fact, the route to Androscoggin from the south was like a long series of wrong turns, all of which went against your better judgment.

The cars that flowed into the state from below, squeezing through the tollbooths at Kittery like they were entering some vast national park, kept to the coastline. Most people drove up the interstate to Portland, where they were reassured by the city skyline and the fact that you could come this far north and still see the temperature flashing on top of a bank tower. At Brunswick, they peeled off onto Route 1 and angled up the coast, dropping down the various peninsulas, from Bath to Bass Harbor, that were like fingers of civility in a place that was otherwise dark and untamed.

But to get to Androscoggin from the south, you didn't go to Portland. I did the first time I came to town, but I was told that I had wasted a good half-hour inching along Route 302 through places like Windham and Raymond and Bridgton. The route of choice, I learned, was right up the Maine Turnpike to Auburn, off on Route 4, with its mini-malls and trailer parks, and on through the crossroads towns of Turner and Livermore. The towns and settlements between them were tired, as if it took tremendous effort to just keep going, and the effort had been ongoing for a very long time.

First-timers would be unsettled by the weight of inertia that had settled over the place and would look to the wooded hills for solace. They would watch the hills as they angled northwest on Route 108, until the Androscoggin River broke through past the village of Livermore, and the river gave the road a purpose and a route. And then the thunderclouds of steam crept over the horizon and the road bent left with the river and there was the mill, all stacks and vast woodpiles, as if all the trees in Maine had been cut down and dumped right there. There were trucks and railroad cars and miles of empty yard dotted with scattered rusting junk, and then, after all that, there was a glimpse of the town hidden behind all of it.

Androscoggin was a paper company town, as industrial as anything surrounding a Pennsylvania steel mill or an aluminum smelter in some bleak stretch of Ontario. This surprised people who had not been there, including people I knew back in the city. From their apartments in the East Village, in Fox Point in Providence, their condos inside the Beltway around D.C., they pictured a tiny town with a village green and old duffers with Down East accents sitting on the porch of the general store.

"This isn't like that," I would tell them, the few who called, the even fewer who cared. "I don't know. It's kind of hard to explain."

Androscoggin had been built in the late nineteenth century by rich men who wanted to become richer by turning trees into paper. They made their fortunes and everyone else made a living and raised families on the tenement-lined streets that grew up around the mill like military housing. More than a hundred years later, people from Androscoggin were still enlisting for lifetime hitches in the wood room, the pulp mill, and on paper machines. They wore St. Amand Paper jackets and bought four-wheel-drive trucks and snowmobiles. Their families were fed and clothed. Some of their children enlisted, too, filling the ranks that retirement never thinned. Others went to college and never came back.

They went to live in cities and towns that did not smell like rotten cabbage, which Androscoggin did, especially on overcast days when clouds sealed the valley. On days like that, the smell was strongest, seeping everywhere, like some kind of poisonous gas. But it smelled every day, every night, a constant reminder that SAP paid the bills—that if you didn't want to work at the SAP, most likely you'd have to go somewhere else to work for less money.

Not that a reminder was needed.

The mill was everywhere, sprawling along the river, fed by lines of wood trucks and railcars that never stopped coming. Pulpwood, cut in eight-foot lengths, was piled so high that from a distance, the stacks looked like silver-gray hills, mountains of twigs. The mill itself loomed over the town so massively that drivers—skiers, hunters, fishermen—coming toward Androscoggin on Route 2 would pull to the side of the road and stare, amazed that anything this monstrously huge could have been built so far away from everything else.

How far? Let's just say we had the last McDonald's for a hundred and fifty miles. The next one was in Quebec.

Androscoggin was an outpost, the big town for a dozen or so poverty-stricken hamlets where a few people scratched out a living, working in the woods, maybe doing a few weeks in the dowel mill in Dixfield at four bucks an hour. When those jobs ran out, there was bartering truck parts, or fixing some out-of-stater's camp, which didn't pay much, but did put beer on the table. And there was always the State, two or three hundred bucks a month from AFDC.

Against this backdrop of hangover to hangover existence, the mill smelled pretty good.

But it wouldn't smell much today, I thought, watching the plume against the blue sky. It would be a good day in Androscoggin. It would be a good day for an autopsy.

By eight-thirty, the Pine Tree had thinned out a little. There were three Canadian chip-truck drivers at the counter, having cigarettes and coffee and eggs before they headed back up through Coburn Gore and home to Quebec. Their loads were dumped at the mill and their rigs were parked out back. I'd noticed the names on the cab doors: Guy Laurent et Fils, Yves Martin et Fils, Marcel Nadeau et Fils.

I wondered what their daughters did.

The three drivers were hunched over their plates and when I sat down next to one of them, I could hear short bursts of French and then a few words in English: "That son of a bitch."

The waitress, the new one named Stacy or Tracy, put a white cup down in front of me and poured coffee without asking or even looking at me. I was looking at her fingernails, which were painted a dark maroon, when a hand touched me lightly on the shoulder.

"Hey, Jackson," Vern said quietly. "How's it going?"

"Okay, I guess. How 'bout you?"

"Can't complain. You go down there last night?"

"Oh yeah."

"Bad?"

"Bad enough, I guess. Arthur on the ground and fifty people staring at him."

"Circus, huh?"

"Yup," I said.

Stacy or Tracy put a cup down in front of Vern. Her lipstick was dark maroon, too. I opened the plastic container of half-and-half and poured it in my coffee. The spoon had a piece of something on it but I picked it off and stirred the coffee, then took a sip. Vern asked one of the Canadians for the sugar, in French. *Le sucre*. He slid it over and Vern said, "*Merci*."

Thank you, Mr. Berlitz.

"So what the hell happened?" Vern said to me.

"They don't know. There's supposed to be an autopsy today sometime. They get a cause of death and then they decide where to go from there. That's what Vigue said, anyway."

"That's it?"

"I don't know. I guess so. They didn't seem too worked up about it. Probably figured Arthur was a little screwy. Probably jumped in. Hard to tell what they're thinking. Going by the book, I guess."

"Why would Arthur jump in the river?"

"The canal, you mean."

"Whatever. The water."

I shrugged. Sipped. The coffee wasn't hot enough.

"Friggin' Keystone cops," Vern said. "Don't want to leave McDonald's. Get their uniforms dirty."

He took a sip of coffee and scowled.

"Just 'cause the guy wasn't a friggin' lawyer or a doctor or some bigwig, they don't give a shit."

"I don't know about that," I said. "Maybe they just need a little time. I don't know. I always thought Vigue was pretty straight. Not stupid anyway."

"Ah, they're all the same."

I didn't say anything.

"So what do you think happened?" Vern said.

I thought for a second.

"I don't know. I really don't. What do you think? I don't know what he'd be doing down there at all. You know? How would he even get there? Walk?"

"He have his camera?"

"I didn't see one last night."

"Maybe they ought to drag that section of the canal there, you know? Check with the taxi people, see if he got dropped off someplace around there."

"In the middle of nowhere?"

"Well, he wouldn't walk down there, half a mile from anything in the friggin' cold. So he had to get a ride somehow."

"Maybe you ought to head up the investigation," I said.

"Who'd do sports?"

"I'll rewrite the *Sun*. That's what you do, anyway, isn't it?"

"Beats leaving your desk," Vern said. "Speaking of which, Jackson. You know we're gonna have to find somebody to do film?"

"Ah, yes, the wake is over. You been in the office yet?"

"Just for a sec. Martin's there. I think he wants a briefing."

"Oh, Jesus. Just what I need. He didn't say that, did he?"

"No, he was just sort of wandering around. Had his column in his hand, doing the old Martin shuffle."

"You ought to show more respect for the editor emeritus."

"Ah, I'm only kidding. We'll all be old and useless someday."

"You're halfway there already," I said.

"Watch it. I'll quit and you'll be covering sixth-grade basketball and taking the pictures."

I shook my head.

"So he's got the latest installment of 'Yesteryears'?" I said.

"His blast from the past, coming at ya."

"Better read than any of your meandering drivel."

Vern nodded solemnly.

"Yessir, we sell out up at the Sunset Home."

Stacy or Tracy bustled by and shamed me, subliminally, into getting to work. I asked Vern if we still needed prints made for the paper that week. He said he had an entire basketball section to finish and, as far as he knew, all the pictures were still in negatives in Arthur's darkroom at home. We didn't have anybody who was really good at processing film or making prints.

"You never did any of that in your checkered career as a journalist?" I asked Vern.

"Any of what?"

"Photos. Processing film."

"Hell, no," Vern said. "Papers I worked for, we took our film down to Photomat. None of this *New York Times* shit. You big boys were sending people to El Salvador, I was hitching a ride on the JV bus. You're writing one story a week, I'm cranking out four a day."

"I thought you always worked for weeklies."

"Weeklies, dailies. All small potatoes."

"*Pa-day-duhs*, you mean. You sound like a flatlander."

"I am, Jackson, I am," Vern said, taking a swallow of coffee. "A flatlander lost in the Maine wilderness."

"A Mormon among the Apaches."

"That's right. A missionary out there with the heathen unwashed." He smiled.

"He was a weird guy, you know?" Vern said.

"Arthur?"

"Yeah. Don't you think? So friggin' solitary, you know what I'm saying? In two and a half years, I don't think I ever saw him talking to anybody as, I don't know, as an equal. You know? It was always whoever would tolerate him. Cops. Firemen."

"Us."

"Yeah," Vern said.

"People who were getting paid anyway," I said.

"Right. If it was part of the job. Did you ever have him over to your place for dinner?"

"No. Maybe I should have."

"And talk about what?" Vern said, holding his cup out for more coffee. "What it was like at the *New York Times*?"

"Maybe he would have liked that."

"Maybe. But I don't think he could take much head-on conversation. A heart-to-heart over a few beers. Up close and personal."

"But you know right away," I said. "You come to a place and you look around and you see that nobody has anything to do with the guy. And these are people who have known him their whole lives."

"So you figure there's a reason."

"Didn't you?"

"I guess," Vern said. "You back off, sort of."

"Unless you're some kind of social worker."

"And I'm not," Vern said. "And you're not either."

Stacy or Tracy came by with the coffeepot and I shook my head, no.

"Where were you right before you came here? To this paper?" I asked Vern.

"In the dairy country of Wisconsin," he said. "Working for a weekly. With my nose buried in the want ads in the back of *Editor and Publisher*."

"Did they have somebody like Arthur at your paper out there?"

"Typesetter named Alice Neilson. Lived with her cat. Had pictures of the old thing all over her desk. She could set type like a son of a bitch, though. What about New York?"

"Are you kidding?" I said. "New York is full of them. The *Times*, too."

"All the lonely people," Vern half-sang.

"You got it," I said.

Vern left, walking up the block to LaVerdiere's drugstore to get the *Boston Globe*, his daily ritual. I let Stacy or Tracy give me a fresh cup of coffee and sat and felt a little guilty about Arthur—that I didn't feel anything that resembled grief.

I felt bad, but it wasn't grief. It was just feeling bad, sort of lousy, as if something had gone wrong. A big mistake in a story. The car breaking down. A guy you know drowns.

Hey, what can you do?

I'd known Arthur since I'd come to town, what, seven months ago. I'd seen him every day—every day I'd been at the paper anyway. He'd come into the office in his thrift-store plaid pants with his hair all greasy and his lenses and camera bodies all clacking together in the Army surplus ammo pouch he used for a camera bag. If I was on the phone, he'd wait, lurking out front in the big room, checking the basket for the prints we'd already published. He'd wipe the grease-pencil marks off them and, if I said it was okay, he'd sell the pictures to the mothers of the basketball players, the fire department, the Ladies' Aid, the officers of the Grange. When I'd come to the paper, the new guy from New York, he'd asked me if it was okay if he kept doing it and I'd said, Sure, as long as it wasn't something we needed for the files.

Arthur had always asked if things were all right. He'd walk in quietly, the way he did, almost infiltrating the office like a terrorist or something, and suddenly there'd be a print on my desk and Arthur standing there, waiting for me to say the picture was fine or good or even great, which his pictures never were. They were adequate for a small weekly. Grainy sometimes. Almost always formula. But sometimes he got lucky, and when I told him I really liked a photo he'd wag like a puppy and ask me if I really thought so, and I'd say I did, and he'd wag some more, licking up every last morsel of approval and then lapping the empty plate until it shone.

It made my skin crawl.

It was sad, this life of groveling, and now Arthur's death had been sad, too. Floating in the ice water in the canal, yanked out with a hook in front of all his acquaintances but not a single friend.

No, this wasn't grief, but in Androscoggin there wouldn't be much grieving from anybody. Maybe a few somber faces, but they'd be outnumbered by the people who were glad to have something happen, something to break up the monotony of the long winter and shift work.

I looked around the restaurant. Four old ladies from the River View up the street. More Canadian truckers. A high school kid eating toast and reading the *Lewiston Sun* sports page. Nobody looked too shook-up.

"Hey," somebody said to my left.

I turned. Saw teeth. Smelled gum and cigarette.

"What happened to your man there? Arthur?" the guy said. "What, was he screwing around, somebody offed him or what?"

He was a union guy from the mill. Bobby something. The last name didn't come to me.

"Where'd you hear that?" I said.

He grinned. Pushed back his baseball cap that said BUILT FORD TOUGH in white letters.

"I'm like you," he said. "I got my sources. Got to. Never find out anything in the paper, right?"

He tapped me on the shoulder. I told him I didn't know much yet, the cops still investigating, blah, blah, blah. He acted like I wasn't telling him the whole story and left when somebody he knew better walked in.

But I was telling him the whole story. A guy had died, somebody who worked for the paper, and what I knew about it would make a two-inch brief. An AP person from Portland who got stuck with the late police check would know as much just from calling the state police dispatcher in Augusta or the Androscoggin Sheriff's Department.

I wondered what had been in the *Sun*. Probably a couple of grafs, inserted on the local page or maybe the jump. There was a paper in pieces at the end of the counter. I walked down and got it and looked through it until I found the brief on the local section front.

It was boilerplate. What the *Times* did when somebody without notoriety or celebrity was killed. The drug runner from the Dominican Republic. The kid from the projects in Brooklyn. The Russian lady from Brighton Beach. In New York, you couldn't keep up. You couldn't keep track. After a while, you barely could care, but in Androscoggin, we didn't have that excuse.

I left the restaurant and, in no hurry, walked down Main Street toward the office.

A couple of old ladies from the senior center smiled and nodded as they passed. Outside Perry's Variety, David Mattson from the school board waved his folded *Sun* and jumped into his double-parked Toyota pickup. One of the secretaries from the municipal building, a very nice grandmother named Toni, swished out of Alfond's Bakery with a bag of something and coffees in a tray and said "Hi" over her shoulder.

I said "Good morning" back and kept walking. I walked the length of the street, all two blocks of it, and turned around at the empty Mobil station on the corner. From there, I crossed the street and headed back toward the *Review* office, looking up at the false fronts of the downtown buildings, thinking, for the thousandth time, that they were like the facades on buildings in the Old West. The names of the original owners were inscribed in granite and cement at the top of each building: Carpenter, Hyde, Bushnell, Burr. The names of the actual builders, the Italian, Scottish, Irish, and, as a result of one of those quirks of immigration, Lithuanian laborers who shoveled and laid brick and nailed down floors, were not inscribed anywhere. I often had thought that this was an injustice, and I thought so again as I walked along, knowing that what I really didn't want to do was run the gauntlet at the office.

But here it was.

"Jack," Cindy said.

"I know," I said.

She came around the counter and walked toward me, her eyes dark with mascara but pink from crying. A couple of feet in front of me she stopped and fingered the gold chain that disappeared inside her blouse somewhere around the unbuttoned third button. There were times when I wouldn't have minded Cindy throwing her arms around me, but this wasn't one of them. I sidestepped and headed for my desk, leaving her in mid-scene.

I knew what they wanted. They wanted me to come out and say a few words, maybe make them feel better, but more likely to give everybody a chance to savor the excitement of this event, to speculate and hear everyone else's speculations about what had happened to Arthur.

They waited out front. Cindy and Marion and Paul and Vern and Martin, whom I could hear talking to nobody but everybody as I took off my parka.

"Awful thing. Awful."

Martin came around the partition and stood five feet away. When I looked over at him, he continued.

"Awful thing. Awful."

I nodded.

"I can't believe it," Martin said, hands in the pockets of his wool car coat, his galoshes doing a little shuffle on the carpet. He took his right hand out of his pocket and pushed his glasses back on his nose. They slid back down.

"I can't believe it," he said.

"You knew him a long time, didn't you?"

"Oh, Godfrey, yes. For . . . I don't know how many years. Way back. I can't believe it."

"Nope," I said.

"You get over there?"

"Yeah. For a while."

"Much to see?"

"Not much. A body and a bunch of firemen. You know what those scenes are like. A little different when it's somebody you know."

"Well, I would imagine, yes," Martin said. He fiddled with the zipper on his coat. "You get an obit yet?" he asked.

"Not that I've seen. Beauceville's doing it, I guess. But Arthur's still down in Augusta. Autopsy."

"Oh, yes. They'd have to do that. Find out what happened, I mean. What will they try to see? If he was . . . if he died before he was in the water, that kind of thing?"

"That kind of thing," I said.

I could hear the others still talking out front and I didn't want to say all this twice. But Martin was still standing there. Martin Wiggins, the retired editor, probably wishing he was back at the big desk, feeling the adrenaline run, that pumped-up, surging feeling you get when you have a big breaking story.

And then he came to.

"Well, I'm sorry," Martin said. "If you need any help fleshing out the obit, let me know. I'll be home. You know, just little things the funeral home might not know. He didn't have any family, you know."

"Why don't you call them, then," I said.

"Maybe I will. Might save everybody some time. Hey, don't mean to talk business at a time like this, but you got any problems with my column? Want to look it over while I'm still here? They really were quite a team. Lost by two points in overtime. Quite a game. Would have been New England champs of nineteen fifty-one. That Waterville team was tough, though. Fast? My goodness, they had some speed. But you got to go. I'll be home, Jack."

Even Martin. Business as usual.

"Okay, Martin. Thanks," I said, and he walked out, saying, "Carry on, troops" to the group that was still waiting for me to come and deliver a eulogy for Arthur Bertin.

"I'm not sure what to say," I said. They still waited.

"What can you say? Arthur's gone. We don't know what happened, but we know we'll miss him and his contribution to this paper. You guys know even better than me. You worked with him for what— ten years?"

"More like twenty," Marion said, hands wrapped around her I (HEART) MOM coffee mug. "He did pictures for Martin forever."

"We've got sports stuff in the files that goes back twenty-five years," Vern said. "Photograph for the *Review* by Arthur T. Bertin. Must've been when he was in high school."

"Maybe we could run three or four pages of his best stuff," I said. "A kind of tribute to the guy."

"The collected works?" Vern asked.

"That'd be fun to sell," Paul said. "Jesus. Right before Christmas."

"Who could say no?" I said. "Without seeming like a real dink?"

"You got time? I'll make a list," Paul said.

"We wouldn't make money on it," I said. "We could take the proceeds, which would be what? A couple hundred bucks? So you could take the money and use it for something in Arthur's memory. Something for the high school. A trophy case or something. They have a darkroom up there?"

"Yeah, they do," Vern said.

He was leaning against the counter next to Cindy, who still looked upset. Once in character, she found it hard to come back out.

"Well, I don't know, but I don't think it's right," she said.

"What?" Vern said. "Selling Arthur's pictures? Using his untimely end as a vehicle for commerce? Hey, look what they do with George Washington."

"No. Being open like this. We should be closed in honor of his memory."

Paul rolled his eyes and blew smoke toward the window.

"But you didn't even like the guy," he said.

"That's not true, and it's got nothing to do with it, whether I or you or anybody else liked him. It's respect, for God's sake. What do you think? We should just say, 'Good morning, Mr. Smith, or whatever.

Yes, it's too bad that Arthur is dead, drowned or whatever, but that will be seven-fifty plus tax, running for three weeks, Autos for Sale.' "

"This is a newspaper," Paul said, exasperated. "It isn't a friggin' jewelry store, Cynthia. It's a public institution, you know? They don't close the hospital 'cause some doctor's mother-in-law kicks off."

"A business is still—"

"All right, all right," I shouted over them. "Here's the way it's gonna work. Business department. Cindy. Marion. Paul if you want. Put a sign on the door. 'Due to the death of Arthur Bertin, the *Review* business office will be closed until tomorrow, Wednesday, November 13. It will reopen at eighty-thirty a.m. Thank you for your consideration.' Or something like that."

"Well, I'm working," Paul said, mashing his cigarette in an ashtray. "I've got about forty accounts to hit—"

"Well, don't make it sound like I just want the day off because—"

"Cindy!" I said. "It's okay. You're right. We should do something. Show our respect. But you better do it quick before you get people in here wanting to know what happened."

"What did happen?" Cindy said.

I started to answer. Stopped.

Even in the throes of grief, they were all ears.

I told the story, trying to ease past the details about Arthur's postmortem appearance, but Marion, of all people, wanted to know how he looked. The maternal side of her coming through.

But Cindy and Marion closed up in no time, flying out the door to go and spend the day shopping or hanging around at home or any other way they could show their respect for Arthur. I set to the job of throwing the mail away, filling my wastebasket with important press releases. On the other side of the room, Vern was on the phone, his big sack of a body slouched in his chair. When I put on my jacket to go to the police station he put his hand over the receiver.

"Cops?" he said.

"Yeah," I said. "See what they know."

"How long does it take to do an autopsy?"

"I don't know. Couple of hours. I suppose it depends on what they find."

He started talking, calling somebody "Coach."

I went back and got the medical examiner's number off the Rolodex, where it had been since an old man had shot his wife over on Oxford Street, last Christmas.

Dialed and waited.

"Hello," I said. "This is Jack McMorrow at the *Androscoggin Review*, the newspaper. I wonder if you could tell me when the Arthur Bertin autopsy results will be available. Right. *Androscoggin Review*. Yup. In Androscoggin. His name? His name is Bertin. Was Bertin. Arthur. You got him last night. The guy that drowned. He was found in the water. Bertin. Right. My name is McMorrow. Jack McMorrow. *Androscoggin Review*. Yeah, it's a newspaper. Well, could you ask him to call me when the information is available? No, I know you don't know when that will be, but I'd appreciate it."

God, I thought. That wasn't a receptionist, that was a guard dog. If she ever broke her chain, she'd be dangerous. But then I supposed somebody had to man the phones so that down the cool halls and through the swinging doors, where the only sound was the whine of bone saws and the clatter of instruments in steel sinks, the good doctors could carve their stiffs in peace.

3

The hardest thing about working for a weekly was sitting on the sidelines while the dailies beat you to your own story.

That morning, the *Sun* had its couple of grafs on Arthur's death. The next day they might have an obit, some stuff from the cops. And the *Review* would still be two days from hitting the streets.

I was used to working in terms of hours, not days. Forty lines by eight p.m., make the upcountry editions. Make some more calls, update it for suburban, make the one a.m. deadline for the metro. That was the routine at the *Times*. The Quincy *Patriot Ledger* in Massachusetts. The *Providence Journal*. The *Hartford Courant*. The *Androscoggin Review*.

Not what you would call your typical career path. And part of me still wondered if I'd done the right thing, stepping out by the side of the tracks and letting the express roar off on its way.

It still happened, usually when I sat still for too long. First the list of papers, the vita with the twist at the end. Then the face of that fat jerk, the words undressing me as I stood in front of the Androscoggin Valley Rotarians, the new guy in town, the guy from New York who had come to run their paper.

Six months later, I could still hear him. I could hear the background noise, mumbling and glasses clinking, and then this silence as his boozy, arrogant, fat-gut, cigar-stink voice echoed around the restaurant.

"Well, I've been listening to this. And it's all very interesting. But I still have a question, which is this: If you're such a distinguished journalistic fellow, and you seem to be, working in New York and all these places, what the hell are you doing here?"

Why didn't he just come out and say it?

Even worse than the question was the answer, a stumbling ramble about changing priorities and the fast and slow lanes and other platitudes that these small-town students of human nature knew were a crock. I knew they were a crock, too, but what could I say?

"Well, guys, I was pretty good at this, but you know the younger guys were better, these twenty-eight-year-old hotshots from the *Miami Herald*, the *Seattle Times*, coming into New York, into Manhattan, even, like they owned the place, writing stories on their try-outs that were pretty good, and then in the first month on the job, coming back from the Bronx, from some godforsaken hellhole in East Brooklyn, with some knock-your-socks-off story on a kid hustling for his crack-addict mother, or with some tidbit that they'd gotten from city hall, having wormed their way in with some aide in the mayor's office and they'd just gotten to the city, the bastards.

"So guys, everybody else is pushed back in line, which is fine unless you're the one who is being pushed, and you get assigned the second-rate stuff, not total crap, because the *Times* didn't do total crap, but just the inside-the-metro-section stuff, borough politics and education policy, and you know that you are on the bench, or at least not leading off, and it's gonna get worse and never get better."

No, I didn't say that; I didn't even like to think it. And when I did, when it snuck up on me, like it was doing right then, I got up and moved. Which I did.

I told Cindy I'd be back and walked up the block to the police station, inside the back door of the big stone municipal building. The dispatcher, Charlotte, was on the phone behind the glass so I waited, glancing at myself in the wide-angle security mirror beside the door, looking at the missing kids on the posters on the bulletin board. They were from California. Chula Vista and Long Beach, a boy, three, and a girl, nine, smiling in the black-and-white pictures. For months I had been saying I would call to see whatever had happened to them, but I hadn't yet.

Charlotte hung up and reached over to turn up the volume on her television, then looked to me and smiled hello. I asked for Vigue and she said he was out and she didn't know when he would be back. She asked if I wanted to leave a message and I said no, I'd come back later on, and she smiled again, and turned back to her soap opera.

So I'd tried the ME. I'd tried the cops. I could hit the fire station, see if the rescue people had anything to add, but the shift went off at seven, so I'd get somebody who had just come on and didn't know anything about anything. Who did that leave? Taxi drivers? A long shot. Arthur's friends? He didn't have any, that I knew of. But what *did* he have? What did he do? What was inside his head?

Or inside his house?

I walked back up the block, saw Vern across the street outside Perry's again, and waved. He waved and I turned off Main Street on to Court, behind the office, and got the car. It started hard, as usual. I was going to have to get it looked at, but I hadn't found anybody yet who had the hang of working on twenty-five-year-old Volvos with dual carbs, one of which was screwed up.

It was a weird car, an old Volvo 144 that you didn't see much anymore, especially in Maine, where the winters chewed up vehicles and spat them out. The woman I'd bought it from, a news assistant at the *Times*, hated it because she got it from a guy who was no longer her boyfriend. I'd thought it had character, which it did, but in Androscoggin there were times when it was a little too conspicuous, an easy way for people in town to know where I was, and when.

Maybe I'd trade it in on a log truck.

I drove out Main Street and took a right over the green steel bridge at the Androscoggin Falls. A half-mile west of downtown, I swung off on Carolina Street, went a hundred yards, and parked in the lot of what had been Carolina Street Service but was now closed up, the lot filled with junks.

The black Volvo blended right in.

I got out, crossed the street to the storefront that had been Arthur's studio. Standing at the front door, I looked both ways and fished for the key in the bottom of the mailbox on the wall. That was where Arthur got it when I dropped him off at night. He'd rattle the box, take out the key and unlock the door, and wave once before disappearing inside. I'd never been invited in.

There was mail in the box. Flyers and junk, then the key at the bottom, loose.

I unlocked the door and gave it a nudge with my shoulder. It shuddered open and I stepped into the dim light. My heart pounded as my eyes adjusted and the studio waiting room took shape.

It was dim but not dark. The storefront windows were covered with paper that looked like it had been newsprint but was now brown from the sun. There was junk everywhere. Newspapers piled in red vinyl chairs. Cartons of books and magazines and stuff along the walls. The place smelled like dust and developer. When I stepped away from the door, my boots grated like sandpaper on the gritty linoleum floor.

Brides had come here with their gowns in plastic bags. Little kids had fussed as their parents had fixed their hair, pulled at their clothes. *Just wait a second. You want to look nice in the picture, don't you?*

But that had been a long time ago. A very long time.

I walked across the room to the counter and picked at the stacks of magazines and newspapers and camera parts. The newspapers were yellow. The *Sun*, June 14, 1986; January 30, 1979. Magazines were in piles, dusty. *Photography*, May 1953. A blonde woman in a red leotard and fishnet stockings. Babies and kids in *Universal Photo Almanac*, 1950. John Glenn smiling in his space helmet on the cover of *U.S. Camera International*, 1963. I put the magazines down and walked to a dark gray blanket hung across a doorway. Stopped for a second and then groped inside for a light switch. The light went on. Red. The darkroom. I pushed the blanket aside and stepped in.

There were bottles of chemicals, brown and frosted with dust. Black darkroom sinks. Trays and a couple of enlargers. Next to one of the sinks was a crinkled tube of toothpaste and a bar of soap, pink, with dirt in the cracks. A toothbrush stuck out of a glass.

Arthur's bathroom.

I swallowed and turned back through the blanket. To the left was a narrow hallway, then another blanket, beige instead of gray. I reached and groped again and found the light switch on the right. I flicked it and froze.

It looked like a hideout for a hostage. There was a bed against the far wall, unmade, with gray sheets. At one corner the bedding was pulled back. The mattress was stained. There was a wooden crate on end next to the bed, with a dirty plate on top and a fork on the plate. On the wall next to the bed was a reflector shade, the kind photographers use to light portraits. It was thick with grime, like a faded dirty parasol.

This had been the studio but was now the bedroom. A studio apartment, silent and still. I walked to the center of the room and stood.

To the right, along the wall, were stuffed toy animals. A teddy bear sat and stared. A light blue bunny rabbit with foot-long ears lay on its side. The tools of the trade, props used to get the little tykes to smile. They looked like they'd come to life and murder children in their beds.

The place was giving me the creeps. I told myself ten more minutes, then out.

Along one wall was a bookshelf. I rummaged through more magazines, more newspapers, folders of old prints of couples and kids and groups lined up and shot against walls, all with ARTHUR BERTIN PHOTO stamped on the back. Dead people, I thought. Folder after folder of them. Arthur's portfolio. His friends from the other side.

I walked the room, picking and poking. The crate beside the bed had stuff that looked more recent, less dusty. There were notebooks, white reporters' notebooks from the *Review*, filled with Arthur's scrawl. Pens and reusable film canisters. A binder with more pictures. I opened it to the middle, a photo of a guy in an Army uniform. He was standing beside a car from the early fifties.

Arthur.

He was thinner, with thicker hair that still looked greasy, even back then. On the next page was another picture of him, standing on the runway of an airfield with planes in the background. It must have been Air Force, not Army. Arthur was looking into the viewfinder of an old 120-millimeter camera. Four smiling guys in uniform were posing in front of a big propeller plane.

The pages went chronologically. An advertisement for Arthur's studio grand opening, May 15, 1958. Arthur Bertin photos clipped from the *Review* and taped to lined paper. A cop beside a wrecked car. A bunch of official types with a shovel.

More pages and more clippings. I went to the back and then turned to the front. A black-and-white wallet-size picture fell out on the floor. I picked it up. It showed a man and woman sitting on a lawn but it was taken at a weird angle, from above and crooked. The man had his arm around the woman's waist. The woman was staring into his eyes, like something from an old movie.

Strange.

The woman was pretty, with dark hair combed back. She was wearing a full skirt with pleats and her legs were stretched out on the grass. They looked like pretty legs. The man looked passionate. I held the picture up to the light. It almost looked like Martin. What? In his passionate youth? In a play? Was that his wife, or was he married before—

I heard a sound.

Scraping. Metallic. Nothing. Then again.

The mailbox. Somebody scraping in the mailbox for the key. But the key was in my pocket.

I listened. Nothing, then another scrape. Nothing. A tap on the door. I closed the binder and put it back on the shelf. Turned and switched off the light. The room went black except for the edges of the blanket at the doorway.

A bang. I stood and listened. Another bang. The door rattled.

I took a step toward the blanket. Fought off an urge to run. Listened.

Nothing.

Was there a back door? I couldn't remember. How would I explain being here in the dark? The landlord? Who would be out there?

There was another bang, then glass breaking, falling on the floor.

I jumped and batted at the blanket and walked toward the front door. Kicked something and stumbled, then ran to the door. There was a fist-size hole near the knob. I waited at the door. Listened. A car whined by, fast. I opened the door but the bottom caught on the glass and I squeezed through the narrow opening and half-walked, half-trotted to the car. Keys. I dug and emptied my pockets. Handkerchief. Change. The studio key. The picture of Martin and the woman. Keys. Get the hell out.

4

So now I had a secret. But it was like somebody seeing a murder while committing a burglary. How did I know somebody almost broke into Arthur's? Because I more or less broke in myself.

When I got back to the paper, I felt myself almost slink through the door. For somebody who prided himself on his basic honesty, it wasn't a comfortable feeling.

I needed to stop and think, to sort things out. I needed a time-out.

No such luck.

The first thing I saw was the back of a tan trench coat, gray corporate slacks, corporate-approved L.L. Bean boots.

"Oh, damn," I said. "Not now."

David Curry didn't hear me because he was up to his eyebrows in Cindy's aura, thinking that just because she was smiling she was buying his act, which she was, but no more so than she did any of the other male revues that came through the door.

Curry was the local flack for St. Amand Paper, a puffed-up flunky who thought he was really something just because he wore a suit to work. The suits were corporate issue, right down to the yellow tie, which, in Androscoggin, was like wearing a cummerbund. But Curry wore them because the big guns in Pittsburgh wore them, or at least they had last time he saw them. Of course, yellow had been replaced by red in corporate fashion, but he didn't know that, and I didn't feel like telling him. If he thought wearing a yellow tie would help him to make it through the ten years he had left until retirement, let him wear it. If there were more women in the higher corporate echelons, Curry would wear a dress.

One could only hope.

Curry was a yes-man, a valet for the people who made the real decisions, and, more importantly, didn't want anything printed about the mill or the company that they hadn't written, approved, preread, or censored.

"Hey, Jack," Curry said, turning around. "How's it going there? On the trail of something hot or what?"

"Not really hot. Arthur Bertin dying. That's probably the biggest."

"Oh, yeah. Oh, wasn't that a tragedy? Hey, listen, if there's anything the company can do, anything, you give me a call. A real tragedy."

"On mill property, too," I said.

"Yeah, wasn't that strange. Where was it exactly? Way down south of the pulp mill, wasn't it? I haven't been down there myself in years."

"No reason to."

"No—hey, what's down there? Some storage. Empty property, really. Off the record, I can't see any reason for Arthur to be there, off the record."

Curry leaned closer. I knew we were talking man to man because I could see the stains on his teeth.

"Now this is really off the record—was he, you know, having problems? Despondent or something, I mean?"

I didn't say anything and he backpedaled.

"I was just curious, you know, if he had some problems and that's what happened. I wondered what happened, why, you know, he'd be there and all. Tragedy, really, 'cause I knew Arthur. He did some work for us years ago, pictures at the retirement dinner. Did a heck of a job, too."

"I don't doubt it," I said. "But I didn't think he had any problems. No more than anybody else."

I paused and looked at him. Waited. Waited some more. Waited for him to get to the point.

Because I knew what he wanted, the slimy little weasel. I was doing a story on the mill and he wanted to run more interference, do a little of what they called damage control. The story was about the mill asking for a tax break from the town. They paid $2.8 million a year and they wanted to knock off $400,000. For weeks, they'd been in "negotiations" with the board of assessors, which was the assessor and four people from the town council. Behind closed doors, they'd been talking about these state formulas which were used to decide how much companies paid in local taxes. In public, there was a shakedown going on, and St. Amand was doing the shaking.

It really was pretty simple.

While St. Amand went for a tax break, it leaked information saying it was considering closing the Androscoggin mill and moving the production of magazine paper to Georgia. In Androscoggin, a leak like this didn't trickle. It hit the town like a thunderstorm, complete with hailstones. Once everybody was good and worried, the company confirmed the rumors by not denying them.

Voilà. Four hundred grand, delivered on a silver platter.

But not by the *Androscoggin Review.*

In years past, the *Review* would have come out with some boot-licking editorial about the company's contribution to the community, about the need to cooperate with the town's biggest employer. Instead, I made a few phone calls, talked to a couple of people at the *Wall Street Journal*, three or four industry analysts on Wall Street, and called the city in Georgia where the Androscoggin jobs were supposed to go. The *Journal* guys sent up some stories about other paper companies using the same ploy to extract tax breaks. The analysts said it was unlikely that the company would move production away from its Maine wood supply. The union guys in Georgia said they'd been told their jobs might be moved to Maine.

Not exactly Pulitzer material, but not bad reading.

And read it was. Three page-one stories and an editorial, accusing the mill of extortion, more or less, and telling the town to tell the mill to take a hike. Curry was on the phone at eight that morning, along with a few readers who had told us what we could do with our muckraking paper.

Nice to be appreciated.

Curry tried the same approach, but I told him to stuff it and hung up. He called back in an hour, apologizing, fearing for his job and begging for a meeting so that I would "be apprised of all the information."

That had been three weeks before and now we were buddies. The *Review* hadn't backed off, but we'd published the reaction of town officials, which had been indignant. We'd had a slew of letters to the editor on the issue. They ran three to one in favor of St. Amand, with the only support coming from a few militant union people, some regular crackpots, and a woman who had run for town council the year before and lost because people thought she was a hippie.

I was damned by faint praise.

"So, hey," Curry said, presumptuously pulling up a chair near my desk. "I think I'm gonna be able to do something to clear this thing up."

"The drowning?"

"No, no. I mean the tax thing. I'd like to put this issue to bed, and I'm sure you would, too."

"Why would I want to do that?" I said.

Curry tried to laugh but it came out a snort or a cough. "No, really. I think I'm gonna be able to do something that will save us both a hell of a lot of trouble, and this town, too."

He said *hell*. That meant we were really talking man to man.

"So are you going to tell me or do I have to trick it out of you?" I said.

Another snort.

"No, Jack," Curry said. "I can tell you, but you've got to understand that it isn't a hundred percent confirmed. But I think I can get you Haze Gavin."

"How do I get rid of it once I've got it?"

"Come on, Jack. Haze Gavin. T. Hazelwood Gavin. He's the CEO of Quinn-Hillson. The parent company of St. Amand. Calls the shots. And baby, believe me, Gavin doesn't sit down and talk with just anybody."

"Must be nice," I said. "What's he want to come here for?"

"Well, he wouldn't come here. But I can get you an interview with him by phone. Maybe a conference call with a couple of the executive VPs. Everything out in the open. The abatement. The Georgia mills. Our long-term plans for Androscoggin. The whole goddamn thing laid right out."

"The gospel according to St. Amand Paper."

"No. This isn't a press release. Ask the tough questions. Dish it out. Do a Q and A. Print the entire interview. If the company isn't forthcoming, the town will know it. But we've got nothing to hide. If we did, we wouldn't be coming to you like this."

"I think you're worried you might lose this one, and you figure twenty minutes of Gavin's time is worth half a million bucks."

"Jack, you are one cynical newsman," Curry said.

Snort.

"No, David, I'm just pulling your leg a little. If T. Hazelwood Gavin wants to chat, I'd be glad to chew the fat with him. But no preconditions."

"Nope. What I've told you is what he wants. You'll like him, Jack. Haze Gavin is a straight shooter. Hell of a good guy."

And doesn't know you from a rat's ass, I was thinking, when Cindy came around the corner.

"Jack, there's a Mrs. Morrison on the phone. From the middle school? She said you were supposed to be there ten minutes ago to talk to the sixth grade?"

"Hey, let me get out of your way, Jack," Curry said, grabbing his coat.

Damn, I thought. I loved journalism.

"Tell her I'm on my way," I said, and I was.

"I'll call you," Curry said.

"No doubt," I muttered as I went out the door.

Mrs. Morrison wasn't pleased. She was a big, tanned cross-country skier type who didn't appear to take anything from anybody, and that included newspaper editors who stood her kids up. I smiled and apologized but she still gave me the chill as we walked down the yellow-tiled halls with the construction-paper pictures taped on them. I knew we were close to the class in question when the pictures had progressed from kindergarten-primitive to fifth-grade postimpressionist. Some of the stuff was pretty good and some of it wasn't.

But all of it was honest.

No, you couldn't bullshit a kid. Not one. Not thirty, which was roughly the number of faces staring up at me as I stood in front of the class. Behind them was a diorama kind of thing with dinosaurs and big, green plants with lots of fronds. I had barely glanced at it when the teacher, a bearded guy about my age, wearing jeans and a western shirt, finished my three-second introduction. I didn't catch his name but I did catch something about milk break being at some particular time.

Belly up to the bar, boys. And girls.

And then I was up there and they were all waiting.

The first thing I did was tell them they could interrupt me at any time with questions. Fifteen hands shot up, which was fine with me. Over the years, I'd learned that the best way to talk to kids was on their terms, in their language, about what they thought was interesting.

"How much do you get paid?" a small boy asked from the front row. He wore big sneakers and a faded Boston Bruins sweatshirt.

"Not enough," I said, and then caught myself. If the kid wanted to know, I'd tell him.

"About five hundred dollars a week," I said.

Somebody out there said, "Wow."

A little girl with big glasses read her questions off a piece of yellow lined paper.

"Do you like your job? What other newspapers have you worked for? Do you write your stories on a computer?"

I said I did like my job. I said I got to meet people like them, that every day was different. That was true at all the papers where I had worked, I said. Did they want me to name all those papers?

"Sure," the bearded teacher said, from his post leaning against the bookshelf under the window.

Who asked him?

So I did. I told them I'd been doing this kind of work for almost fifteen years, longer than they'd been alive. They looked at me like I was Methuselah. I told them I'd worked at the Quincy *Patriot Ledger*. A boy asked me what a ledger was, and I told him it was a book that you used to keep track of things. Then I went on. The *Providence Journal*. The *Warwick Beacon*, which was also in Rhode Island. I started there writing sports. The *Hartford Courant*, I said. And then the *New York Times* in New York City. I was something called a metro reporter there, I told them. I covered police stuff, which there was a lot of in New York. After that, I wrote about borough politics.

"Do people in New York live in burrows?" a rambunctious boy in the back said.

The class tittered and I said no.

"Did you ever go to a murder?" a girl asked.

I said yes, I did. There were a lot of murders in New York.

"Did anybody ever shoot at you?" a boy asked.

"Yeah, did you ever get shot at, like with an Uzi?" his buddy asked.

I said no and saw my approval rating plummet. Reporters didn't usually get shot at, I said. No more than anybody else. I didn't tell them it was criminals and poor people who usually got shot at, that the punishment for being poor in the city sometimes was death.

A girl in the front, small and sort of pale, asked, "Do you like it here better than New York?"

Hey, these kids had a future. As therapists.

"This is a better place in a lot of ways," I said. "You get to know people easier and they know you. It's safer, and in New York you can't go skiing as much. You can't go hiking in the woods, except in Central Park, and that isn't really woods. It's more like paths and ponds and places to ride bikes."

"Why did you work for so many papers?" the Uzi kid asked. "Did you get fired a lot?"

The kids snickered. I smiled.

This wasn't analysis. This was primal-scream therapy.

"Well, you don't really get fired in the newspaper business," I said. "Not usually. But people like to sort of move up to bigger papers. It's sort of like in sports. Baseball. Who likes baseball?"

Most of the hands went up.

"Well, it's sort of like in baseball where you're on a high-school or college team. Then Single A. Then Double A. Then Triple A and the majors. If you're good enough. Newspapers are like that for a lot of people. They want to keep moving up from little papers to bigger and bigger ones until they get to places like the *New York Times* or the *Washington Post* or maybe a magazine. *Time* or *Newsweek* or one of those. But it takes a few years to get that far. And some people never do."

The same kid raised his hand, the little brat. I glanced at the teacher to see if he would tell the kid to let somebody else ask a question, a nice simple question, but the teacher looked like he was enjoying himself.

Why teach long division when you can see the newspaper guy interrogated by the KGB?

"So why did you go from the—what is it?—the *New York Times* to the *Review*?" my nemesis asked, looking me straight in the eye. "Isn't that, like, sort of going backwards?"

The little bugger.

"Who is this guy?" I asked, giving him a big grin and biding for time as the real answer raced through my head.

I left because I wasn't the best. I could tell him that. I could tell him about the younger reporters getting the choice stuff, the investigative stuff, the foreign stuff, the bureau chief jobs. But I didn't.

"I needed a change," I said, as the teacher seemed to listen more closely. "New York can wear you out. And I like the people here. When I came up to do a story on the paper here, the people were so nice I decided to come back."

There was a moment's pause, then another question, this time from one of two smirking dark-haired girls.

"Are you married?" one blurted out.

"She thinks you're cute," the other one said.

"Crystal!" the first girl said, and everybody whooped. I waited for the teacher to step in and referee but he still hung back. Not somebody you wanted with you in a foxhole.

"Am I married? You sure you guys haven't been reporters? I'm gonna hire you to work for me. No, I'm not married. Never have been."

"You have a girlfriend?" Crystal asked, while her friend giggled.

"Do I have a girlfriend? Boy, you don't give up, do you. Well, I do have someone that is sort of my girlfriend. Sort of."

"Is she pretty?"

God, man, I thought. You gonna let these kids dissect me or what?

"Yeah, she's pretty," I said. "Sort of like you."

More whoops, boys snorting.

"What's your girlfriend's name?" Crystal called out over the din.

They quieted down to listen, the little buggers.

"Roxanne," I said. "She lives in Portland. Only she might not be my girlfriend. Not like you think. We've only gone on a couple dates."

Both of which ended in bed, I thought.

I tried not to think about it, not up there in front of the kids. Roxanne smiling at me and shaking my hand, when we met at a party at the home of a guy I had known back in Providence who had moved to Portland and the *Press Herald*. The guy was a photographer who liked sailing the Maine coast and filled his house with beautiful kids and, on that night, beautiful people. One was Roxanne, and I could still see that look she gave me as we met, a look that went right through me, warm and open, as if she'd known me for years, as if she knew everything about me.

We'd talked and gone out late for a drink and more talk and then we'd climbed in her little yellow Subaru and gone to her apartment in an old brick building on the chic Western Promenade, where we did not talk much at all.

So I could tell the kids that. I could say she was a social worker who worked with kids like some of them, that she was young and bright and great-looking, with long dark hair, and that making love with her was the most fun I'd had in ten years.

But I didn't. Instead, I looked at my watch, which had reached the witching hour of 11:43 a.m. I said I had to get back to the paper to make some phone calls and write some stories. They clapped to thank me, with boys in the back stomping on the floor until the teacher told them to stop.

Where was he when I needed him?

I had a blank yellow legal pad in front of me on the desk. The number of the medical examiner's office was ringing and Vern was shouting to a coach over the phone. I covered my right ear with my hand and waited.

A woman answered. I asked for the medical examiner, Dr. Richard Ritano. She paused, as if I was trying to peddle him some embalming fluid, then asked my name.

"Jack McMorrow," I said. "I'm with the *Androscoggin Review*, the weekly paper in Androscoggin, and I have a question about the Arthur Bertin case."

Nothing.

I waited, wondering if she'd hung up on me very quietly. Then there was a click, then another silence, then more clicks and a guy who said, "Yeah?"

I identified myself again, identified the paper.

"Have you issued a finding on the cause of death?"

"Haven't issued anything."

"You mean you haven't come up with anything yet?"

"Did I say that? No, I said I hadn't issued a finding yet."

"So you have come up with something?"

"Like what?"

"A cause of death. Accidental or homicide or whatever."

"What paper did you say you were from?"

I told him again, told him I'd seen him testify in a murder trial about two weeks after I came to Maine. A guy had been shot by his wife and left in a closed car in a garage for a month. In the summer. Ritano had related all of the grisly details about the advanced state of decomposition. He was cool. Arrogant. Condescending.

A real jerk. Then and now.

Would he have taken me more seriously if I'd said I was from the *Boston Globe*? The Associated Press? Like a lot of people, Ritano probably thought bigger was better when it came to newspapers. Sometimes that was true. Sometimes it wasn't.

I could hear him breathing and shuffling papers. Finally, he coughed.

"Well, I can't tell you much," he said. "Preliminary findings, and I would ask that you stress that these findings are preliminary, if you would do me that much of a courtesy. Preliminary findings show that the deceased, Arthur Bertin, died of accidental drowning. Secondary cause, hypothermia. He got cold in the water and drowned."

I scribbled as he spoke.

"No evidence of foul play?"

"Not at this point. That's why I said accidental."

"Any scratches or bruises that might indicate that he fell or was assaulted?"

"Nothing inconsistent with a fall from the height of the riverbank there."

"It's not really a riverbank," I said. "It's a canal. A stone canal. It channels water through the mill."

"Whatever."

Whatever. Whoever. Some schmuck from the sticks as far as this guy was concerned.

"Maybe you could explain something to me, Dr. Ritano," I said. "Let's say somebody, hypothetically, somebody is pushed in a river or a canal or whatever. How does your office or you decide that he didn't fall, that he—"

"Whether it was accidental or a homicide?"

"Right."

Ritano let out a long sigh. Another dumb question from a dumb reporter.

"It's very complicated," he said wearily. "There are things we look for in conjunction with—"

"What kind of things?"

"There's no hard-and-fast rule. Each case is taken on an individual basis and examined in the context of the circumstances of the death, the identity of the victim. His character. Listen, I could, and have, taught entire courses in forensic medicine on this subject. I could talk for hours."

"Do you check the area of the death, the scene, to see if, let's say, there is a sign of a struggle? Check the body to see if there are any signs of a struggle or whatever?"

"Sure, you do. Police do some of that work. They confer with this office and we come up with a finding. But I really don't see how this broad kind of generalization is going to help you with your story."

How kind. He was concerned about my story.

"Well, specifically then," I said. "In the Bertin case—"

"Hey, listen," Ritano interrupted. "I'm not gonna beat around the proverbial bush here. I'm not gonna get into a discussion of what we did or didn't do in a case that is still pending, so that you can take something out of context and make a story where there isn't one."

"I think the story is that you found that Arthur Bertin's death was accidental."

"Preliminary. I said preliminary. I stressed that."

I kept scribbling, now on the third page of legal pad.

"So what might change?" I asked.

"Hey, I told you. I'm not going to speculate on that. With the evidence we now have, that's the ruling."

"I understand that. And I appreciate how forthcoming you've been. But is there more evidence coming from someplace? The police?"

"I can't comment on that. I've already given you more than I do ordinarily."

Big deal, I thought.

"I appreciate that," I said.

"Yes, I'm sure you do," Ritano said. "What did you say your name was?"

"McMorrow. Jack McMorrow. The *Androscoggin Review*."

"Been with the paper long?"

"Not too long. About six months."

"Where were you before that? Other papers?"

"Oh, yeah."

"Like where?"

First the kids and now this guy. Talk about the public's right to know.

"Around New England. New York area."

"New York City?"

"Yup. For a while."

"What, the *Post* or something?"

"No, the *Times*," I said.

Ritano sniffed.

"That explains a lot," he said.

The ink was still wet on Ritano's rubber stamp.

I'd seen it work that way before. A homeless guy. A bag lady. A drug dealer with no ID. In the city, they'd turn up dead and some junior member of the coroner's staff would show up and ask the cops what they thought.

"Who the hell knows?" the cops would say.

Why waste time on somebody nobody cares about? Why waste time on a possible homicide when there are very definite ones stacked up in the fridges down the hall?

So it didn't surprise me that Ritano wasn't fired up to do a full investigation of Arthur's death. But I was surprised that Vigue and the other local cops weren't pushing it more. They didn't have anything else to do. But it was like the word was out. Hands off. Let it die.

If they didn't push it, the ME wouldn't. The AG's office wouldn't. Nobody would. Except me.

I went over my notes from Ritano, underlining the best quotes and filling in the gaps where he'd gotten ahead of me. I could leave it alone, too. A couple of routine stories from official sources and the case would disappear from the news pages and end up in a file in our morgue. We'd get on to more-pressing issues, like the cost of the town's new backhoe or the building of the new animal shelter. Maybe a nice photo of the town council at the groundbreaking.

Or maybe we'd keep pushing for a little while. Maybe something would break. Arthur deserved that much. For us to give his death a little bit of a whirl.

5

The fire truck was parked in the middle of Main Street, with the diesel clacking like a city bus and the ladder jerking spasmodically between the light poles.

I stood on the edge of the crowd of kids and old men and focused the camera on the ladder. Five rungs from the top of it, a fireman named Honey Rancourt was leaning out, trying to hang a big plywood candy cane onto the top of the light pole. I shot as he leaned out, just before he missed and grabbed back at the ladder, cursing. The annual cursing of the Christmas decorations. A New England ritual.

When I'd first come to town, it had amazed me that these kinds of things really happened. In the suburbs of Jersey, where I grew up, they didn't get the town together to hang Christmas decorations. Christmas decorations were something that just appeared at the mall. Around Halloween.

So when the town brought out the fire truck to hang the plywood candy canes, it was like it was the prototype of the cliché. But nobody saw it that way, with the big-city cynicism that comes from being too hip or cool. For Androscoggin, hanging the candy canes was like putting up the tree at Rockefeller Center. With Honey Rancourt, your master of ceremonies.

I moved back through the kids to where the fire chief, a calm, wise sort of guy named Will Dubois, was standing by the cab of the truck. Dubois was a nice guy. Very sure of himself and his place in the community.

"You're the cameraman now?" he said, standing there in his big rubber boots.

"Don't have much choice."

"Shame," Dubois said, like he meant it.

"Hard to believe," I said.

"Yeah."

Dubois ran a hand through his hair and watched as the ladder swung across the street. He had handsome white hair, like a fireman in a cigarette ad.

"What do you think could have happened? You've been to a few of these things," I said.

Dubois watched Honey on the ladder. Another candy cane went up.

"I've given up trying to figure out some of the stuff that goes on around here," he said, over the idling diesel. "There are some of these things where you just never know. I don't know that this will be one of 'em, but it wouldn't surprise me. Not at all."

An older man came up and spat tobacco juice on the street. He grinned at me and poked Dubois in the ribs. His face had liver spots on it and his hat said A&A AUTO PARTS, with a picture of a wrecker truck.

"What's Honey's real name?" I asked Dubois.

"Clarence," he said. "But if you put that in the paper, nobody will know who you're talking about. Been Honey since he was in grade school."

"And useless as tits on a nun," the old man said. "What are you doin'? Taking pictures of these bums?"

I walked. It was only 3:30, but the sun dropped behind the mountains early and the buildings on Main Street made a chilly shaded canyon that was turning my feet cold. I walked up toward the municipal building, past Ducharme's Department Store, where they had plastic canes full of green and red candy piled in a shopping cart outside the front door. Two gray-haired women were looking at the canes and one woman held one up and shook it. I smiled and they smiled back and I kept walking, thinking I'd seen one of them in one of Arthur's pictures. The Daughters of Isabella? Beano at the elderly housing?

I was thinking about it when a police cruiser hissed by fast, blue lights on.

By the time I turned the corner at the municipal building, up the block, the cruiser was parked by another one, and two cops were leaning into the backseat. As I got closer, I could see somebody in the backseat, thrashing. Then I could hear the guy's muffled bellowing as one of the cops, Vigue, reached in and yanked him out by the neck and shoulders and dropped him headfirst on the pavement.

The guy was thirty, maybe thirty-five, with a beard and long dark hair tied in a ponytail. He had on black biker's boots, and he tried to kick Vigue and the other cop, LeMaire, J., as they dragged him toward the door by the chain between his handcuffs. I stood next to the door as they moved past me and down the hallway, to the windowless door to the holding cells.

"He's upset," Vigue grunted.

It was fifteen minutes before they came out of the cell area. I could hear the ponytailed man hollering inside.

"I'll kill you. Come on, Vigue, you pussy. Take off that gun and come in here, you wuss. You pussy, you wuss. You pussy, you wuss."

It almost had a rhythm to it. A cell-block mantra.

Vigue waved me into his office as he crossed the hall. I stood and waited as he fished for cigarettes, first in his jacket and then in the top desk drawer.

"You want to interview my friend?" he asked. "Nice fella. His girlfriend called. Trailer out in East Overshoe, past Androscoggin village. Girl calls when he says he's gonna cut her up and feed her to the Doberman. Gonna cook her, she says, and feed her to the dog. One rugged son of a bitch, I'll tell ya. Friggin' blotto, and it still took four of us to take him down. A couple of country boys came by and helped us out. I'm telling you, I'll take a drunk over one of these cokeheads anytime, mister. When we got there, he was cutting a hole in the bathroom door with a knife and the girl had gone out the back of the trailer. Maced the bastard, I mean but good, and he still wanted to fight."

Vigue sat down on his desk and lit a cigarette.

"Getting too friggin' old for this, I'll tell ya."

He exhaled.

"What do you want anyway. A story?"

"If you've got one kicking around."

"Got one kicking the cell around, if you want."

I smiled. Waited.

"No, I talked to the ME a while ago. After lunch. He said Arthur was an accidental drowning."

Vigue inhaled and waited.

"So I have a couple of questions."

"So ask 'em."

LeMaire, J. walked by in the hallway, wiping his hands on a paper towel.

"Were the state cops here at all?" I asked. "And two, does this mean your investigation is finished?"

The guy in the cell stopped yelling. A door slammed. Vigue glanced past me toward the cells and then back at me.

"I don't keep tabs on the state boys," he said. "They don't ask for my help, if you know what I mean. But they did call and I told them what I had so far. As far as their coming here or going to the scene, you'd have to ask them."

"Who was it who called?"

"Hoag. Detective."

"So who did go to the scene?" I asked.

"We did."

"Went to the scene?"

"Yeah. We inspected the scene. SOP."

"Looking for what? What do you look for in a case like this?"

My notebook was out of my parka pocket. I reached for a pen from my shirt. Vigue glanced at the notebook, then looked back at me.

"They teach it at the academy. Crime scene. My first job is to keep it secure. That was our primary job here. But we also look for any sign of a struggle. You know, rocks missing off the wall, scuffs in the dirt. Anything. Pieces of clothing. Footprints."

"Find anything?"

"This for print?"

"I'd like it to be."

"Can't tell ya. Ongoing investigation."

"Come on," I said.

"Can't do it. I'd like to but I can't. AG would have me by the balls. I'm telling ya."

"Okay. Off the record."

Vigue hopped off the desk, showing me that he was almost fifty but still in great shape.

"There wasn't much to see. That's the truth. That wall is all friggin' granite. Granite blocks. You don't get sneaker prints off granite blocks. Besides, there were fifty friggin' people there, including the press. Boat came in and busted the ice into a million pieces. You beginning to get the picture?"

"So you've got nothing?"

"Nothing at the scene. Except Arthur."

"And they say nothing on him says anything except he got cold and drowned."

"You're telling me that one," Vigue said.

His radio went static and he fiddled with the squelch knob.

"We couldn't see anything. Couldn't even tell where he went in," he said.

"Coffee, Lieutenant?" LeMaire, J. asked, poking his head in the door.

I could see the end was in sight.

"Okay, Lieutenant. For the record. Are you still investigating the Arthur Bertin death?"

Vigue stubbed out his cigarette. I could hear the coffee machine buzzing and rattling in the hallway.

"The death is being treated as an accidental drowning at this time," he said, speaking as if the words were from a language he was just learning. "At this point, in light of the medical examiner's ruling, we welcome any information from the public, but do not consider this, the incident, a suspicious death. At this point in time."

I wrote in my notebook.

"Now let's have that in English," I said.

"Hey, if I could tell you any more, I would. You know what I know. We're still looking into it, but unless something new comes in, it appears to be an accident. As far as what happened to him, that's anybody's guess."

I put my notebook in my pocket.

"Just doesn't make sense," I said.

"Hey, you're in this business as long as I am, and you know that not much makes sense."

Not much made sense. It was a nice way to put it. Sort of backward, but it was about the way I felt. Unsettled. Uneasy. Not sure why, or even if *unsettled* or *uneasy* were the right words.

It was almost dark and the mill traffic was moving, lots of trucks backed up at the light before the bridge. I walked back to the office, checked my messages and found only one, from a lady at the regional health agency. Cindy was on the phone, Marion had left, and Vern and Paul were around, judging by the work on their desks, but not in. I looked around and got out while the getting was good. It had been a bad day and I'd had enough.

I got in the Volvo, choked it and it started, sputtering in the cold. I flipped the useless heater on and circled the block on the mill side, then inched my way up Main Street to the Food Stop, where I went in and grabbed a six-pack of Ballantine Ale from the cooler. I was the reason the store stocked Ballantine; the manager called it "rocket fuel," and the clerks always had to stop and look up the price, while they knew Budweiser by heart.

I forgave them their ignorance.

The night started to take shape a couple of blocks from the house. I'd cook brown rice and stir-fry some vegetables, watch the national news, Peter Jennings, and listen to Dave Brubeck or Bill Evans. And I'd drink a couple of beers. Maybe I'd drink all the beers.

But then my plans changed.

The yellow Subaru was in the driveway behind the house. The smell of chili greeted me in the downstairs hallway, and Roxanne met me at the door. She handed me an ice-cold Molson ale and kissed me quickly on the lips. In that order.

I followed her into the kitchen and put my Ballantines on the counter. Roxanne opened the refrigerator and took out a bowl of guacamole dip. She was smiling, happy and excited. Neither of us had said anything; we just beamed with anticipation of chili, and more.

"I didn't expect to see you this week," I said.

"I didn't expect to be here," Roxanne said.

She was picking the foil from the top of a bottle of red wine.

"Were you working over this way?" I asked.

"Nope. Waterford."

"So what brings you to scenic western Maine?"

"You."

I took a long swallow of ale.

This was Roxanne's second visit to Androscoggin and our third meeting. She'd stopped in town the week before on her way from Burlington, Vermont, back home to Portland. I'd shown her around, and then we'd come back to the house and talked and gone to bed. I thought of it often. Until Arthur had died, it had kept me smiling like a fool.

Roxanne was refreshing, rejuvenating, energetic, uninhibited, and, unlike the last woman I'd been involved with, in New York, didn't make me feel like I was needed to act out a fantasy from the pages of *Cosmopolitan*. With Roxanne, I didn't feel like a foil. She didn't pattern herself after some abstraction of the ideal woman. Roxanne was the way she was. If you didn't like it, that was tough.

But I liked it.

Her hair was pulled back and her cheeks were flushed from cooking. She was wearing ripped Levi's and a blue-and-white-striped sailor's jersey from L.L. Bean.

"Did you wear those clothes to work?" I asked.

"I changed in the guest bedroom," she said, pouring the wine.

We clinked bottle and glass and walked into the living room. Through the bedroom door, I could see a skirt and blouse and stockings strewn on the bed.

"So go ahead and mess up my house," I said. "I've been cleaning all week."

"You could clean up all year and still not make a dent in this place. I'd go crazy if I lived here."

"I'd go crazy if you lived here."

She put the guacamole and tortilla chips on the table and sat down on the couch. I put my beer down and eased her back on the cushions. She laughed and quickly turned to me and we kissed. I loved the taste of her, the smell of her, soap or perfume or whatever the hell it was.

"Do you want to eat now or later?" she said, pulling her mouth away.

"What are you serving?"

"You're going to smell it burning if I don't turn the stove down."

"Turn it way down," I said.

I grabbed my beer and her glass and went into the bedroom. Roxanne came behind me and sat on the edge of the bed and kicked off her running shoes. I unlaced my boots and tossed them toward the door.

"So how was Waterford?" I asked.

She pushed me down on the bed and rested her chin on my chest.

"If I'd wanted to talk about Waterford, I would have gone back to work," she said.

"What do you want to talk about?" I asked.

"You," Roxanne said. "And how good you're going to make me feel."

"Is that an order or a prediction?"

"I brought my crystal ball."

She pulled her shirt off over her head and slid out of her jeans as I did the same. We sat on the bed and kissed, and I leaned back a moment to look at her. She smiled and raised herself up, arching her back and lifting her breasts. I grinned.

Roxanne knew she was beautiful. She reveled in it. She knew I thought she was beautiful, that I wanted her. She turned her head to let her long dark hair fall across her shoulders. No coyness. No self-consciousness. Just that open smile, delicate white shoulders, a statue's breasts, strong smooth legs.

I shook my head as I leaned toward her.

"I think I'm developing a taste for younger women," I said.

"Taste this younger woman," Roxanne said.

She smiled.

I gulped.

We made love deliberately and steadily but with a gathering momentum, like a wave moving toward shore, an offshore roller. Before it broke, we were face-to-face, sitting up with her hair falling on my chest and shoulders. She was forceful. Intent. Then out of control.

When I finally reached down to the floor for my beer, it was warm. I drained it anyway, but Roxanne said she'd get me a cold one. She went over to the closet and took a faded tan chamois shirt out of the closet and put it on. I watched.

She went to the kitchen and from the bed I heard the refrigerator door open and shut. Outside, shriveled oak leaves rattled against the dormer window. Roxanne came back into the room with two bowls of chili, another Molson, the wine bottle, and two candles. The candles were lit. The flames wavered as she put the tray between us on the bed.

"That's a fire hazard," I said.

"You're a fire hazard," she said, smiling.

We sat and ate the chili. It was hot enough with the cumin and red pepper and chili powder to make the beer taste great but not so hot that it scalded your esophagus. We talked between bites.

"I took a funny way over today," she said. "I think I went too far. I just kept taking signs that said north or east and I ended up in places like Temple and Madrid and Phillips. I almost ended up in Rangeley but I turned around."

"Rangeley is nice," I said. "We should go there sometime and rent a cabin on the lake. Maybe even leave the cabin for short periods of time. You have beautiful legs. Have I ever told you that?"

Roxanne pulled the chamois shirt down over her knees and pursed her lips disapprovingly.

"So what were you doing in Waterford, or can't you talk about it?"

"Sometimes I feel like I can't think about it," Roxanne said, suddenly quiet. "Oh, let's see. Same stuff. This morning I had to go tell this four-year-old girl's mother that we're initiating an investigation. The girl came to the daycare center with a bump on her head and bruises on the backs of her legs. It was the bruises that did it. Pattern was too regular."

"What did the mother say?"

"Not much. It's the second time we've looked at a child from the family. Different boyfriend now. The first one was inconclusive. Nobody knew anything. Kid wouldn't talk about it. This time, I don't know. The little girl is awful young, even for her age. Scared of her shadow. Chances of her talking about what happened are slim to none."

"Think the mother will straighten out?"

"If it's her? I doubt it. She probably got the same treatment herself. Maybe still gets it. I didn't see the boyfriend."

"They probably don't care what happens," I said, picking at the Molson label.

"It isn't that they don't care. I don't know. So many people in this situation feel like they have no control. They just get kicked around. Lousy jobs, illiterate. When they get a chance to have some power over somebody, they get their revenge."

"On a little kid."

Roxanne sipped her wine.

"You know what else? She was pregnant. The mother. Seven months anyway. When she came to the door she was smoking a cigarette."

"God," I said. "Some of these people should be sterilized. The kids don't have a chance, and their kids won't either."

Roxanne held her wineglass on her lap.

"You sick of talking about it?" I said.

She shook her head.

"It isn't that. I don't know. It's just that I don't like it when people say things like that. 'They should be sterilized.' 'Take 'em out and shoot 'em.' It means you've stopped thinking about the problem. A lot of people do that and it's—"

"I know. It's an easy out. Doesn't accomplish anything."

She leaned over and kissed me softly on the neck.

"You're still sexy, even if you're a reactionary," she said. "So how's the paper. Raking any good muck?"

I managed a bit of a smile.

"Nothing too juicy. We had, I guess you could call it, an unfortunate thing happen. Sort of awful, really."

She paled.

"Not to me," I said. "To Arthur. Arthur Bertin."

"The little photographer guy who came up to us in that restaurant?"

"Yeah. Well, he's gone. Dead. They found him in a canal down at the mill. Near the mill. Yesterday. He was drowned."

"My God," Roxanne gasped.

I told her about the kids, the fire truck, the boat.

"I can't believe it. He seemed nice that day. Remember how sort of shy he was? He had been at a football game and he was having hot chocolate to warm up, and it was like he didn't want to look me right in the eye but he kept almost peeking at me."

"He was afraid of women. Especially young, attractive ones."

"Well, what happened?"

"I don't know. They say—the medical examiner, I mean—says it was an accidental drowning. But I don't buy it. Where he was is in the middle of nowhere, and he didn't even have a car. So what did he do? Walk down there in the middle of the night to look at the view and get too close to the edge?"

"What do the police think?" she said.

"Accidental death until they find something that says otherwise."

"They must have their reasons, don't you think?"

"Yeah, like they don't feel like worrying about it, like it might involve some work. It's a big rubber stamp. Bang, bang. Case closed."

"Did he kill himself?" Roxanne asked.

"I don't know. Maybe. He seemed fine to me, though. Strange, the way he was, but happy enough. Basketball is about to start up and he really liked shooting basketball photos. It was warm, which is why he hated football. He said he had bad circulation, and he'd freeze standing around outside like that.

"But it's not just that. He wasn't the type to do something dramatic like that. I don't know. Something so final. He hemmed and hawed over everything. Which shot was better, which one to print, did I like this one, did I like that one better. Drive you crazy."

I finished my beer and ate a spoonful of chili.

"This is really good. You don't cook bad for a sexpot."

Roxanne sat with her legs crossed. I was glad she didn't paint her toenails.

"So what are you going to write?" she asked, fiddling in the chili with her spoon.

"I don't know. A news story. Write it straight. That's all I can do right now. I'll do some kind of profile, too. 'Stobit,' they call it. Part story, part obituary. But I'll keep pushing. Do an editorial. Maybe if I write enough nasty things about the cops and the medical examiner, they'll reopen the case. Bow to media pressure. Appoint a special commission to investigate allegations of neglect of duty and corruption."

"Have you ever had that happen?"

"Written stories that resulted in commissions being formed?"

"Yeah."

"Actually, I was involved in one. The *Journal*, in Providence. They had this hotshot investigative reporter who did some stories on a Mafia judge. Guy ended up being booted off the bench. I was just a gofer. But that was the *Journal*. This is the *Androscoggin Review*. There's something called the clout factor, and I don't know how much we have."

I finished my beer and put it down on the floor by Roxanne's shoes.

"I guess I'll find out," I said.

"You've got clout with me," Roxanne said.

"Just so you don't want me to tie you up."

"Do people really do that?" she giggled.

"Don't ask me. I just know what I see in Times Square."

"And what's that?"

"Nothing as nice as what I see right now."

"You didn't really go there, did you? To those movies, I mean."

"Hell no. I just went there to buy heroin."

"What am I getting myself into here?" she said, putting her arms around me.

"I've been asking myself that question," I said, kissing her deeply, and then deeper than that.

6

I really had worked on a story like that. It was back when I was a young would-be hotshot working eighty hours a week at the *Journal*. The story had to do with bid-rigging and the construction industry and this judge who was on the take, but I didn't actually write it. I was what they called a contributing reporter, doing groundwork as part of the investigative team and getting my name at the end of the story in agate. The reporter who did the writing later won a Pulitzer for his work on the Mafia. He accepted it and packed his family off to Miami to work for the *Herald*. Rhode Island was a small state, and a lot of people didn't like him.

But I had never felt that I was in any danger back then, meeting construction-company sources in shopping malls and rousting Mafia types in their offices. Nobody went after reporters, and besides, I was twenty-four and I wasn't afraid of anything.

In eleven years, I'd changed.

Over the years, I'd gotten the late-night phone calls, the notes nailed to the door of the apartment. Bad grammar. Atrocious spelling. Threats of violence and a sad commentary on the state of public education. But even then, I'd had the protection of being one of millions. I could disappear into the crowd, hide behind the big security guards who stood in the *Times* lobby. In Androscoggin, there was no place to hide.

It was morning and I stayed in bed and thought about things. The *Journal*. Roxanne in bed. God, she was voracious in a single-minded, almost athletic sort of way. After the self-doubting neurotics I'd been with, it was almost baffling. Could she really be that well-adjusted?

She had left while it was still dark, a figure in a skirt and white blouse, bending over me with shoes in her hand. She'd said she'd call me, and then there was the faint whir of the Subaru motor and the sound of gravel and leaves crunching in the driveway.

Exit, stage left.

Her assessment of Arthur was interesting. That he was polite and nice. With Roxanne, there were no snide remarks about his clothes, his hair. Ridiculing wouldn't have accomplished much, she'd probably say. And if you didn't make fun of his clothes, there wasn't much more to say.

Arthur was very private. He never talked about himself, his family. He'd never given me a clue of what he did when he wasn't shooting pictures for the paper. I hadn't seen a television or even a radio in his studio. Maybe photography was his life. His photography. The Knights of Columbus bowling champs. The Garden Club and the Androscoggin High School basketball team.

The phone rang once and stopped, jarring me loose from the bed. I stood in front of the window for a second, naked from the night before. Outside, it was cloudy and raw and looked cold enough to snow. I grabbed my robe, picked up two empty Molson bottles from the floor, and went to the kitchen to make breakfast.

I was out of the house at 8:30. The Volvo started hard, and I sat for a minute to let it warm up. It was a car that taught you Nordic discipline. A good student, I waited for the temperature gauge to inch past the line next to "C" and started downtown through the back streets.

Lawns were covered with a film of frosted oak leaves and a light tentative snow was beginning to fall. I drove down streets lined with old Victorian houses, the town's showplaces of the last century. Some were faded but intact. Others had been chopped into apartments, the intricate detail yanked off as it rotted. The doctors and lawyers and lumber and paper barons were gone, and another era had come to a not-so-graceful end.

The new money did not build mansions. The new money was mill money, and it was earned at sixteen dollars an hour, time and a half on weekends and holidays. It built ranch houses on slabs with oversize garages for ski boats and snowmobiles and new four-wheel-drive pickups. It bought security and luxury that hadn't even been dreamed of by earlier generations. It was hard-earned union money, and sometimes I wondered how long it would last.

At the west end of town, I cut in on a convoy of pulp trucks lumbering toward the mill. On the upgrades, the drivers downshifted and the trucks shuddered under the strain, coughing big clouds of diesel smoke. I followed the dirty orange warning flag that dangled from the waving tip of the longest spruce log in the load of the truck in front of me. The tree was spindly, maybe eight inches at the stump and thirty years old. That was what they were cutting now because most of the bigger stumpage had been cut. The country wiped its noses and kitchen counters faster than trees could grow in the Maine woods.

Where the pulpwood procession went straight on Route 108, I took a left and drove past the boxcars and storage sheds down to the canal road. When I pulled up to where Arthur had been pulled out, two kids, thirteen or fourteen, were standing on the wall. They looked over their shoulders at me when I got out of the car. One of them flicked a cigarette out into the water.

I walked up and said hello. They looked at me suspiciously, then grunted a guttural greeting. We stood there, the three of us.

They were wearing high-top sneakers with the laces undone. Their blue denim jackets had designs scrawled on the back with ballpoint pen. Red bandannas hung limply from their back pockets.

We looked down at the black water. The jagged chunks of ice broken by the rescue boat had refrozen in a zigzag pattern like the fruit in Jell-O salad.

"You a cop or something?" one of the kids suddenly asked.

He looked at me defiantly, one eye covered with a swatch of blond hair.

"No," I said. "I work for the paper."

"The paper here? I worked for the paper. Had a route but quit it."

"Too much work?"

"Naah. I didn't feel like doing it."

We looked at the water some more. It looked bitterly cold but deadly as hot tar. The walls were sheer granite slabs, stacked on top of each other. There was no easy way out, and the water wouldn't give you much time to think about it.

"A guy bought it here," the short kid said.

"Yeah, I heard," I said.

"Friend of mine saw him. In the water there, with his arms out like this."

He held his arms out in front of him and stuck out his tongue and tilted his head. His friend snorted. The short kid grinned at me.

"My friend knew he was dead. He freaked right out, man."

"Scared him, huh?"

"No, it didn't scare him or nothin' like that. It was just, like, gross. Like the guy was in there floating and everything, and he was dead. It was some old guy. He bit it, man. Big-time."

We stood and looked down at our feet. Four dirty sneakers. Two tan leather boots.

The kid turned toward the Volvo.

"What kind of a car is that?"

"Volvo."

"That from Japan or someplace?"

"Sweden."

"What?"

"It's Swedish. Made in Sweden. It's a country in Europe."

"What is it? An antique or something?"

"It's not that old. It's a sixty-four."

"That's old. Me and him weren't even born yet."

"Nope."

"I've got a dirt bike. Suzuki two-fifty. I bet it's faster than that."

"Maybe," I said. "But the car's warmer."

We still stared. They seemed mildly fascinated by the idea that a man had died here and their friend had seen him. Maybe it gave them a sense of their own mortality, the frail thread from which all life hangs.

"What do you think happened to him?" I asked them.

"I bet he got drunk and passed out and fell in," the taller kid said, speaking for the first time. "Probably some old wino. Probably puked on himself and fell in."

The short kid made a gagging sound and leaned over the edge. They both laughed, and I was reminded of the boys whooping in the classroom the day before. I left them there and went back to the car and drove back up through the junk and shacks toward the highway.

So that was the crime scene. No cop. No cordon. Nothing that could ever be introduced as evidence without noting that it had been trampled by truants and firemen and any of the other countless people who had wanted to come down and see where Arthur Bertin had died. The old guy. The wino.

He might have been old by the kids' standards, but he wasn't a wino. He never drank that I knew of. In fact, he seemed as terrified of alcohol as he was of women.

No booze. No women. No family, and no one I would really call a friend. What did that leave?

It was almost nine o'clock and everyone would be in at the office, drinking coffee and waiting for the caffeine to seep into their bloodstreams so they could function enough to begin the day's business. They wouldn't need me for a while. They certainly wouldn't miss me for at least two cups.

I drove back slowly, passing oncoming pulp trucks. When I came to the turnoff to Court Street and the downtown, I braked, thought for a second, and then drove straight, over the bridge and out Route 2.

In five minutes, I turned off the main road and slowed as I passed Arthur's studio. A piece of cardboard had been stuck in the window that had been broken while I was in the building the last time. The place looked even more deserted, more forlorn.

I made one pass, then turned around in the vacant gas station and came back. This time I made it more official, pulling up in front of the door for anyone to see. If anybody asked, I was looking for negatives Arthur had processed for the *Review*. Important negatives. To make important prints. I checked the front door and then remembered that I was still carrying the key from the last time. The key turned and I went in.

The room seemed even more dank. The air smelled unclean. I flicked on the bare overhead bulb and wondered who paid the electric bill when the customer was deceased. Maybe Arthur paid in advance.

From the front room, I pushed through the blanket to the darkroom and fumbled for the switch. The safelight went on and the room glowed amber. I waited for my eyes to adjust and then started rummaging in the half-dark.

I wasn't sure what I was looking for, but it wasn't negatives for the paper. It was something, anything, that didn't have to do with the *Review*. Something that would tell me about the rest of Arthur's life. Something that would tell me why he was in the drawer at the morgue when he didn't drink, drive drunk, chase after women, or climb mountains.

The darkroom was filled with supplies: paper, dark brown jugs of developer and fixer, boxes of rejected prints. Arthur's stuff wasn't horrible but it wasn't good, either, and it was interesting to see how hard he had worked to come up with even mediocre results.

I flipped through the prints—football, clubs, people passing a giant cardboard check—and opened the cupboards. More jugs, empty and coated with dust. Pieces of enlargers. Lenses. Unidentifiable junk. I weeded through it.

Nothing.

I pushed through the blanket and into the bedroom and found the light. The murderous bunnies and teddy bears eyed me as I picked through a couple of cartons and found nothing but photo magazines, old yellowed copies of the *Review*, and more dirt and dust. On the bunny shelf, it was more of the same. Years of accumulated, worthless junk. I inched along the shelf, squatting and moving things aside until something stopped me.

It was a three-ring binder, blue, with the Androscoggin High School seal stamped in gold on the cover.

And it was clean.

I opened the binder and took out a wrinkled manila envelope. There was white lined paper in the binder, but I flipped through it and it was blank. I put the binder down and opened the envelope. In it was a stack of prints, eight-by-tens, black-and-white. I pulled them out and froze.

A woman, naked from the waist up, her breasts silhouetted by a lamp. A couple standing beside a bed, the woman nude and the man wearing boxer shorts. They were pressed together, embracing.

A girl, fourteen or fifteen, shot in daylight as she walked beside an in-ground pool. She was naked. A towel hung from her left hand and her hair was dark and wet and slicked back behind her ears.

Another one with the figure blurred, though you could tell it was female. A woman wearing a dress, bending down. That one was blurry, too.

Arthur. Arthur the voyeur.

I felt sick. Clammy and nauseated. I stuck the pictures back in the envelope and tucked the envelope under my arm. Sticking the binder back on the shelf, I got unsteadily to my feet and headed for the curtain.

Everyone was in when I got back to the paper. Even Martin, waiting for me by the partition, a sheaf of hard copy in his hand. I walked by him and headed for the bathroom, where I stood at the sink and looked at the pictures again under the light.

They were more chilling than erotic. Ghostly, almost. I went through the whole stack and thought I recognized only one of the figures. It was a woman in a slip or something, and I was pretty sure it was one of the waitresses at the Pine Tree. She was in her thirties. Blonde and sort of tough. I looked at the picture, the figure framed by curtains, the camera pointed through the window to the lighted room. I turned off the light, opened the door, and walked to my desk, where I slid the waitress into the top middle drawer, under some papers and notebooks. The envelope still under my arm, I waved to Martin again, said I'd be right back, and walked up the street to the police station.

Charlotte the dispatcher was watching a soap opera on the television above the radio console. A blonde woman in a strapless black dress was kissing a guy in a tuxedo. Charlotte was drinking diet cola from a can. I asked her if Vigue was in and she nodded toward his office in mid-sip.

He was on the phone, a file open in front of him, photocopied checks spread out on the desk.

"Yeah, I could find him if I wanted to spend a month in Florida. I'd go in a second, but something tells me the taxpayers would see things a little different . . . Yeah . . . I know . . . So one of these days he'll get picked up. These guys can't stay straight. Yeah. They got asshole genes . . . So he'll get picked up and then we'll go after him. No, it isn't gonna happen tomorrow. Next month, I don't know. Yeah . . . Yup."

He hung up the phone.

"Another happy customer," he said.

"I've got something to show you," I said, and dropped the envelope on the desk in front of him.

"What's this, your diploma?"

"Arthur's. Arthur Bertin's. Stuff I found at his studio."

"Playing cop or what?"

"Somebody's got to do it. Open it up."

He looked at me like I'd pushed him too far, then slowly picked up the envelope and opened the clasp. He pulled the prints out, with the couple embracing on top, then deliberately thumbed through them.

"So?"

"They're Arthur's. I got them at his studio. In the bedroom. I was looking for some prints he took for us. I found these."

"Should I arrest you now or later?" Vigue muttered, but he lit a cigarette, then started thumbing through them again.

"So this is how the boy got his jollies, huh? If the girls didn't come to him, he went to them."

"Through the bushes."

"Better than knocking at the front door, I guess. Hey. This babe works at the Savings."

He was looking at the picture of the couple embracing.

"Wouldn't kick her out of bed, would ya," Vigue said.

"Anybody else you know?"

He shook his head and kept looking, stopping at each picture for a few seconds. As he looked, I told him about the narrow depth of field, the small portion of the photos that was in focus.

"Shot with a telephoto," I said. "A two-hundred, maybe. The prints are grainy, so he probably pushed the film to sixteen-hundred. Especially shooting at night through a lighted window."

"We get a lot of prowler calls. Maybe they'll stop."

"Maybe Arthur took one of these too many and somebody decided to get rid of him."

Vigue didn't appear to have heard me. I was about to rephrase it when he shook his head slightly, side to side.

"Nobody gets that pissed off about some guy taking his old lady's picture," he said. "If he does, he kicks Arthur around the yard, busts his camera over his head, maybe. The wife calls the cops and we charge them both with disorderly conduct."

"No swim in the canal?"

"Not in my book. Blow his head off from the back porch, maybe. But nothing like you're thinking," he said.

Vigue had come back to the photo of the couple, the woman from the bank.

"What's he got that I don't got," he said.

"So what happened?"

"You tell me, Sherlock Holmes."

There were voices in the hall, cop voices, and then the door rattled and LeMaire, J. and a reserve kid named Kelly pushed through, laughing. Vigue stuck the pictures back in the envelope and started to hand them to me. I put my hands in my pockets.

"For your investigation," I said, nodded to the boys, and left.

I sat at my computer terminal and ran my hand over my face. I'd missed a spot shaving, leaving a strip of stubble under my jawbone. I ran my fingers over the spot and stared at the photograph in the top drawer of my desk.

Vigue had known the bank teller. I'd known the night waitress from the Pine Tree.

Her name was Joy and she worked the counter. I'd never paid much attention to her before, but then, I'd never seen so much of her before.

The photo was slightly out of focus and very grainy, like the rest of the stuff from the blue binder. The waitress was standing, apparently looking into a mirror. She looked like she might be saying that she didn't look bad for thirty-eight or thirty-six or whatever she was. And she didn't.

She was naked, lean and trim from all that waitressing. Lift those trays, serve those coffees. I found myself scrutinizing her figure and, for a second, wondering what she would feel like, what she would say. Was this what Arthur had felt?

I caught myself. Maybe I shouldn't have kept this one out. Maybe I should have given them all to Vigue, washed my hands of it. Or maybe I should have made copies of all of them. If I wanted some evidence for myself, why just one? Well, it was done now, but for the first time I began to feel like I was getting tangled up, that I wasn't in control. I wondered if Arthur had that feeling, too.

What made him do this? He was a strange sort of asexual guy. What did people like him do to sublimate their sex drive? Did they have one at all? Did he feel as left out as he really was?

In high school, did he have dates? He was in the service. Did he ever go with bar girls in Manila, meet a shy, sort of homely girl from the secretarial pool? Or did he always just watch?

His buddies serve their hitches and come home and get married, going on honeymoons where they flop around in heart-shaped tubs. Not Arthur. They have kids and more kids and driveways littered with broken toys. Arthur doesn't, and over the years, he does a lot of watching as women pair off with men of all shapes and sizes. If you're used to watching, maybe taking pictures of women undressing might be a logical progression.

I'd known reporters who were real wimps who were fascinated by the cop beat, sportswriters who were uncoordinated kids. We all live vicariously, some more than others.

I looked over at Vern. He was eating a cream-filled chocolate cupcake while he talked to someone on the phone. The cream was on his fingers and he wiped them on his maroon coach's jacket. He wasn't a coach. Never had been. He'd found the jacket on the ground after a football game. He'd made a halfhearted attempt to return it and now wore it every day.

Never look a gift fantasy in the mouth.

So what was mine? To be a great reporter and win a Pulitzer? From Androscoggin, Maine, even I couldn't keep that dream going. To go back to New York and save somebody from a mugging in the subway or someplace? Write a book that would put me on the cover of *The New York Times Book Review*? Marry Roxanne, build a log cabin in the woods, and live happily ever after, still having great sex at seventy?

Roxanne could be part of it. But not all of it. I'd run on country roads in the fall, ski alone for days in the White Mountains. Get home and have a fire in the fireplace. Read John D. McDonald and listen to Django Reinhardt. Drink good beer before, during, and after all of the above.

The first night we went to bed, Roxanne said I was professionally lonely. Solitary was more like it. Lonely was somebody like Arthur, making his way through the yards in the dark, standing motionless outside windows, escaping with a blurry erotic image on four-hundred-speed film.

A lonely hobby and a lonely life. And a lonely death.

"Zen and the art of weekly newspapers?"

I looked up, startled, quickly slid the drawer shut. Vern was grinning over the top of my terminal.

"I was thinking of checking for a pulse but you blinked," he said.

I smiled and leaned back from the keyboard.

"Just a lot to think about, I guess. I'm trying to write about Arthur."

"The news story?"

"News story. Stobit. Maybe an editorial."

"You sending him out in a blaze of glory?"

"I don't know about that," I said. "But God, he worked here. For a long time. I'll have to call Martin and find out just how long. But you figure everybody in town knew him, or knew him by sight. God, think of all the team pictures, the installations at the Legion. Twenty or thirty years of this stuff."

"An institution."

"Yeah. Just because he was a little eccentric doesn't mean he wasn't part of the fabric of the town, the community."

"And he died unexpectedly."

"And suspiciously."

"You come up with something?"

Vern came around the desk and stood close.

"Not much, really," I said. "Not that I would be the one to come up with things. But everybody else around here—the ME rubber-stamped the thing, you know. That makes Vigue say the case is closed. 'Until the department receives new information.' Blah, blah, blah."

"What about off the record?"

"Not much more. He thinks it's weird, but what can he do about it? That kind of thing."

"And if it was a homicide, state cops would handle it," Vern said.

"But it isn't, so nobody handles it."

"Catch-22."

He stood with his hands in his jacket pockets, big and doughy and rocking back and forth on his white high-top sneakers.

"That's funny, because it really isn't like Vigue. Guy can be a son of a bitch, but I wouldn't call him lazy."

"No," I agreed.

"I remember one time. Before your time. Four years ago, I guess. Kid gets shot hunting up in Roxbury or Byron, one of those places. He was from Mass., or some place, and this other out-of-state guy shoots him. The shooter was from Pennsylvania, I think. So anyway, Vigue finds the guy from Pennsylvania was related to some guy who is in the Mob, with one of those names like Johnny 'the Homicidal Maniac' Cappaccino, so he decides that it might have been an execution. So the staties come in and they're here for two or three days, and we run all these stories that are libelous as hell about this guy, who turns out to be a schoolteacher who felt like hell already for shooting this guy. The miracle was that the guy didn't kill himself in jail. Thing wasn't cleared up for months."

"So what happened?"

"Oh, he paid a fine and got probation or something. Turned out the other guy, the guy who got killed, was driving deer, and he had a blaze-orange handkerchief and the rest of his clothes were camouflage."

"So he deserved it."

"More or less. But Vigue was running around like we should reconvene the Warren Commission."

"Nobody's reconvening anything for Arthur," I said.

"He's not from out of state," Vern said, now leaning against the partition.

"And the ME says it's an accident. I guess that means Vigue can't launch an all-out investigation, but Jesus. He hasn't done anything. Nobody has done anything. A guy supposedly walks two miles from anywhere in the freezing cold to a place that is nothing but rubble. Goes to the edge of this ten-foot wall and slips and falls in. And he's not suicidal, that anyone knows."

"Just a little weird," Vern said.

"So?"

"I know. I agree. The guy's idea of a big adventure was shooting an away basketball game. Go all the way to South Paris. If he stayed at the Pine Tree and had a third cup of coffee, we heard about it for a week."

"It stinks," I said.

Vigue. The pictures. The medical examiner. Why was Arthur down at the canal? Who cares? What happened? Who knows? Toss the spare parts back inside the old thoracic cavity and staple the little runt back together. We've got work to do here. Bring in the next stiff.

The front door banged and Paul stormed in, tossing his briefcase on the light table.

"That idiot knows my deadline is tonight at five, but he says he has to have it. Has to get it in. It isn't in from the agency, but he'll bring it over. He'll bring it at two minutes of five and I'll be here all night."

He took a breath.

"Hello. Fellas," Paul said.

"The Furniture Shoppe?"

"You got it. Fletcher the dink."

"All you have to do is stick to the deadline," I said. "Teach him a lesson."

"Yeah, a quarter-page lesson. Three-hundred-buck lesson."

He sat down at his desk and shuffled through insertion orders.

"Hey, I'll tell you," Paul said. "I'll work here forty hours a week. Maybe fifty. But not sixty. I'm not spending my whole life in this place. Life is too goddamn short."

Vern turned back to his desk.

"Some of us are trying to put out a newspaper," he said. "If the advertising department can't behave appropriately in the workplace, it may face disciplinary action."

"Discipline this," Paul snarled.

"Now children," I said, and turned to my screen and began to write.

> Preliminary results of an autopsy performed on the body of Arthur Bertin showed that the Androscoggin man died of accidental drowning, Chief Medical Examiner Richard E. Ritano said Tuesday.
>
> Bertin also was suffering from acute hypothermia at the time of his death, Ritano said.
>
> Bertin's body was found Sunday in a canal on the property of St. Amand Paper Co., between the Androscoggin mill and Route 108. Ritano, who performed the autopsy at Kennebec Valley Medical Center in Augusta, said there was no indication of foul play in the death of the forty-six-year-old freelance photographer.

Ritano emphasized, however, that the findings were preliminary. He said he could not say when a final ruling would be issued.

Bertin's body was first discovered floating in the canal at 3:55 p.m. by youths playing in the area. Fire and rescue units were dispatched and recovered the body using an Androscoggin Fire Department rescue boat. The body was found lodged against the canal wall about a half-mile west of the St. Amand access road off Route 108.

A longtime Androscoggin resident, Bertin was a freelance and studio photographer for many years. He was a familiar figure at area sports events, which he often covered for the *Review*.

I grabbed the phone and dialed the police department.

Charlotte the dispatcher answered, with the television blaring in the background. I asked for Vigue and she put me on hold. I waited and Vigue answered.

"Lieutenant. Jack McMorrow again."

"Yup."

"I know we talked about this already, but I wanted to get, make sure I had the latest information."

I could hear him breathing.

"You there?" I asked.

"Oh, yeah."

"I couldn't hear you."

"That's because I didn't say anything. Hey, listen. What can I tell you. Nothing's changed."

"What about those pictures?"

"Those pictures don't mean squat. What'd you think he was? A priest? Just because he was a weirdo doesn't mean somebody killed him. That was true, we'd have ten homicides a week. He ain't the only one with a skeleton in his closet."

"But he's the only one who ended up in the water."

Silence. Vigue was not happy.

"Listen. I'm not—this department is not gonna be railroaded into commencing something as important as a homicide investigation. Just because the stiff worked for your paper doesn't make it the crime of the century."

"But the pictures—"

"The pictures are interesting. I will make sure they are considered should any other information come to our attention. And—"

"Is it gonna come to your attention, or are you gonna go out and find it?"

"Listen, Sam friggin' Spade. This is what I am gonna tell you. This is for the record: You can do whatever you want with it. This death is under investigation. This department is always looking for information that could potentially involve criminal activity. But at this point in time the medical examiner has ruled it an accidental death. At this point in time we do not have any information that would indicate that this is a homicide. At this point in time. I don't know any other way to say it."

"Well, I'm not a cop, but—"

"You bet you're not a cop, and I am. So are a lot of other people around here, and they are doing their jobs and they don't need people like you interfering with this investigation. And I'd like to know just how you found those pictures."

"Subpoena me when the killer is brought to trial."

"Jesus! You are—you are almost enough to piss a man off. That's off the record."

"Be that way," I said. "Thanks for your time. I'll talk to you later. Oh, and if you really want to know more about the pictures, I'd be glad to talk."

"I know where to find you," Vigue said, and he hung up.

In front of me on the desk were two yellow legal-pad pages covered with scrawled notes. I went through them, rewriting where the handwriting was illegible. I looked at them and began typing.

> Androscoggin Police Lieutenant John Vigue said police are continuing their investigation of Bertin's death. But Vigue on Tuesday said police had no evidence that would lead them to view the death as suspicious.
> "This department is always looking for information that could potentially involve criminal activity," Vigue said.

I wondered if I should use the railroading quote or any of the other stuff. Vigue would hit the roof, but did I want him completely turned off on me and the paper? Would he get so mad at me that it would make him back away from the Arthur thing even further? Or had I already crossed that line?

Flipping through the pages, I decided to wait. But I took the Vigue notes and stuck them in a folder with the picture of Joy. I took the photo of the woman with Martin and put it with the other stuff and stuck the folder in my file cabinet under "N," for no reason. I shut the drawer and for the first time since I'd been at the *Review*, locked it.

7

It was late Tuesday afternoon and the shift had changed at the mill, releasing a stream of cars and pickup trucks that flowed down Main Street as if it had been squeezed out of a tube. I was sitting at my desk with my hands on the keyboard but my gaze on the traffic under the Christmas lights. When I looked back at the screen, nothing had changed. The slug read SIDEBAR-ART and the rest of the glowing green screen was blank.

I looked around the office. Vern was drawling into the phone with the southern accent that he fell into every once in a while, usually when he was really waxing on about something or when he was drunk. I wondered about that. Was it just sports macho, or had he lived in the South at some point? He never said much about his background. Nothing that really told you much. A private person who never shut up.

Paul was cursing as he picked at a roll of border tape for an ad. He'd been in a nasty mood all week, but that was the way he usually was when he was under a lot of pressure, which pre-Christmas was. Or when one of his two-month flings was on the way out. Then I'd hear him talking to Cindy, man to woman. "She doesn't understand.

I adjust my life to hers. But if I ask her to make some adjustments for me, she acts like I'm pushing her around. I don't know how long it's gonna last." Within a week, he'd be with somebody else. Two months later, he'd be talking to Cindy again.

I took a breath, stretched my shoulders, and started typing.

> Arthur Bertin didn't leave much behind when he drowned last weekend. There are stuffed bunnies gathering dust in his studio on Carolina Street. They are left over from years ago, when Arthur used to get kids to smile for the camera. Many of those photographs are probably still treasured by mothers and fathers who by now are grandparents. Their grandchildren won't be able to go to Arthur to have their photographs taken.
>
> There are pieces of old Nikkormat cameras scattered around his studio, too, cameras cannibalized to keep one camera in operation for Arthur's work at the *Review*. Most of those pictures have disappeared with the papers, but a few probably have survived. They turn yellow in scrapbooks. Perhaps Little Leaguers still have them taped to their bedroom walls.

I thought of the stack of Peeping Tom photos, the bank teller in her slip. It really didn't change anything—or did it? Arthur took child portraits. He was practically an institution at the *Review*. I knew of his other side, but most people didn't. And they would be expecting that his career be acknowledged somehow. But could I do it without feeling like I was lying to the public? As I sat, I heard Dave Curry's booming Dale Carnegie voice.

Maybe I'd ask the opinion of somebody who lied for a living.

"Jack, sorry to bother you again, but something came up, and I thought you'd want to know about it."

Overdressed and overbearing, he shook my hand and pulled some typed pages from his leather folder. He handed one to me and the way he waited made me think I was supposed to read it. I looked at the Philadelphia letterhead, the phrase, "reaffirming our commitment to the community." There was more about the company pledging to do everything in its power to retain jobs in Maine, but the "extremely competitive marketplace, the responsibility to the shareholders, the burgeoning environmental costs . . ."

"What's this say in English?" I said.

"Ha, ha," Curry said. "Always right for the jugular. Well, you want a quick answer, I guess, and if I may paraphrase Haze Gavin, St. Amand and parent firm Quinn-Hillson are both reaffirming their commitment to the community. Gavin knows that you have been making some inquiries about the company's actions in other contexts, and the company is just saying that each of those actions is taken independently, and we are not in a mode where we make any of these decisions easily. But we are in a mode where some difficult decisions may have to be made if the community, the town, the employees don't recognize the marketplace we're working in."

"So what does this have to do with me?"

"Ha, ha," he said. "No, Jack, we are serious. We recognize that you have legitimate concerns about the company's moves and the way they might impact Androscoggin. You have a responsibility to get all the information out to the community, and you are doing a great job of that. But we want to make sure that you *do* have all the information. So Haze Gavin wants you to look at this statement. Consider it talking points. Then we can get together, do a conference call, and really lay it out for everybody to see. What's your deadline for this week?"

"Deadline is Thursday morning to make the streets early Friday. But that's in North Conway at the printer's. In theory, we should have everything set to go Wednesday night."

"Hey, I remember deadlines at the college paper. University of Oklahoma. Boy, did we bust some deadlines."

Bust some deadlines? Spare me.

"When does Gavin want to talk?" I asked. "Tomorrow? We have had some other things going on."

I waited. One, two, three . . .

"Oh, yeah, the Arthur Bertin thing. Well, I know, I'll call you. We can work around that, I'm sure. Terrible thing. I didn't mean to . . . No, you take care of that, of course. If there's anything that the company can do, we'll—"

"What's down there? Where he died, I mean?"

Curry's expression changed, almost as if he'd been asked a real question for a change and could give a real answer.

"Nothing, really, Jack," he said. "A lot of storage. Nothing really. If we put in another paper machine, not that we have any firm plans, but if we ever did expand, that would be the direction we'd head. But nothing. Just . . . I don't know, just a lot of junk."

Junk and a dead man who had been very lonely.

Curry finally left and my stomach grumbled. I closed Arthur's editorial and shut off my machine. I got up and looked out at the traffic, looked at Marion's note on the community news copy and briefs, with thirty-six inches in the system. Marion was very efficient. It was good to have at least one grown-up in the operation.

Vern was still on the phone, talking basketball. He was a funny guy, able to talk for hours about nothing or, when he was drinking or hungover, come out with something that cut to the absolute heart of a subject, a verbal stiletto. It was unsettling, as if he thought more than he ever let on, as if the veil was always down. Almost always.

The shift-change traffic had thinned, which meant there were no cars on Main Street. My stomach grumbled again and I decided to head home, and within minutes I had caught both of the lights on Main Street on green, swung over the bridge, past the park and up the hill. At Penobscot Street, I went left, slowing to let a group of high-school kids saunter across the street. When I got to the house it looked bleak and cold, with the lights out and the driveway empty.

I parked the car at the door and rifled the mailbox on the way in: *Newsweek*, a bank statement forwarded from New York, and a letter from a friend in Oshawa, outside Toronto, also forwarded from New York. I ripped the envelope open as I climbed the stairs two at a time. At the landing on the second floor, I stopped.

The door was open. The frame was splintered, all bare and jagged. I pushed it gently and it swung partly open.

In the middle of the kitchen, the refrigerator lay on its side. The door hung open and milk and orange juice had mixed in a yellow pool on the floor. A loaf of bread was sitting in the pool, stomped flat. Counters were covered with cereal and rice and sugar. Red wine had been splashed on the wall.

I walked stiffly to the living room.

My stereo was upside down on the floor. Chairs were tipped over and books were strewn everywhere. In the bedroom, the bed was on its side and all my clothes were in a pile in the middle of the floor. Someone had urinated on the pile, making long sweeping yellow streaks on white sheets.

I felt weak, short of breath. I swallowed and looked at the room. Record covers were thrown into the bedroom. I could see Miles Davis,

Dave Brubeck in a tie. Bill Evans, with something to be depressed about. I started to reach down to pick them up, then straightened up and stepped to the kitchen. The telephone receiver dangled from the wall. I picked it up by the cord and called the cops.

"Somebody's trying to tell you something, chief," Vigue said, still standing in the doorway. "Boff anybody's wife? Late on some bills?"

I shook my head and kept mopping. LeMaire, J. was in the living room, taking pictures with an automatic Canon so the carnage would be recorded for posterity and the insurance company.

"Nobody you've offended?" Vigue continued. "Maybe just pissed off?"

"How the hell should I know?" I said. "Maybe we left somebody's name off the honor roll."

LeMaire, J. sloshed through the pale orange pool. Vigue walked to the end of the kitchen and looked through the door.

"They missed the bathroom," he said.

"Great. I'll sleep in the tub and eat off the toilet seat."

"Could have pulled the toilet off the wall. Then you'd have the neighbors pissed off, too."

"There aren't any. They moved out," I said.

"Maybe you got them pissed off."

"They loved me like a son."

I almost mentioned the St. Amand story but held back and wrung the mop in the sink. Curry and his people wouldn't go for this sort of thing. Maybe a few of the workers would, if they'd had a few, but this wouldn't keep a story from going. If they wanted to slow things down, they'd have to hit the office.

LeMaire, J. crunched back into the living room with the camera dangling around his neck. He looked like a demented tourist. A paramilitary Smokey Bear.

"How you gonna secure it?" he asked.

"Secure what?"

"The premises. Lock the place up."

"I don't know," I said. "What's left to protect?"

"They could burn the building down," he said.

"They can do that in the hall."

I put the mop headfirst in the sink and bent to look. We had stood the refrigerator back up but the door wouldn't close. In the back, next to an overturned tub of cottage cheese and a cabbage, were three cans of Ballantine, lying on their sides like ejected mortar shells.

"Wasn't kids," Vigue said, over my shoulder. "With kids, beer's the first thing to go."

I reached in and tipped the cans back on their ends. One small step for man . . .

"I'm not kidding, chief," Vigue said, almost cheerfully. "Somebody picked you out for this one."

8

Dinner that night was part of a loaf of oatmeal bread and a hunk of bright orange cheddar cheese, the only real cheese they had at the store at the bridge. I was the only one at the office, and I ate at my desk and worked, editing releases, rereading the Arthur editorial, shuffling papers, and wondering what I was being warned away from.

At nine o'clock I got up and locked the door from the inside.

At nine-fifteen, Mrs. Beauceville from the funeral home called and said she had an obit. I took it—four inches of copy to sum up the entire life of a man named Randall Pelletier. He was born in St.-Prosper, Quebec, and moved to Androscoggin when he was fourteen. He worked in the paper mill under various owners for forty-seven years, retiring due to ill health. He died four years later at sixty-nine, and was survived by one daughter, Imogie Brant of East Hartford, Connecticut. There was no mention of Imogie's mother. Friends could call Friday from two to four p.m., Saturday from one to three.

Good-bye, Mr. Pelletier. *C'est la guerre.*

It was beginning to pile up, Pelletier and Arthur and all the rest. Stacked on top of me, an awful dragging weight.

I got up from my chair and turned off the lights, then went over to stand in front of the window. It was flurrying and the snow blew like dust in the gutters. Most of the stores were dark, with fluorescent lights left on to discourage burglars.

How desolate.

A northern outpost with me sitting in a little storefront office writing about people no one else had ever heard of, people who would live and die here without ever venturing into the outside world. Whole lives played out in Androscoggin, Maine, with generation after generation coming and going like the issues of the *Review*. Inevitable. Unstoppable. Fading into the deepest, darkest obscurity in the blink of an eye.

Oh, how I hated this feeling. I hated the questions that I couldn't drive away when I felt like this. Was this it? Was I kidding myself when I found this rewarding? Was I on some long downward slide? Was I some kind of washed-up loser at thirty-five?

Jack McMorrow. Small-town reporter, laboring away in the ragged nameless mountains of western Maine, typing in the night. Alone.

Maybe that was most of it. I was lonely. It had been a bad day, as bad as I'd had in quite a while. And Arthur dying. It was natural to be let down about all of this. But was that all it was? I didn't know. I just didn't know.

I looked out at the street. A pair of headlights rounded the corner by the fire station and drew closer until the form of a pickup materialized. The truck was dark, sagging in the rear with loud exhaust. As it rumbled by I saw that it was a Chevy, very rusted. The driver glanced up and saw me in the window. I saw a beard, a cigarette, and then he gave me the finger.

How could he have known?

I worked until three in the morning, mostly to keep from going home. Roxanne called at eleven-fifteen to say hello. She was in bed, she said, curled up with a magazine, wearing a warm flannel nightgown.

"Everything okay?" she asked.

"I guess," I said. "Somebody broke into the house. Messed it up a little, if you can believe that."

"What? My God, what did they mess up?"

"Not much," I said. "Just sort of threw things around a little. Nothing too terrible. So don't worry about it."

"Well, I will worry about it."

"Well, you shouldn't."

"Well, I will."

"Well, don't," I said.

She said good night, sounding worried anyway, and I wished I hadn't told her. We hung up but not on a romantic or sexy note. Then the coffee wore off and I felt exhausted, so I got everything ready for the morning, page dummies in one folder, copy still to be set in another, photos in a third. I left the stories on Arthur in the computer for a final check when I was fresher, then unlocked the front door and walked out in the still night to my car. My shoes made a crescendo of crunching noises in the snow on the sidewalk. Up and down Main Street, nothing moved. Stars moved in and out of the clouds, and I didn't see a single other car on the way home, if you could call it that.

With the windows open, the house was near freezing, but it still smelled like a school cafeteria, sour milk and faintly sweet fruit.

I opened the kitchen window wider and, keeping my parka on, got one of the three beers out of the refrigerator. I drank half of it leaning against the counter and then went into the living room and stared at the remains of the stereo. From the rubble of books and papers, B.B. King stared up at me. It was an old album, early sixties, and B.B. was wearing a yellow tuxedo and a huge diamond pinkie ring. I left him on the floor and went to bed. In my sleeping bag on the floor, the beer beside me, I could see my breath in the air.

Paul sucked the last half-inch off his cigarette and flicked the butt out onto the road. Vern roused himself in the backseat and I watched him in the rearview mirror. Under the maroon coach's jacket, he was big and formless, like a sack of sand. His hair was still slick from his morning shower, and it looked like he had cut it himself. Blindfolded.

"Hard night?" I asked.

"Not really," Vern said, yawning. "Couple beers and hit the sack. Just resting up for the home stretch, Jackson. Saving myself for the last kick, over the Alps, down the plains, and under the Arc de Triomphe."

"Victorious?"

"*Mais bien sûr.*"

The morning was clear and cold and icy bright, with banks of green spruce pointing to garish blue skies. We were following Route 2 along the Androscoggin River, which at this point, fifteen miles west of town, ran fast enough in the shallows to keep all but the little backwaters from freezing. As I drove, I looked out at the shimmering water, rising and falling over the rips and eddies, and thought of Arthur. His shoes must have weighted him down. His socks and pants, his belt and jacket. Wet and heavy as lead. Did he have a camera? Could they drag the canal? Would they care enough to even consider it?

I knew the answer to that one.

Vern and Paul had sunk into their seats, no small feat in the spartan Volvo. Vern was probably nursing the closest thing he ever got to a hangover. Drinking slow and steady, he didn't get drunk enough to feel sick but didn't get sober enough to feel good. Paul could have had a fight with either of the two women he saw on a rotating basis, migrating from Darlene to Laurie like a Bedouin follows water holes. I'd met both of them and Laurie got my vote. She was attractive in a robust sort of way, but direct and open. She would have made a good wife or a good mother, but Paul would say she was tying him down, or she didn't understand him or some other manufactured excuse and go back to Darlene, when she was split up with her boyfriend, which was most of the time. Darlene was attractive in a provocative sort of way, a little too much makeup, sweater too small, a defiant look that dared you to undress her with your eyes. She would not make a good wife and was a terrible mother, from what I could tell, with a three-year-old daughter she left most of the time with her mother. She was weak and spoiled and had learned too early to get her way by moving her hips.

Darlene, I mean. I didn't know about the daughter.

The car whizzed between the trees. I downshifted on the corners, weaving between the ledges that jutted out of the banks. The ledges were the skirts of the mountains, the very edge of the steep ridges that climbed to the mountains to the west. The steeper the terrain was, the more life was squeezed into the valleys, trapped in the narrow catwalks along the rivers, the occasional deltas where the river jogged and a farm could be squeezed under the blue shadows. I had a theory that the mountains were the reason people here turned to ice-fishing in the winter. It wasn't the fish. It was the only chance to walk out on terrain that was absolutely flat. On the snow-covered plains that were the ponds and lakes, the fishermen sat by their shanties, stood in clusters by the holes in the ice as if they were oil men waiting for gushers. They drank beer and whiskey and waited for the little flags on their lines to trip, tossing the fish on the ice to freeze as they breathed. Pickerel and perch and lake trout were frozen before they were dead. Tissues freeze from the outside; the brain is the last to go.

The woods gave way to farmhouses and trailers and then a small development with ranch houses lined up in a former pasture like tents in a Civil War bivouac. Another five miles and we were on the outskirts of North Conway, New Hampshire. Fast-food restaurants, strip malls, real estate offices built like ski chalets, and factory stores selling Scandinavian dishes.

Civilization.

"Here we go, team," Vern said, as we pulled into the parking lot of the low brick building that was Conway Printing. "Look sharp. On and off the field."

It took all day. We stood over light tables, the wooden benches with slanted opaque plastic tops over fluorescent bulbs. Our computer discs were popped into a terminal like the one in the *Review* office, and for nearly an hour, the pieces of the newspaper—news, sports, ad copy, classified ads—spewed from the typesetter in the next room. We hunched over the pages with razor knives and moved columns of copy around the pages, slicing stories into blocks and sticking borders on with narrow black tape. The photos were reshot in the camera room and the PMTs—blurry reproductions of the original pictures—were run through a waxed roller and slapped on the pages.

It was a funny process, primitive and painstaking all at once. There were a million and one mistakes that could be made and we'd made most of them, hacks at a craft that people honed over decades.

But that day, it went pretty smoothly. There was a minor snag when Paul realized he'd forgotten to dummy a four-column ad on an inside sports page that Vern had finished laying out. So they called each other names, the woman who ran the operation, Lois, called us children, and we slammed the thing home in near record time.

"Lois, baby, give me five," Vern said, lifting his hand high over her head as we stood outside the press room waiting for the first run to end.

"Vernon, baby," Lois said, "grow up before it's too late."

We stayed long enough to take a few copies as they came off the press, damp and smelling of ink. I still considered the whole thing a minor miracle, seeing my words in print, and I stood and scanned the pages while the pressmen, a couple of nice old Finnish guys in blue coveralls, waited to see if there were any problems. The older guy, Milt, picked up a paper and started reading the story about Arthur.

"Booze?" he asked me.

"Never touched it," I said, and he said "Humph" and tossed the paper down on the stack.

Page dummies and photos and boxes of supplies went in the trunk. We got in the car and Vern and Paul traded places, with Vern in the front and Paul in the back. I liked it better that way because Vern was easier to not talk to, and I was tired.

We drove to the other side of North Conway, past the worst of the tourist traps, and pulled into a country store on Route 202. Vern got out and shuffled inside and came back in a couple of minutes with our weekly order: a six-pack of sixteen-ounce Budweiser cans, a big bag of pretzels, and a *Boston Globe*. I pulled back out into traffic and Vern pulled out three beers. I put mine between my legs, waiting to open it until we were well out into the woods. When the lights were behind us, I opened the beer and the ritual of postpress relaxation began.

Vern looked at the *Globe* sports section, using a flashlight from the glove box. Paul smoked a cigarette in the backseat, opening the window a crack to flick out the ashes. I turned on a country-western station and drove along at the speed limit, one hand on the steering wheel.

Our reward. Sometimes we'd talk. Sometimes we'd ride in silence, with the black woods running along both sides of the car and the radio connecting us to the rest of humanity. My brain would shut off for an hour. Usually.

On this trip, it switched back on after half of the first can of beer. It sorted the events of the past few days. It sorted and resorted, shuffled and reshuffled. Arthur's photos. My house. The canal. Vigue and St. Amand. I tried to grasp something from it all, something I could take as fact—true, irrefutable fact—and build on.

That Arthur had a kinky hobby that could get him in trouble?

That I couldn't think of any reason for him to be down at that canal?

That he wasn't suicidal, as far as I could tell?

That somebody had wrecked my house for a reason?

That St. Amand would rather that I stopped writing about them and went away?

Were those facts? I wasn't even sure of that. I wasn't sure of anything except that I was tired and confused and couldn't stop things from happening long enough to figure them out. I'd won awards for investigative reporting. I'd spent weeks poring over people's expense vouchers and canceled checks to find payoffs and kickbacks. How complicated could this be?

When I finished my beer, I dropped the empty can in the bag at Vern's feet and took another. I opened it, took a sip, and looked in the rearview mirror, where I could see Paul's cigarette glowing in the dark.

9

I'd never liked the Base Camp. It was a bar, a pickup joint, and I liked pubs, places with pigs' feet in jars and bartenders who knew everybody by name, including the old men who had their own seats at the bar. Besides, whoever had named the place had been mistaken. The only expeditions mounted from this place were to the next bar down the block. The mountaineers eyed each other lustfully through the blue cigarette haze.

We sat at a table near the bar, facing a line of dungarees and derrieres. The Celtics were on the television above the liquor bottles and Vern squinted to see the score. The waitress came and blocked his view.

She was small and bleached-blonde and tough-looking. Paul called her Lindy, and ordered a pitcher of Bud and a large pizza.

"Mushroom, green pepper, and pepperoni?" he said.

"Fine," I said.

They were the ones pushing to stop for something to eat. I felt like just going home.

Vern nodded to the waitress. She sauntered off like she was doing us a huge favor and we sat in silence and watched the crowd. It was a little after seven and the place was already filling up. No homework to do.

The beer came in a couple of minutes, thumped down on the scarred table by the same blonde charmer. Paul did the honors. I told myself I'd drink my share of the pitcher, eat a couple of pieces of pizza, and go right the hell home. It had been a long day over the light tables, a longer night at the terminal, and I wanted to call Roxanne and climb in bed. Ideally, she'd be there for both, but that probably wasn't going to happen.

We drank. Vern watched the Celtics and Paul eyed the women. I sipped my beer and watched no one in particular.

To my right, toward the rear of the room, a half-dozen guys were playing pool. They moved back and forth from the pool tables to a counter where their beers were lined up. They weren't very good pool players, from what I could tell, and they cursed after each shot.

To my left, three guys were talking to two women. The women were worn and weary, the kind who would look fifty when they were thirty-five. They'd probably spent the last five years in places like this, where just breathing the air would cut ten years off your life.

One woman was blonde, white blonde with black eyebrows. She was about twenty, wearing strategically torn dungarees and a sleeveless T-shirt with thin straps, and her breasts sagged. Her friend was shorter and wider from the waist down. Her hair was dyed, too, but it was reddish and brown at the roots. Both of them were smoking long, dark-colored cigarettes and drinking white drinks, probably coffee brandy and milk.

As I watched, one of the guys leaned close to the blonde and shouted something. She laughed and spit out some of her drink.

He grabbed her rear end and then grabbed her friend, too, and the friend smiled and pretended to slap at his hand. He took a swig from a Bud longneck.

The guy was big, with a beer gut and muscular arms and shoulders. His hair was just long enough to show some vanity, and he had a weak chin. The fatal flaw.

I watched and tried to pick up the words over the Celtics and the music, which was loud and metallic. As I listened, the guy suddenly turned and looked at me, then turned back to his friends. They laughed and looked back at me and I felt a rush of blood hit my face. I turned to the pool players and then the pizza was slapped down, with three paper plates. Vern grabbed a piece, pulled the string of cheese toward his mouth, and then watched as a lump of cheese and sauce fell on his lap. Paul guffawed. Vern looked unhappy. I said I'd get some napkins.

Swinging wide of the big guy and the girls, I walked toward the end of the bar where there was a metal napkin dispenser. I pulled a wad out and swung even wider on the way back.

The big guy seemed to be moving toward me between the tables. I detoured toward the wall but he detoured, too, until he was standing in front of me. I stopped to let him by but he just stood there.

"Excuse me," I said.

"You're not excused," he said.

His T-shirt said BIG JOHN'S, HOUSTON, TEX. He hadn't shaved in a few days and he was scowling. Not that I was any prize.

"Could I get by?" I said.

"You like to horn in on other people's conversations?" he said.

"Not particularly. Mostly I just want to get back to my table before the guys with me eat my pizza."

"Screw your pizza."

I couldn't believe it. People around us were watching. A girl at the closest table got up and took her drink. I stopped smiling.

"I don't want any trouble. Hey, I don't even know who you are. Whatever you're all worked up about, it's got nothing—"

"I'm not worked up. I just don't like some candy-ass listening to my conversation, you know what I'm saying? Why don't you mind your own goddamn business?"

"That's exactly what I'm trying to do."

"You better try harder."

I swallowed drily and looked at him. He was a good two or three inches taller than me, forty or fifty pounds heavier. His hands were at his sides and his eyes were both intent and vague. He smelled like stale beer and cigarettes. I realized my heart was absolutely pounding.

"I'm too old for this crap," I said, my voice far away. "If you want to screw around, do it with somebody else."

"Somebody who isn't scared, Mr. Newspaperman?"

"No," I said. "Somebody who is as big a moron as you are."

I dropped the wad of napkins on the floor. Chairs scraped as people pulled away. My heart was slamming now, like a basketball on concrete. I remembered that my father had told me to guard with my left and keep my punches close to my body. No loopy swings, he had said.

I was eight then. Maybe nine.

The right came first. My left went up to block it. My right shot straight out, aimed at his face but it hit his throat, scraping under his jaw. His teeth clacked and he swung the right again and tried to grab my arm with his left hand.

Everybody was yelling. Screaming. He was against me, trying to push me back. I staggered and the right came around again and crashed into my ear. I heard myself say "Ow," and bent my head lower and moved inside his next swing, jabbing blindly in the direction of his face.

One jab missed.

The next three connected and made a crunching, slapping sound. With the third, I felt something snap. Maybe his nose. His arms closed around me and he flung me sideways into the tables.

I hit my head on something, saw a white flash, and heard him panting as he came toward me. I rolled to the right and pulled myself up on a table, but he was coming at me.

There was blood all over his mouth and chin. The yelling was everywhere, so I couldn't think. I forgot my father's advice and swung a sidearm right. Hard.

I got a lot of air, then as he pulled his head back, my fist grazed his eye and his nose. The eyeball felt wet.

He bellowed and raised his hands to his eyes. I stood and waited. He started for me, then stopped and put his hands to his eyes again. A cop crashed through the crowd of bodies and slammed him to the floor. I was relieved for a moment and then I was on my stomach on the wet linoleum floor with a nightstick pressing into the back of my neck so hard that it hurt.

There was dried blood on my upper lip. I felt it with the tip of my tongue and then touched it gently with my finger. A piece broke off and landed on the desktop. I flicked it on to the floor.

Vigue hung up the phone.

"Badly scratched cornea and a busted nose," he said. "What do you think, Muhammad Ali? Should we stick with the simple assault or go with aggravated? Aggravated's a felony. Look more impressive on your résumé."

I took a deep breath.

"I told you. I couldn't just stand there. He started it, took a swing at me. I haven't been in a fight since third grade, for God's sake."

"Beginner's luck, I guess," Vigue said.

"Come on, Lieutenant. I didn't want to hurt the guy. He was huge. I was just trying to keep him from killing me."

Vigue didn't look up from the form he was filling out.

"Happens," he said. "You get a guy who hasn't been in a fight in his whole life and someone goes after him and he goes berserk. We had one guy break half the bones in another guy's face. Stove him all to hell. Just couldn't stop punching once he got started. I think he was a librarian or something. Looked like a wimp."

He kept writing. I slouched in my chair and looked at the cuts on my knuckles. On Vigue's radio, I could hear the dispatcher calling the Androscoggin ambulance for an elderly man with chest pains.

Vigue yawned.

"You want to know who he is?" he said.

"Sure."

Vigue pulled a torn piece of computer printout from under the form.

"Let's see. Ah, yes. The Dirtbag Hall of Fame. Cormier, Roger D. Twelve eighteen sixty-one. Address used to be fifteen and a half Hancock Street, but he said he's been living with friends. In town and up in Roxbury. Some shithole, no doubt. Let's see. Weight, one eighty-five. Eyes blue."

"Black and blue," I murmured.

Vigue looked up, then back down.

"Mr. Cormier was laid off from the maintenance department at St. Amand last July. They laid off ten people or something back then, if I remember. I don't think he was in the mill long. Works in the woods, mostly. Those boys tend to get a little rambunctious when some flabby foreman tells 'em what to do. So that didn't work out. He said something about wanting to leave town, go work in Oregon or someplace. A big loss for the community. Now, let's see. Arrested for OUI and operating after suspension. But it's been almost, let's see, almost five years since he's been arrested for assault."

"Turned over a new leaf," I said.

Vigue folded the printout and attached it to the report with a paper clip.

"He's a minor-league dirtbag," he said. "Gets drunk and mouthy. Used to like to beat on people, if I remember correctly. May have taken our attitude adjustment course once or twice."

"Needs a refresher."

"He doesn't think so. Mr. Cormier says you cold-cocked him. He asked you about some story about the mill and you cold-cocked him. He informed us that you want to shut the mill down."

"He what?"

"Shut down the mill. A wise-ass New Yorker, I think was the way he put it. Guy from the paper trying to shut down the mill."

"Is that what this is all about? St. Amand stories?"

"I'm just telling you what he said. You called him a moron and took a swing at him. I think, personally, you're running with the wrong crowd."

Vigue stopped and lit a cigarette.

"You shed any light on this?" he said, talking smoke.

I thought for a second.

"I'm writing a story on the mill and the tax-break deal. Just looking at other cases where towns did the same thing with the parent outfit. Not that big a deal."

"Maybe Mr. Cormier thinks it is."

"I don't even know how he'd know about it. He doesn't work there anymore."

"Small town. Hard to keep a secret."

Vigue got up and left the room. I heard a filing cabinet drawer sliding in the booking area. I slumped in the metal folding chair and slid straight again. It hurt no matter how I sat.

My face and head ached. The chair was torture. They probably used it to extract confessions from prisoners who couldn't be broken with rubber hoses and cattle prods.

Vigue came back and I thought I caught a faint smile before he sat down. He was enjoying this, watching the reporter, the know-it-all who was always pestering him for information, squirming, at his mercy.

"I'll tell you what I'm gonna do," he said, feet on his desk, hands on his hips. "I'm not sure you did everything you could to prevent this altercation, but it is a first offense. I think you've learned a lesson."

"Give me a friggin' break."

"What do you want? Special treatment?"

"I think I'm getting it already."

"Maybe you haven't learned that lesson."

"What? Turn the other cheek?"

"Just walk the hell away. Leave the tough-guy stuff to the guys on the TV."

"Yeah, right. So what does he get? Cormier."

"He's been charged with disorderly conduct. That's ours. If you want to file an assault complaint, he'll get that, too. That means you testify as to his actions in the incident. You want to do that?"

"Hell, yes," I said, and winced as the cut on my lip started to open.

"Well, Mr. McMorrow, you can come in here between eight and five tomorrow and fill out a complaint. That complaint is reviewed by the DA, and then we most likely would serve a summons. He would be required to answer the charge in court."

He smiled.

"I testify?"

"That's the way it works, chief. You come to court and say what happened. That's sort of important, since you're the one alleging the offense. We could ask around at the bar, but we don't do real well in getting volunteer witnesses out of that place."

"So if I don't show up, he walks," I said.

"No. He probably pleads on the disorderly, unless he gets a total bozo for a lawyer, which is a pretty good chance. He gets a hundred-dollar fine. You come and play witness and he gets a week in jail, six months chitchatting with probation and parole. He gets one of those good-lookers and he may even thank you."

He gave me a big smile.

"Welcome to the system, friend."

I got up stiffly.

"Yeah, right. I'll let myself out."

And I did, stepping out into the hall, where Vern was reading WANTED posters.

"See anybody you know?" I said.

"Hey, you out?"

"I tied sheets together and crawled under the desks. The car running?"

"And pointed toward the border."

We went outside to where the car was waiting like a faithful spaniel. I got in and reached across to unlock the door for Vern. He reached in and took a box off the backseat and handed it to me. Four slices of cold, congealed pizza.

We drove through town to Vern's in silence. I couldn't think of anything to say. He apparently couldn't either, until we pulled up in front of the apartment house, big and dark with old-lady curtains silhouetted by dim lights on the first floor.

"Myrtle's in bed," Vern said. "Rev this thing and let's watch the curtains move."

I smiled, barely. Vern looked over.

"So when's your next bout?" he said.

"I'm retired. I want to get out now. No lingering Ali decline."

"He retired and then declined. But you took less punches. And that guy was no hack. Hey, Jack, he was the heavy favorite. An upset. Bookies hate it when this happens."

"Yeah, right. Hit him in the eye by accident. I don't even . . . The whole thing is crazy."

I shook my head, felt almost like crying, which would have been awkward. Vern cleared his throat, then reached up to wipe a porthole out of the fog on the inside windshield. Goddamn feeble defroster. Goddamn friggin' town.

"Hey, Jack, don't be so hard on yourself," Vern said, his sympathetic face turned toward me. "It isn't like it was your fault or anything. Guy picked a fight. You weren't hitting on his wife or mouthing off or whatever. Whaddya supposed to do? Stand there and let some meat-head punch you out? Guy could have killed you, you know? It's true."

"It sucks anyway."

"Suck a lot more if you got all your teeth knocked out. Try that on the *Review* dental plan."

"There isn't one."

"Right. Hey, come on. You won. What's the matter with that?"

I shook my head and looked toward my window. It was foggy and I wiped it with my hand. The hand was cut on the knuckles. Vern reached out and squeezed my shoulder, then popped the door and swung out. The pep talk was over. The windshield was fogged. Myrtle's bathroom light came on, then the light in Vern's living room. I'd only been in his place once or twice, just a quick stop while he put on his jacket. It was neat but in a transient sort of way, with a chair, a table, a bed, books in wooden crates. That's all I'd seen.

For a friendly guy, Vern was very private.

I sat in the car and . . . just sat. The pizza box, white with grease spots, was on the passenger seat. I opened it and pulled out a piece of pizza, which was thick and cold and oily. I took a bite, then another, and with the rest of the piece clenched between my teeth, put the car in gear and drove down the block. At the corner, by the Andro-scoggin Elementary School, I turned right and headed back through downtown, left on Route 108, and then on into the darkness beyond the glare of the mill.

Four or five miles out, on the outskirts, where the house trailers were in darkness, I tossed the crust of pizza into the box and let out a long sigh that ended as a shudder.

10

───⟊───

When I woke up, Roxanne was kneeling beside the bed.

"What time is it?" I said.

"What happened to you?" she asked.

"Why aren't you at work?"

"I called and told them I'd be in at noon."

"Cushy government job."

I closed my eyes and a bell rang in Roxanne's kitchen. She left the bedroom and I eased my way out of bed and went to the bathroom. I peered in the mirror at the scabs on my upper lip and the scrapes on my forehead and left cheekbone. My neck was sore to move and there were dark brown bruises on my upper legs and knees. There was a crusty cut on my scalp but that wasn't sore to touch.

My scalp burned when I stepped into the shower so I kept my head out of the spray. I stood and let the hot water run down my neck and back, moving my head in a circle until I could feel the muscles loosening.

I'd make a lousy linebacker.

The fight didn't seem real. Not here, in Roxanne's bathroom, with the dried flowers on the back of the toilet, the dappled Renoir poster, the herbal shampoos and conditioners lined up on the side of the tub. Things were nice here. Safe. Soft. A different world.

I brushed my teeth with Roxanne's toothbrush and found a pink plastic razor in the cabinet. It was dull, and by the time I detoured around the scrapes, it wasn't worth doing at all. Still looking like hell, I searched for my clothes and couldn't find them. I went out into the kitchen in my shorts and stood there like an invalid while Roxanne, still in her bathrobe, finished scrambling eggs, grabbed English muffins from the toaster oven, and pulled the coffeepot from under the machine.

She put a plate down on the table.

"Don't tell me you want an invitation now, after barging in here in the middle of the night," she said, grinning and pulling her robe tie tighter.

"What time is it?" I said.

"It's nine-thirty, and your watch is on the counter where you left it. What the hell happened to you?"

I sat down and she waited. I drank most of the glass of orange juice and put butter and jam on a muffin. Lots of butter. When you might be beaten to death any day, you don't worry about cholesterol. I took a bite and chewed. Roxanne was still waiting. I took another bite and she waited some more.

"I got in a fight," I said, reaching for the juice. "In a bar."

Her jaw didn't so much drop as sag.

"That's it. A fight. A guy tried to punch me out. This big guy."

I drank the juice. Started on the eggs.

"Why do you go to bars like that? You're not in college," Roxanne said, then cut herself off.

I kept eating, trying to chew without moving my upper lip. It slowed me down, but not by much. Roxanne watched me and sipped her coffee.

"You're proud of yourself, aren't you. Men."

I shrugged.

"What'd you do, knock him out or punch his lights out?" she asked.

I smiled. Vern said it. Cormier was no pushover, and I'd won. For a second I pictured him with his hands over his eyes and the blood running down his chin like glaze on a doughnut.

"I don't know what's going on, Jack, but this isn't what I thought I was getting myself involved in. Is this what you do, or is something really wrong?"

I put down my fork. Felt worse instead of better. In the kitchen, there were teal-blue plates on a narrow shelf under the cupboard. Pottery stuff. Spices in jars and a nightlife section of the *Casco Bay Weekly* stuck on the refrigerator.

Normal.

"Do you want to talk about it?" Roxanne said, speaking more softly.

"Yeah," I said. "Maybe we'd better."

I talked for a half-hour and had the rest of the coffee from the pot. Roxanne nibbled a muffin and listened. I minimized the damage to the house and the shock of being in a fight.

"I don't think anybody would kill him over those pictures," Roxanne said. "Not because he took pictures of them. I mean, that isn't their fault. They're victims. They might be mad, and if they caught him in the yard or something, maybe they'd beat him up or call the cops. But what does that have to do with that canal place?"

"I don't know. Maybe nothing."

Roxanne shrugged, then got up and put the dishes in the sink and ran water over them. The pipes of the old house shuddered when she shut off the faucets.

"You know," she said, still facing the dishes, "you could just go by the medical examiner's report."

She paused.

"You're not a cop. You forget that sometimes, I think."

"No, I don't."

"Yes, you do. Sometimes."

No, I don't, I said to myself.

"Sometimes," Roxanne said.

She dried her hands on a dish towel and came back to the table. I pushed my chair back and she leaned on my lap and put her arms around me.

"Could you stop remembering you're not a cop long enough to relax for a couple of hours?" she said. "You're not hurt that bad, are you?"

Her hair glistened and her robe had parted enough to show the white skin of her breasts. I parted it a little more. She waited for me to answer.

"I've got to get back and hand out the checks, and I've got calls to make and—"

"You know the old saying," Roxanne said, sliding into my arms. "All work and no play . . ."

I kissed her.

"I'm glad they didn't name you Leonard," she said, and kissed me again. "Or Raymond. Or Alex. Or Ronald."

It was later, much later, that I considered the rest of the day. We were up and dressed: Roxanne in jeans and a red cotton jersey, me in my jeans of the day before and a big white T-shirt she said had belonged to her brother. I didn't believe her, but I wore it anyway.

Roxanne suggested we go out for lunch in the Old Port, Portland's gentrified waterfront. They'd pushed the fishermen's bars out and replaced them with shops that sold wicker chairs and antiques and elegant clothes. The stores had names like T. Boothby Ltd. and Snap's. The streets were filled with new Volvos and Saabs and people from L.L. Bean catalogs.

The fishermen weren't missing much.

I didn't say this to Roxanne. She was younger and, like all young people who live in cities, liked little restaurants that served up pseudo-ethnic food. She wanted to go to a place that was supposed to be Caribbean or something and served spicy broiled fish. I could picture us eating broiled Mahi-mahi, drinking Jamaican beer that was fifty cents a bottle in Kingston but four bucks a bottle in Maine. What was wrong with clam chowder and a Budweiser?

It just didn't thrill me, the idea of sitting in some place where all the men were good-looking, the women white and blonde and of obvious good breeding. And then there'd be me, the guy with the cuts on his face, who was wondering where they put all the mothers and grandmothers, much less the poor people.

So I said I had to get back to Androscoggin, which I did. Roxanne looked disappointed but beautiful, and went into the kitchen to mix up some tuna salad for an early lunch. I had mine on whole wheat, with a Labatt's from the back of her refrigerator. Roxanne had hers on a small rye toast. With spring water.

"You see what I mean?" Roxanne said, taking small, surgical bites. "If Arthur's down there and he's killed, it's premeditated because somebody had to get him down there. Like an execution. You don't execute somebody because he takes dirty pictures."

"Not usually."

"He was weird," Roxanne said. "Maybe he was into something else. I don't know. Maybe he did more with these pictures than just look at them."

Well, we knew what *something more* meant. Blackmail. Get a shot of the guy with his secretary and then squeeze them for cash. But Arthur? What did he want? Certainly not money.

"I just can't picture it. There wasn't anything greedy about him. He didn't want, I don't know, things. God, if you could see how he lived."

"Was it awful?"

"No; you see worse, I'm sure. It wasn't that it was a shack or anything. It was just this back of what had been his business. Like me sleeping in the back of the newspaper office."

"For years."

"Right," I said. "It isn't poverty. It's existence."

"It's a different world," Roxanne said.

I finished my beer and nodded.

"You're telling me," I said.

"But it was nice of you to visit," she said, a soft smile bringing back instant images of the morning.

"Sure beats the phone, doesn't it?"

I was halfway to my desk before I realized I was supposed to be in traction or on crutches, or at least battered beyond recognition.

"Jack!" Cindy called, squeezing as much concern into the one word as any Shakespearean actor ever could. "Are you all right?"

"Yeah, fine," I said, but it was too late.

They crowded around, Cindy helping me with my coat, and Paul and Vern and Marion hovering as if to help me to my seat.

"Paul said you kicked his ass—whoops, sorry," Cindy said. "I knew Cormier in high school. He was this big goof, and he went out with this girl I knew, but she couldn't stand him, so she finally dumped him, and then he started seeing this girl from Dixfield, so none of us saw him much after that. Thank God. You're lucky he didn't break your hands or something; you wouldn't be able to type."

I stood there and felt my Roxanne glow drain away.

"Okay," I said. "I appreciate it, the concern and everything, but it really wasn't that big a deal. Really. Nothing. Foolishness I wish I'd never had anything to do with. Thanks, but let's just forget it."

"Come on, Jack," Paul said, tapping me on the shoulder. "It isn't every day the editor of the paper gets in a friggin' fight and actually wins."

"I wish it was no day."

Oh, God. They looked hurt again. I gave them a smile and thanked them for carrying on without me for the morning.

"Any messages?" I said.

"You got a call," Cindy said. "Correction from last week. In the sentences? Guy says we put him down for six months in jail when it should have been six days. He was ripped. And I think maybe he'd been drinking. He said he'd call back."

She headed for the counter.

"And Martin was in for his check," Cindy said. "I told him you'd be in later, and he said he'd be back. And another thing, you might think this is queer, but I didn't know what to do. Arthur got a check. You want me to send it back or what?"

To where? His estate? Probate court?

"Leave it and I'll take care of it," I said.

She high-heeled her way back to me and handed over two blue envelopes.

"All yours," she said.

I stuffed them in my pocket and walked out the door. Better to drop Martin's check at his house than get stuck talking with him all afternoon. And better for me to get out of Roxanne's brother's shirt. He might need it for the family reunion.

Martin's house was on Monument Street in a neighborhood of small brick Victorian houses originally built for middle management people at the mill. They weren't grand, but they were on a hill overlooking the town. What was more important was that they were downwind.

I left the car running in the driveway and went up the steps to the glassed-in porch. As I raised my hand to knock, the inside door rattled and dogs started yipping on the other side of the door.

"Michael! Tillie! It's Mr. McMorrow. Now you behave yourselves. Oh, these dogs. Now get down before I have to . . ."

The door opened and two dachshunds flashed out past me and then back on to the porch, barking the whole way but at nothing in particular. I stepped in and saw Pauline Wiggins standing at the inner door that went into the house.

"Hi, Mrs. Wiggins," I said, and offered the envelope. "This is for Martin. His check. I was going home and I thought I'd save him the trip."

She opened the door wider.

"Come in now, Mr. McMorrow, don't worry about your shoes. I'll get Martin. What do you take in your coffee, dear?"

Martin's voice came from inside the house.

"That Jack? Well, have him come in, Pauline. Have him come in. Jack, come on in, good to see you. Get you a cup of coffee? Pauline, get Jack a cup of coffee. Mike. Tillie. No. Get in there."

Outnumbered and outflanked, I surrendered.

The house smelled old, like Martin's coats and old tweed jackets, and even like his breath. I'd been there twice before, but had never come in this far.

"Coffee cake, Martin," Pauline was saying, leading the way into the kitchen. "Did you finish that coffee cake? I told you not to eat all of it. Sometimes I wonder. Oh, good. That's enough. I won't have any."

She was a retired high-school English teacher and she ran the house like a study hall. I remembered that from the last time when she had been nagging Martin about the garden hose and leaving it out, and how she had told him to put it away and he hadn't, and now he'd driven over it and she didn't know if it had a crack in it and it was practically new.

Pauline was like the dogs, nipping and yipping at Martin's heels. He was deferential but resigned, like somebody who'd once thought of rebellion but had buried the idea deep over the years.

"Sit down, Jack," Martin said. "Give me your coat."

I handed him the coat and the check. He folded the envelope and put it in the breast pocket of his flannel shirt.

"Keep the bill collectors away another month," he said.

Pauline put coffee in mugs and cream and sugar on the table. Everything matched, with salmon-colored flowers that went with the wallpaper. She went to a drawer and took out matching cloth napkins with embroidered W's and put one at each of three seats.

Oh, Lord, I thought.

The last time I'd been at the Wiggins house, we'd sat on the porch and looked at bound volumes of the *Review* from the thirty years when Martin was editor. The papers were folksy, with correspondents from each little hollow who made sure that the readers knew everything everyone had done in the past week, whom they'd seen, where they'd gone after church on Sunday.

After that, Martin had taken me into the den to see his guns. They were oiled and polished and displayed on racks on the wall like trophies: rifles, shotguns, revolvers. A Parker twelve-gauge shotgun he'd inherited from his father. It didn't mean much to me but I'd tried to seem impressed. Nothing like an old gun to get your blood moving.

The guns and old papers were nice, but what really made an impression on me was Pauline's pride in her husband's work, and the implication that I had a big pair of shoes to fill. It was like he had to be somebody to be married to her. It was small-town status-seeking mixed up with affection and pride, and it was interesting to watch and listen. Interesting to a point.

"You working today?" Martin asked.

"A little," I said. "Yesterday was long, going to press and all."

"Oh, yeah. The big crunch. We used to get back at dawn, sleep for an hour, and then have to go back in to open at eight o'clock. But we loved it."

"We didn't have these computers," Pauline said, handing me the plate of cake. "It was all typewriters and hot lead and all the rest of it. But I'd be down there every night after school. Couldn't keep me away. Sometimes I think I chose the wrong career, don't I, Martin?"

Martin didn't answer.

"You'd go down after teaching every day?" I said, sipping the coffee.

"Oh my, yes," Pauline said, warming up. "I started going down to the *Androscoggin Review* back when I was still in high school and Martin and I were keeping company, back when I was a junior. I was just a girl, and my father, he was a manager at the mill; he thought this newspaper business was really not the most reputable thing, but I insisted, and he wanted me to be happy. Papa always did want me to be happy."

"So you've been together ever since high school?"

"Oh, yes," Pauline said, while Martin watched and perhaps listened. "High school and then teachers' college, and then it was that next summer we were married. That was right after the Depression, and then there was the war, but we survived, with the grace of God."

"That's a long time to be together," I said, finishing the coffee.

"Fifty-one years," Pauline said. "We weren't blessed with children, but we were blessed in other ways. These young people today—oh, you'll think we're old codgers or something—but these young people today. Divorces and not getting married and fighting over the children and this and that. We were lucky, I think. Martin had the paper and I had my teaching. Felt like half the town was my children, what with the school. But it was much smaller then. Oh, a different town. A different time, but that's life, right?"

"Surprised you never tied the knot, Jack," Martin said abruptly.

I smiled. How did he know I hadn't been married five times?

"I'm waiting for the right one to come along," I said. "This girl I saw in the office last week. She looked like the right woman to me. Pretty thing; you would have thought so, Pauline."

"Local girl, Mr. McMorrow?" Pauline asked.

"Portland," I said.

The doorbell rang and the dogs went skating across the linoleum on their claws. I got up and drifted that way with Martin. An older woman was at the door with an empty dish that she gave to Pauline.

Martin and I went out on the lawn, where a man in a pickup truck was waiting.

"Martin," I said. "I was going to tell you. I was at Arthur's, and I saw this old picture of you—at least, it looks like you. I don't know. You're sitting with this girl. I figured it was back when you were a swinging bachelor."

He looked at me funny and didn't say anything.

"I took it by mistake, looking for some stuff for the paper. I was going to give it to you."

Martin still looked funny.

"Oh, yeah," he said vaguely, and then the dogs had bolted out the door and he was calling them and I walked to the car, which after a half-hour was still running. Nothing like Swedish technology.

I got in, waved, and drove off.

I went home, and at four-thirty, was back at the office in a clean shirt and corduroys.

Martin was waiting on the sidewalk.

11

He was at my side as soon as I got out of the car.

"Jack," Martin said. "I was just wondering about that picture. The one with me in it. I was wondering if I could have it now. Probably wouldn't mean much to anybody else, so long ago. Nice to hang on to, you know? I know you're busy, but I'll go in with you and get it, take it off your hands."

I shut the car door. A four-wheel-drive pickup with loud exhaust blared by, and I waited.

"You knew what I was talking about? Which one?"

"I think so," Martin said.

He looked cold, with pale cheeks.

"You and a girl," I said. "You're sort of hugging. Maybe not hugging. Sort of leaning. And she's got her head on your shoulder."

"Old friend of mine. Nancy, I think. We were part of the same crowd, way back when."

"How would Arthur end up with something like that, of yours?"

"Oh, you know him. Pack rat. That place out there. You know he's lucky he didn't have a fire, all that stuff in there. That way for years."

"So he picked it up someplace?"

"Could have been anywhere. In the office. The old office, I mean. On Cross Street. Upstairs; you don't remember that."

His voice trailed off and we stood there on the sidewalk with the cars going by and every once in a while, somebody waving. It wasn't supposed to be important, but I got the feeling that it was. That something very important was going on in this awkward little conversation.

"Pretty girl, Martin," I said.

"Oh, yeah," he said.

He looked distressed.

"I'll just run in," Martin said.

"I don't have it," I said.

"But I thought you said—"

"I had to give it to the cops. I told you I was going to give it to you but I couldn't. It was part of Arthur's belongings."

Martin stammered, "But it belongs to me. It didn't belong to him."

"Cops don't know that. I didn't know that. It's old. They probably won't even know who it is."

A woman walked by and said, "Hi, Mr. Wiggins."

Martin didn't seem to hear her.

"What will they do with it?" he asked.

"I don't know. Maybe put it in with his estate. All that other stuff. Depends on how long the investigation takes. You could ask them."

I took a couple of steps toward the office door. Martin started following me, then stopped. I said, "So long," and went inside.

First fighting, I thought. Now lying.

More beginner's luck.

The picture was in the manila file folder in the drawer in my desk.

Young Martin and the pretty girl. Embracing and mooning at each other. A soulful gaze. Not an old buddy. And the girl was not a girl.

It was quiet in the office. Everybody had been paid and they had left, except for Cindy, who was on the phone to a friend, and Marion, who was setting copy. I sat at my desk and looked at the picture more closely.

The girl was not a girl. She was a woman. She had long slender legs and she was wearing clunky white shoes. Not shoes from the early thirties. Shoes from the forties. Postwar shoes. Martin would have been in his early thirties.

And married.

So Martin had been screwing around. That intimacy in the gaze. Complicity. Knowing eyes.

Fifty-one years, they had been together. From high school to the war, through two other wars to today. With a little something on the side, as they used to say.

I stuck the picture in the folder with the picture of Joy the Wonder Waitress, shut and locked the drawer. I was in deeper. But maybe I wasn't alone.

Martin didn't want that picture to hang on the living room wall. He knew what it was. He'd known exactly what I'd meant, even back at his house. I'd seen the look in his eyes. The look was fear and it was immediate, more immediate than it would have been if he hadn't seen this picture in forty years.

I thought of Roxanne's questions. Why would Arthur take pictures of women? For fun or blackmail? Now, why would Arthur have a picture of Martin? Why would it be in his private collection?

I got up and, with a wave to Cindy, who was still on the phone, walked out the door.

The questions were with me all evening. I cleaned the kitchen and the bathroom. I picked up all the soiled clothes and put them in trash bags and brought them to a Laundromat in the Village Shopping Center, just west of town, miles from anything that resembled a village. The Very Edge of Civilization Shopping Center, maybe, but not a village.

While I was waiting for the laundry, I went two stores up to a stereo shop, walked in, and cut the clerk off before he could tell me they were closing. I said I wanted something basic and I could spend five hundred dollars. Fifteen minutes later, the backseat was filled with cartons and I was again on the road to music.

Whoever the apartment trashers were, I owed them one.

I drove home, dumped the laundry in the bedroom, and set the stereo up along the living room wall. It was higher-tech than my old one but did the same thing. It played Dave Brubeck and I cleaned. The moon was rising behind the bare trees, and in spite of the music, I felt very much alone.

Or maybe because of it.

Gerry Mulligan's sax was playing, low and soft and rippling like muscles. I put down the mop and went to the window and looked out.

It was ghostly in the moonlight, with the silhouettes of the black trunks of the trees and the black ridges that ran along to the west of the house. It got darker here than it did in the city, and it did it abruptly, always catching you off guard and leaving you thinking that the day had been abbreviated, called home early, that it had left without a formal good-bye. In the city, when the sun was jerked down behind the next block, lights went on to replace it. Here, in this town on the edge of wilderness, there were no lights. Or maybe just one or two. A lone streetlight that flickered with the wavering branches. A faraway lamp in somebody's den that showed dim in the distance, and when that somebody pulled the shade, showed dimmer still.

I stood and looked, leaning on the windowsill, my face near the cold glass, and wondered what the hell I was doing here. It was a feeling I had gotten only once or twice before, on bad days when I was lonely. I knew more people now. I had taken a lover, taken her just that morning. But I still felt alone. And worse than that, deep down, when everything stopped and I wasn't working or talking or drinking, I felt afraid.

Staring, I tried to shake it off. It had been a lousy week. The apartment. The fight. Arthur. Only a numb fool could be unconcerned, right? But then the feeling crept back, the one that was worse than the fear itself. It was the realization that it was the same feeling I'd had in the city. The feeling I got when I saw the younger reporters passing me on their way to the far reaches of East Brooklyn and the Bronx. The same fear that had brought me to this town, where I talked to school kids and told them I had just needed a change.

The fear that I'd made some giant, irreversible mistake.

I could stay, alone with myself, or I could leave. At eight, I drove back downtown and circled Main Street. The lights were out at the *Review* and all the stores looked closed, not for hours, but for a decade. I drove around again and circled back to the police station, parking the Volvo next to the police cruisers, where it looked like a refugee from Eastern Europe.

Vigue was there, with LeMaire, J. and a couple of reserves, young kids whom I had not formally met. LeMaire, J. was sitting at a desk reading an equipment catalog and Vigue was standing, one black boot up on a chair.

"I'm not knocking it," he said, as I came through the doorway. "Don't get me wrong."

One kid, short and squat with a red nose, nodded.

"I'm not knocking it. I got no complaints. I'm just saying, hey, there's a few things I've learned. Like, mister, don't expect a pat on the back. You know why? 'Cause it ain't coming. No matter what you do. And it don't come in the paycheck, either. Work in this place almost twenty years and you make what they get in that mill to start. Sometimes I think I should have my head examined. 'What do you do?' 'I chase shitheads around, and every once in a while, one of 'em tries to take my head off.' 'Oh, how nice.' "

The kids shifted in their uniforms and looked unhappy.

"You know where it's got to come from?" Vigue said. "It's got to come from inside. If it doesn't, you might as well take off that badge and all that equipment and go over to that mill and fill out an application. I mean it. Take it right off tonight and go over to that mill. If you don't have it in here for this job, forget it."

"Forty-five bucks for a little belly-band holster," LeMaire, J. said, peering at the pages of the catalog. "Maybe I won't put in for detective after all."

Vigue looked at me.

"And these guys," he said. "Only two words you need to know. *No* and *comment*. Don't turn your back. They'll whack you good. Speaking of whacking, that lawyer get hold of you yet?"

"Nope," I said.

"Cormier's. They want you to drop the assault charge. Poopsie doesn't want it on his record."

"Tough."

"Hey, it's up to you. Just one more dirtball. State pays for the lawyer. Lawyer gets him off. He goes out and does it again. We pay for another lawyer. He goes on welfare. System works just fine."

"So if I don't file the complaint?"

"He gets the disorderly, Class D. Misdemeanor. Pays the hundred bucks or whatever the judge decides on. The lawyer said something about him being ready to go back to work in the woods. I guess they don't take dirtballs."

"The rest of it just gets dropped?" I asked.

"Righto, chief. And I don't care one way or the other. I get paid every two weeks. You afraid of the guy or something, get the jitters, let him walk. But just one thing: Don't complain that the police department isn't doing anything about crime in Androscoggin. 'Cause you'll know what we're up against. Every friggin' day."

"Second the motion," LeMaire, J. said.

The kids looked puzzled, as if they weren't sure if I was the enemy. One made up his mind and gave me a cold stare. Vigue took a portable radio out of the charging rack and went out the door. I followed and stood behind him as he scraped the windshield.

"So anything on Bertin?" I asked.

Vigue scraped.

"Off the record?" he said.

"Sure."

"It'll take time."

"Talk to any of the people in those pictures?"

"I will. The ones I can make out. But don't look for much, all right? And don't come down here every day to bug me about it. Every couple days, maybe. Go easy on yourself."

"So you're gonna track those people down?"

"Jesus, don't make such a big deal out of it. We'll make some inquiries. But they won't say much, I promise you that. I go to that waitress at the Pine Tree and say, 'You may not have known it, but this guy you didn't know took your picture through a window when you were taking off your clothes, and now he's dead.' She says, 'Great. What's the bad news?' "

He put the scraper in the trunk.

"Think they knew him?"

"Doubt it. But what do you think? I told you we can't do it alone."

"What about state cops?"

"Staties? As far as they're concerned—and this is off the record; if you print it, I'll hang you—they think Arthur is some chump who fell in the water. They've got enough real live homicides with guns and knives to worry about some jerkoff who goes for a swim in friggin' November."

Cindy had left me a note and my messages before locking up. A lawyer named Richard Roberts had called from Auburn. Probably Cormier's court-appointed. A dirty business, that.

Somebody named Mrs. Gilbert wanted me to call her before five. It was quarter to six. I put the messages on my desk and put my feet up.

On Main Street, snow flurries showed in the strings of colored Christmas lights, and passing cars left black tracks on the whitened street. Across the street, the girl at McLaine's Fine Fashions was struggling to lock the door. She was probably swearing like a trooper, but I couldn't hear her.

Turn off the sound and the town looks quaint. Get too close and you hear the cursing, feel the hopelessness and discontent. I felt like somebody was turning up the volume, louder and louder. If I stayed very still, I could hear the sound of Arthur hitting the water.

12

I tried to find something to do that night but nothing felt right. After looking at the *Lewiston Sun* and a day-old *Boston Globe*, I went home to the carnage and made my usual tuna sandwich, opened a can of Ballantine Ale. I ate half the sandwich and felt full. The beer tasted funny, but I forced myself to finish it as I leafed through the manuals for my new stereo equipment. The writing in the manuals was ungrammatical and depressing. I put them down and put Brubeck back on. Four guys playing a song a long time ago, plinking at a piano, tooting on horns. I turned it off.

After I cleaned up the kitchen a little more, I got another beer and stood at the counter with the unopened can in my hand. I took the phone and dialed Roxanne's number but it rang busy. A pang of jealousy came and went, a flash of some pretty-boy skier. But could he write an editorial?

I turned off the lights and pulled a kitchen chair up to the window by the table. With the lights out, I could see the snow falling behind the house. It was snowing softly and deliberately, and I sat with my feet up on the table and watched. For an hour, the only sound was the creaking of the joints in the chair when I shifted my weight. And then I heard something in the hall.

I got up slowly and moved quietly to the kitchen door. I heard it again. The scrape of a shoe. I waited. Listened. Waited. Then yanked the door open.

A man in a dark overcoat was standing in the hallway. His back was to me but then he turned. And smiled.

Martin.

"What are you doing here?" I asked.

"Didn't want to bother you, at home, at night," he said.

So he'd just stand in the hallway until I came out?

"You're not bothering me," I said. "You want to come in?"

"You're not doing anything?" Martin said.

"Just watching the snow."

"Just watching the snow, huh," he said.

What, I thought. An echo in here?

Martin was wearing a fur hat, the kind Russians wear. I'd heard that he had one, that people in town called him Khrushchev when he wore it. It was a gift from somebody, I thought, but I couldn't remember the whole story. I didn't feel like asking.

"Coffee?"

"Okay. Sure," Martin said.

I turned the burner on and put some water in a saucepan, then took two mugs from beside the sink and put instant coffee in them from the jar. We stood and waited for the water to boil. I stayed by the stove; Martin leaned against the counter about six feet away. The water on the burner began to hiss.

"So what's up?"

"The picture."

I waited.

"I'd really like to have it. You've got to get it for me, if you would, I mean. Could you? Just tell them you need it for the paper. I thought you could tell them that. You need it for the paper for . . . I don't know what for. You could think of something."

I got the mugs and put them on the stove.

"They'd give it to you," Martin said. "They know you."

I felt like a priest or a politician or a Mafia don, hearing a request from a supplicant. Martin watched me for any faint glimmer of agreement.

"Martin, what's the big deal?" I said, pushing at the saucepan. "I don't understand why this is such a big thing."

He started to speak and stopped and looked away, toward the living room. I could smell his big old overcoat. It was starting to dry and it smelled like damp wool. The water started to simmer, and I poured it into the mugs and put one on the counter beside him. It was a Mets mug, but Martin didn't notice, or at least didn't comment.

We stood for a minute. Martin hadn't moved from his spot against the counter. I looked at him. He seemed smaller and older here, out of his natural setting and in mine. The newspaper—the office, the atmosphere—added to his stature somehow. Here he seemed small and tired, so much so that I almost decided against asking him about Arthur.

Almost.

"Can I ask you something, Martin? Another topic, but I wanted to ask you. Arthur. I was wondering if, when you were working with him, if you thought he was sort of funny about things. About women and things like that."

He looked at me.

"Martin, I can talk between us, right? Well, the cops think Arthur took pictures of women. Between us now. He took these pictures of women without their clothes on. They think Arthur hid in the bushes at night and took pictures of ladies getting undressed, that kind of thing."

Martin looked at the floor.

"I don't know," he mumbled, turning his hat in his hand.

"You sure he never did anything like that? Anything even sort of like that?"

He looked down. I waited. He looked some more and I waited some more. Any reporter knows that sometimes you filled the gaps in a conversation and sometimes you just waited while the person squirmed, searching for an out.

I sipped the coffee. It was awful because the water hadn't been hot enough.

"Well, hell," Martin said.

I waited. Martin tried the coffee and ran his hand over his mouth. I wondered if he even had the words in his vocabulary: voyeur, sexually repressed, stunted social development.

"I don't know, Jack," he said, finally. "Arthur was never much for the ladies. I don't know. The only thing I can think of is this time when there was this thing with the cheerleader girls at the high school. But that wasn't like this that you're talking about."

"What was it?"

"Pictures of basketball cheerleaders. You know, the little girls in their little skirts and what all."

"He took pictures of them?"

"Well, yeah. Nothing wrong with that, but he kept 'em in a book."

"A scrapbook of cheerleader pictures?"

"Well, yeah. Like a notebook with these prints pasted in it."

"How'd you find out about it?"

"He had some on his negatives one time. Five shots of the game and fifteen of the girls. I asked him, and he said it was for them, that they wanted some pictures, and he did it just to be nice. Then a couple of the kids complained to their parents and the parents called me and I had to have a talk with him. Known each other forever. I don't know if that made it any easier. But he told me he kept pictures of the kids over the years in a book sort of thing. Didn't mean any harm. This one mother said she was going to the police if he kept it up, and I told him that, and that put the fear of God in him, I'd say. I didn't hear much about it after that. But this wasn't like you're talking about."

"How long ago?"

"Oh, five years. Maybe more. These days, when I say something was five years ago, it's more like ten."

I took a drink of coffee and swallowed.

"That's like your picture, isn't it, Martin," I said. "Taken without your permission, I mean."

I said it directly and let it hang. Martin looked away and opened his mouth, then closed it. I waited. I wasn't going to help him and he knew it. He could either turn around and walk out the door or tell me. I looked right into his face, counted the pores on his red nose. He stayed.

It took a half-hour and another cup of coffee, but I got an answer —at least as much as I could expect.

He had heard she had died ten years before or more, and he hadn't seen her in forty years. He said he never knew her very well. When the picture was taken, he was thirty-five, and she was about five years younger. They were both married.

Martin called it his "episode." Pauline never knew about it, he said, but Arthur did. Arthur knew because the woman in the picture, with the dreamy Hollywood gaze and pretty legs, was his mother. Arthur's mother. Her name was Meredith, and her husband drank and didn't come home. She was pretty and it happened. Martin pronounced her name as if it hurt.

"So we used to sit," he said, his voice raspy. "That's what we did. Young people today don't just sit anymore. They roll around in the back of some car, and that's why you see these babies being born all over the place. But back then, you could just see somebody without getting into bed right off the bat, and that's what we did. In the afternoon, by the eddy of the river up in Byron. I told Pauline I had to go out on an assignment. I always took my notebook. It wasn't that much. We'd just sit and talk, mostly. I'd talk and she'd listen and she'd talk and I'd listen and we'd sit there and she'd . . . she'd hold my hand. We'd kiss and sit close together. Just sit. That's it. It wasn't this terrible thing."

His eyes had a deadened look, as if he'd had this conversation with himself a thousand times over the years.

"Never did it before and never since," Martin said. "Not like today, everybody and his brother having affairs and dumping the wife for a new model."

"What about the picture?"

He flinched.

"That goddamn picture. Goddamn thing. I didn't even know there was one until a couple months ago. Oh, God. I get this letter in the mail; Pauline is downtown. It's from Arthur. I saw him every day on the street for forty years and he sends me this letter saying—oh, I couldn't believe it, still can't—saying I'm his father. His real father."

"Where did the picture come in?"

"He said he had a picture of us in the backyard on Center Street. We sat over there one time, fools. He says in the letter he took it from the roof. What was he? Twelve? Younger? I didn't know him much then. He was in school when this went on. After all these years . . ."

"So what did he want?"

"I don't know, Jack. That's what was so terrible. Like torture. He never said what he wanted. Money. Or whatever it was, who knows. I just didn't know what to say, so I didn't say anything."

"And you want the picture back so Pauline won't see it?"

"It wasn't anything. Jack, today they swap wives like fishing stories. Don't like the one you have, trade her in. This was nothing."

"But Pauline wouldn't think that?"

He shook his head.

"Did you ask Arthur for it?" I said.

"I tried to, but he'd just walk away. Wouldn't talk about it, or at least he didn't try. I didn't either, I guess. I don't think he was all right in the head. I think he was having some sort of breakdown. Imagine coming up with something like that after all these years. Who knows what went on in his mind?"

"I'd like to, but I can't give the picture back," I said.

Martin looked stunned.

"That's the way it is, Martin. It's a police case. Arthur's dead. His stuff is all evidence, and that picture was part of his stuff, his belongings. I'm sorry, but . . ."

"Well, Jack," Martin said, his voice slow and hard like I'd never before heard it. "Do you know what this will do to an old lady? Do you? This whole goddamn town will know. You know what this place is like. It will be out, and that woman, after all these years, will be a laughingstock. Don't you know what this town is like? Don't you?"

I just looked at him, my mug still in my hand in front of me. I looked and he suddenly put his mug on the counter and turned and went out the door. From my place in the kitchen, I stood and listened to his footsteps on the stairs.

For a little guy who didn't say much, Arthur sure knew how to make trouble.

Maybe I should have told Martin that his secret was safe. It was locked in the drawer with the Wonder Waitress. The waitress was safe, too.

It was Saturday morning, and I was sitting at my desk looking at the two pictures, the works of a lifelong voyeur, the bookends of a long and secret career. Arthur Bertin, a retrospective.

The logical thing would have been to turn both of them over to the cops and go about my business. But it would not be that easy. Would I tell the cops about my conversation with Martin? Who would I tell? Vigue? Go over his head to some state cop who would go right to Vigue with the information? What would Vigue do? Go right to Martin and ask him? Say Jack McMorrow says you had reason to want

Arthur Bertin dead? How the hell did I get stuck in the middle of this mess?

And now Vigue wanted me to go to court, or at least that was the way it seemed. I went over the conversation again in my mind. I don't care, he said. I used to, but I don't . . . Go in the mill and start at what I make here after eighteen years . . . Scraping the snow off his car . . . I'll make some inquiries but don't push me . . . What do I do, go up to the waitress at the Pine Tree and say, Hey, some guy was taking your picture, and now he's dead, and she says—

The waitress. I looked at the picture, the shape of her thighs, the wide shoulders. The waitress.

I felt sick.

He had said *waitress*. He had said the waitress at the Pine Tree . . . He had said it, and I had never given him the picture. I had kept it and he had said *waitress*. I had shown him the others, the girl at the bank, but not this one. The waitress was right here in front of me, and *waitress* was what he had said.

What was going on; what was happening? I knew it. I didn't have notes, but I could remember his voice as he said it, the sound the scraper made on the windshield of the police cruiser, the sneer in his voice as he pictured walking in and saying this to the waitress.

She says, Yeah, what's the bad news?

The door slammed open.

"Hey, Jackson, baby. Dig those scoops. Unearth that news. Jackson, I see a Pulitzer in your future."

"Hey, Vern baby," I said. "You hung over or just glad to be alive?"

"Jackson, I love my job," he said, hopping up on Paul's desk and sitting on top of a couple of camera-ready ads worth eighty or ninety bucks. "You know, you and me are lucky to have found stimulating careers in journalism here in this news hot spot we call western Maine. Some people only dream of such a fate."

"They're called nightmares."

"Oh, Jack. Don't tell me you're feeling pangs about leaving the big city. The glitter and glamour. Dinner with the Saltzbergers."

"That's Sulzbergers," I said. "Them, too."

I paused to break his stride.

"You're in rare form. What's up?" I said.

Vern swung his legs.

"Nothing much, but then again, it doesn't take much to make me embrace life on this planet. I thought I'd start my column, my basketball crystal ball. This afternoon, off to Lewiston for a round robin."

Vern took a toothpick out of his shirt pocket.

"Mint," he said.

"Nothing but the best," I said.

"Nothing but."

He sat on the desk and worked the toothpick around in his mouth.

"Martin as straight as he seems? Pillar of the community and all that?" I asked.

"Polly pure," Vern said. "Church on Sunday, passes the plate."

He didn't ask why I wanted to know. It was a curious thing about Vern. I could stop in the middle of a conversation about the Red Sox and ask him if he had ever been spelunking. He would say no, or yes, and we would start up with baseball where we'd left off.

"They never had kids?"

"Nope. Pauline scared the sperm cells away," Vern said. "No, that's not nice. No, they don't have children. No, I don't know why."

"She pretty tough in the classroom?"

"I guess she was," Vern said. "You know. The ramrod-tough teacher who the kids respect and all that. I guess she was a good teacher. I've been told she got a lot of kids to go to college who otherwise wouldn't."

"Robbing the mill of the best and the brightest?"

"Snatching them out of its gaping maw."

Vern opened his mouth wide, threw the pick in, and chomped it. I grinned.

"Martin ever get upset with her? He seems sort of henpecked or something."

"Oh, she kept him in line," Vern said, looking through the stuff on Paul's desk. "I think she probably wrote three-quarters of the editorials, but who knows now. Martin wasn't a great writer. Really had to work at it. He's written a couple of things for me that took mega-editing."

He waited as a pulp truck downshifted out front, sending out a cloud of blue diesel smoke.

"Martin used to put the phone down sometimes. This is way back, I don't know, five years, when I first got here. I'd hear him say, 'Who the hell does she think she's talking to? A child?' But he kept it to himself. Funny thing was, she was nice as pie to him whenever I saw them together. Motherly, almost."

The phone rang and Vern jumped down off the table. His gut shook when he hit the floor.

"You never know what people are like in the privacy of their own homes," he said, walking to his desk. "Good morning! *Androscoggin Review*. What can we do you for?"

Vern talked, something about a club notice that hadn't been in, and I thought about Martin and Pauline. My time in their kitchen told me that she was the dominant one of the pair, but there was something motherly about the way she treated him. And he seemed to care about her. Maybe that was true love. True love with one brief lapse, long ago but not forgotten.

Vern spotted somebody walking across the street and took off out the door, his jacket in one hand and a notebook in the other. I tried to work but ended up answering the phones, taking three briefs and scheduling a photo of the fifth-grade science fair at Androscoggin Elementary. The teacher said we did it every year, and she was probably right.

We aimed to please, after all.

Arthur had liked those assignments. He'd line up all the kids and get them to smile Norman Rockwell smiles and then bark at them to stay in line until he got their names down in order in his grimy little notebook. He printed in tiny letters and used the same notebook for months, putting everything down: assignments, hours, expenses. I wondered if he'd had a notebook on him when they found him.

Arthur.

The bushes rustle. He strains to focus the Nikkormat in the dark. The shutter clicks, the winder turns. Click. Turn. Click. Like a twig snapping over and over, the same sound, and clothing falls away as the figure passes in front of the window.

Leave those cheerleaders alone, Martin says. Arthur says nothing. Sees the swish of pleated skirts, hears the squeak of sneakers on the polished gym floor.

Arthur in the ice water, turns blue and white. Hauled out by the ankles, some chump who goes for a swim. So I go to the waitress, Vigue says.

I'd like to give you your picture, but I can't.

The phone rang again. I sat with my pictures and stared.

13

Ten miles north of Androscoggin, the road turns into a dipping, twisting, two-lane strip with treacherous iced patches where the pavement is shaded by thick banks of dark green spruce trees.

I drove slowly, between thirty-five and forty-five, occasionally taking the beer can from between my thighs and taking a sip. I had no destination other than a vague plan to head north to Andover and swing west until I hit a road that would take me back to Route 2, either in Maine, near Bethel, or over the border in New Hampshire. There was a road that went that way, coming into Route 26 somewhere north of Grafton Notch, but I'd never driven it. I hoped it was passable for the Volvo, but up this far north it was hard to predict. Maps told you there was some sort of road there, but not whether it was filled with potholes or washed out, or, in spring, turned to muck. It was uncharted territory and I liked it.

It was midafternoon and I'd worked at the office for three hours, rewriting press releases and putting them in the system. Marion couldn't handle the load herself, and that left me, the Renaissance man of Maine newspapers. I had dutifully typed in notes from the Daughters of the American Revolution and announcements from the

Androscoggin Center Calvary Church and then had gone and bought three beers, a bag of pretzels, and a tank full of gas. I had left town like a captain leaving the harbor.

A woman I'd been involved with when I was a little—but not a lot—younger had said these jaunts were an indication that I wasn't able to cope with the pressures of my life. She suggested counseling. I disagreed. The rides were my way of putting things in perspective, I had told her. She never approved, and one day, not long after one especially probing discussion of my problems, we decided to go our separate ways. One less thing with which to cope.

She never complained about my grammar.

In the first hour, I passed through the town of Andover, a wood-mill town with a store where pickup trucks were drawn up like horses outside a western saloon. I drove to the center of the village, turned left at the flashing yellow light, and drove west toward the White Mountains. For the next thirty miles, the Volvo was the only car in sight. Roadside ledges gave way to splintered cliffs, and the sun flick-ered in and out in an early mountain-style sunset.

Without the sun, it got colder. There was more snow here, and the woods looked black and deep. It was starkly beautiful but deadly in winter, especially to someone who had no survival gear. Twelve hours in these woods in winter without matches and you could be dead or maimed. Frozen, like Arthur.

I sipped my beer and turned up the heat.

Arthur was pushing his luck before it ran out in the canal. The voyeurism that began with the cheerleaders was getting out of hand. How long could he have expected to skulk around people's houses in a small town without being caught? It must have been an obsession, a compulsion. But the letter to Martin. Why force the situation after all those years? Did he worry that Martin would die before he could tell him that he thought he was his father? Meek, mild Arthur had been on a collision course with something. Or someone.

I drove southwest on the third leg and third beer of my loop. The road cut through Grafton Notch State Park, a jagged craggy ridge where a mountain climber or hiker died every few years. The rock peaks were high above the road, and I pictured the cold, the wind, the scoured bareness high above me. Today, it would be silent up there. Hawks had gone south. Hikers had packed it in and ice climbers were yet to come. These rocks hadn't been tamed for people to slide down them. They didn't bristle with gondola towers and microwave transmitters. There were no condos, no restaurants, no bars for the skiers who knew the mountains as a diversion from their lives in offices and classrooms to the south. There was just rock and wind and scrub.

I drove along through the gathering darkness and felt reassured.

Back on Route 2, I headed east with my lights on, meeting other cars now, many with skis on roof racks. They were headed west for Sunday River, and the ski areas of the Mount Washington Valley. Roxanne had said she loved to ski. She had this idea that we could go off for a weekend in New Hampshire or Vermont, ski all day, and hit the hot tub at night. Good skiing, good food, good . . . times. When she had said this, I didn't tell her that I didn't own a neon racing suit or the hottest skis. That I was too old to try to be hip. She was younger and hipper, without trying. And when I pulled into my driveway, her car was there.

"All right," I said, whooping softly to myself. The mountain had come to Mohammed.

The door opened when I got to the top of the stairs. Roxanne was wearing jeans and an Irish knit sweater. The sweater gave me a hug and she gave me a long kiss and then an even longer kiss after that. Her mouth was warm and soft and strong. She broke for breath and beamed.

"Déjà vu all over again," I said.

"It ain't over 'til this lady sings," Roxanne said, pulling me toward the living room.

"I think you're the wrong lady."

"I'll ask you about that later," she said. "Sit down and I'll be right back."

Was she going to slip into something more comfortable, just like the movies? What had I done to deserve all this? I hoped I wouldn't pay for it later. Somehow, somewhere.

Roxanne came back from the kitchen carrying a pizza box and an open bottle of Samuel Smith's Nut Brown Ale, imported very carefully from England.

Oh, I would pay for it in another life.

"Pizza," she said, putting the box on the now-wobbly table. "And I brought you this beer even though you lied to me about the state of this apartment."

"I didn't lie. I misspoke myself," I said.

"Ronald Reagan misspeaks. You tell whoppers."

"Tiny white ones."

She looked at me and went back to the kitchen for the wine and a corkscrew. It was red Italian table wine. I popped the cork and poured her a glass. We toasted.

"To England," I said.

"And pizza and you," she said. "In that order. I'm starved."

Roxanne was bubbly, chatty, and she seemed young as she talked about a case she'd won in court that week. *Won* was not the right word in her business, though. Sometimes she lost, and sometimes she lost big.

The decision kept an eleven-year-old girl in state custody rather than handing her over to a supposedly reformed stepfather who had served six months for molesting the girl's older sister. I remembered my last discussion with Roxanne, the one that nearly kept us out of bed, and bit my tongue.

"So with Tiberson, you never know," she said. "Some judges you do know. They lean one way or the other. Tiberson depends on what he had for lunch or the color of the kid's hair or something. I've seen the same evidence presented, the identical situation, and he goes with the guy or the child."

"Nice," I said. "A crapshoot with a kid's life as the payoff. The defendants don't go with jury trials?"

Roxanne pulled a long string of cheese off her pizza and dropped it in her mouth.

"Uh-uh," she said. "They're learning. The ones with any brains or money to get a decent lawyer know that the judge is a better bet. Hey, you figure he's seen a thousand of these things. You get a jury that's never heard all this stuff about semen and penetration. Little old lady sitting up there wishing she could plug her ears. Sometimes she lowers the boom just because she had to sit through all this crap."

I sipped the beer. It was not Ballantine Ale.

"You okay?" Roxanne asked. "I came up here to cheer you up. Keep you off the streets and out of the slammer. Something else happen?"

I shook my head, no.

"Just a lot of little stuff," I said.

"What do you call little," Roxanne said. She pulled her sweater off over her head, stretching so that her breasts were taut under her T-shirt. I lost my train of thought.

"I've just been talking to people a little," I said.

"You're not a cop, Jack," she said.

"I know that. Let's not get into that. It's just that . . . This sounds funny, but there are a lot of people here who really are better off with Arthur gone."

I told her about Martin, between bites, then got up and got another beer from the refrigerator. I told myself this would be the last one.

"Why don't you just give it to him?" Roxanne asked, as I sat back down.

"Because it's evidence."

"If it's evidence, why is it in your drawer? Why don't you give it to the police? Like you told him. You'd be out of it, and they could take over. Why get into all this stuff deeper?"

"Who am I gonna give it to? Vigue? He knew about those pictures. He had to. He talked about the waitress and I never—"

"Never what?" Roxanne said.

"I never gave him that one. I, well, I put that one aside."

"Why'd you do that?"

Her voice had chilled, just slightly.

"I don't know. Just to keep some control of the thing, I guess."

I didn't mention that the waitress was very attractive. Even without that, Roxanne was finishing the wine in her glass. She wasn't smiling.

"You know, Jack, I was going to say that this town was nuts. It is. But I think some of it is rubbing off on you."

She got up and went into the kitchen and I heard the water running in the sink. I took a gulp of the Sam Smith's but it didn't taste good anymore. I put it down and picked up an old *Newsweek* from the floor and flipped through it, stopping at the gossip page, which was about all I could handle. The water stopped running and Roxanne came back into the room and picked up her sweater and put it back on. She pulled a copy of *Farewell to Arms* from the shelf that had been flipped on the floor and started reading.

I got up and got my jacket and gloves.

"I'm going out to get some air," I said. "Want to come?"

"No, thanks," she said, and turned a page.

I hadn't intended to go far. Maybe just go out behind the house for a while and look at the stars. The stars were beautiful in Androscoggin when the wind wasn't blowing the wrong way. When it did blow the wrong way, from the east, the paper-mill steam blotted out the stars like a cloud.

The stairs were dark and I walked carefully. When I got to the door, I turned to my left and looked up.

"Hey," Cormier said.

"How's it going?" I answered.

He was with another guy, smaller, in his late teens or early twenties. The younger guy was wearing a dirty baseball cap with a picture of a truck and the Ford logo. Cormier's hat was blaze orange, a hunting hat. His eye patch was white.

They stood side by side. Both held longneck Bud bottles.

We looked at each other for a moment. The buddy cleared his throat and spat on the snow-packed driveway. He had a stringy mustache that looked even stringier when he pursed his lips to spit. Cormier took a sip of beer and let the bottle fall. The buddy did the same.

Beer up. Beer down. Like an oil rig.

"I wanted to know if you've been thinkin' about it," he said. "You know where I'm comin' from?"

"Out from under some rock?" I said.

The buddy took a step forward, his chin out, mouth hanging open. I took that to mean that he was offended.

"Hey, I came to talk to you," Cormier said. "Don't start in, 'cause I'll end it this time."

"That why you brought shithead here?"

"Come on," the buddy said. "Let's do it."

"I'm not gonna do anything. I live here, remember? I want you to go. Or do we have to talk about how Cormier doesn't want to go to jail?"

"Who does?" Cormier said. "Hey, I didn't come for this bullshit. I came to say somethin'."

"So say it."

Cormier looked at me for a second. I looked back at him. Army fatigue jacket. Brown leather boots. Shirt open at the neck despite the cold. He shifted his weight from one foot to the other.

"Hey, I got a reason to not want this to go to court," he said.

"Oh, yeah."

"If it does, it screws me up with somethin' else. My son. His mother. She sees an assault and she goes to the judge, says I'm danger-ous. We got joint custody, and I don't want to lose it."

"So who's this guy?" I said. "Your lawyer?"

"Ah, don't mind him. He's a buddy. He ain't here to do nothin'. He's just . . . come on, man. Cops make it sound like you killed somebody. It wasn't friggin' nothin' and you know it. I got a chance to make a grand a week cuttin' wood out in Washington, man, and I don't need this hangin' around my neck. What do you want? Friggin' blood?"

No more bar brawler. This was a young man concerned about his future. His son. If I didn't agree to erase this black mark from his otherwise-pristine record, the poor kid would end up . . . end up like his father. If you can't stomp authority, talk your way around it.

The survival instinct was a wonderful thing, responsible for some of the best dramatic performances you'll see. A guy pounds his girl-friend, puts her in the hospital with her nose all mashed in and her ribs broken, spits on her bloody face. And when he gets up before the judge, he's all shined up like the Kiwanis man of the year. Yessir. No, sir. I'm very sorry, sir. I guess I just lost it.

Cormier and friend still stood there.

"So you won't get the big job in Washington with an assault charge on your record?"

"I won't get the job, waitin' around here for lawyers and cops to get their shit together. Come on, what's the big deal? You weren't even hurt, man. Gimme a break."

I said nothing. The buddy eyed me, then looked away. The street was hushed. Cormier watched me closely, probably trying to fight back his natural inclination to beat my head in until I would agree to testify to his nonviolent character.

Then he broke.

"Jesus, who the hell do you think you are? A goddamn fight in a goddamn bar and you're tryin' to put me away for life, for God's sake. Forget it. You're okay. I'm the one who had to go to the hospital."

For a moment, déjà vu, the real kind. Martin, his back against the wall. Now Cormier.

We stood there, the three of us, spouting steamy breath into the cold night air.

"Why me?" I said. "Why'd you pick me out? I don't even know you."

"I told the cops that."

"Tell me. Now."

The buddy's eyes were fixed on mine, like a snake's. I stared right back at him, then at Cormier. The buddy took a long pull on his beer.

Did Cormier not want to talk in front of him? Maybe the word would be out that he wimped out. Begged instead of threatened. Some pussy hits him in the eye and he runs scared.

"They were talkin' about it at the mill," he said, almost softly.

"You don't work there anymore."

"I still see those guys around," Cormier said.

His beer was empty. My feet were cold.

"What'd they say at the mill?" I asked.

"That this guy at the paper was trying to shut the place down."

"Not true. Crazy," I said.

"Hey, it's what they said. These guys got families, car payments, you know? They don't screw around when it comes to their paychecks."

"Who does?"

The buddy's beer was gone, too. He looked restless, bored with the talk.

"How'd you know who I was at the bar?" I asked.

They both grinned.

"We just knew. We know a lot of stuff. Like you got a couple tickets in that black piece of crap you drive. Like the cops know you drink and would love to bag you for OUI. You ought to junk that pecker box and get somethin' that isn't so friggin' noticeable."

"What, you a deputy now or what?" I said.

They grinned. Joe and Frank. The Hardy Boys.

The balance of power had shifted a little. They were cocky, talking too much. But the cop thing made me feel surrounded.

I had my back to the door. They stood between me and the cars.

"So whaddya say?" Cormier said.

We were buddies now. The three of us.

"I'll think about it."

"About what?" he exploded. "About what? 'I'll think about it,' he says."

Cormier said it like he was imitating a sissy. We weren't buddies anymore.

"You keep talking and you're gonna have tampering with a witness. Class C. What will that do to your kid?"

"I'm not tamperin' with anybody," he said. "I tamper with you, you'll friggin' know it, peckerhead."

"Cops'll know it, too."

"Frig the cops," he said.

Cormier looked at me and then turned and flung his beer bottle toward the trees at the back of the yard. The bottle clanged but didn't break. His buddy turned and whipped his, low and hard, and it shattered.

I looked at him.

"You know you throw like a girl?" I said.

He jumped at me, but Cormier pulled him back. I looked at them and the buddy spat. A gob of saliva and mucus landed next to my right foot. I turned and took two steps to the door and stepped inside. As I walked up the stairs, I heard the buddy's voice.

"Chickenshit wimp," he called.

"Redundant moron," I said, and I walked up the stairs and into the kitchen and Roxanne was standing there against the counter, her arms folded and her face gray.

She didn't look mad. She looked scared.

"What's the matter?" I said. "Are you sick?"

She shook her head and took a shallow breath. The phone was off the hook on the counter.

"Somebody call?" I asked.

Roxanne nodded.

"Twice," she said.

"Who was it? What's going on?"

Roxanne bit her lip and started to cry.

14

"It sounded like maybe it was a woman at first," Roxanne said. "Maybe a woman who smokes a lot. That raspy kind of voice."

She sipped her wine twice. I hung up the phone and went and sat beside her on the couch and waited.

"I thought maybe it was somebody you worked with. She said, at least I thought it was a she, I don't know. She said she was a friend of yours and she'd heard a lot about me. That's what she said. I said, 'Oh, that's nice.' Oh, God."

Roxanne stopped. She looked small and vulnerable.

"And then the voice changed a little. Like it wasn't as much like a woman."

"What did it sound like?"

"Oh, I don't know how to describe it. Not a normal voice, that's all. Like a neuter or something."

She sipped.

"He, it, it said I should come to town more often because . . . because he liked to see me in my blue panties. I was shocked. I thought I hadn't heard right, like it didn't sink in. I said, 'What?' It said, it said I had a nice ass and he'd seen me take my panties off."

I put my arm on her shoulder.

"Jack, I have—"

"I know," I said.

"God, Jack! What kind of a place is this? That's what you said Arthur did, isn't it? God, this place is sick. Oh, that voice, it was . . . I can still hear it."

I gave her shoulder a squeeze and told her to take it easy. I couldn't tell her she shouldn't worry because that was not true. There was reason to worry. I felt outnumbered again, like I had felt talking to Cormier about the cops. I felt that way again, only worse.

Roxanne leaned on my shoulder, her legs pulled up underneath her on the couch. I didn't tell her about Cormier. Maybe the two things were related. Cormier and his friend get me outside. The third person calls Roxanne, knowing she's alone. But who even knew she was here? I hadn't known she was coming. They had to be watching the house. Would Cormier have that kind of patience? That temper? Could he just sit and wait like that? Set something up that took more planning than picking a fight?

And this took planning.

Unless the caller had been just lucky, he—or she—had been watching Roxanne. She had a pair of medium blue underpants. She had worn them the last time she had come to see me. But Roxanne didn't cavort around the house in her underwear. It was too cold. She might have walked through to the bathroom off the kitchen. I tried to remember and couldn't.

The caller must have had a clear view. Maybe into the bedroom. He must have used binoculars.

Or a telephoto.

Roxanne was saved by the bell. The phone. It was one of her supervisors, and he said somebody was "in crisis," which meant something in the jargon of the social worker.

Roxanne pulled herself together, said she would come but it would be about an hour and a half.

"Yeah, I know forty-three Chestnut," she said. "Oh, do I know it."

She left with her eyes still red, her skin still pale. I walked her to the car door, locked it when I closed it. She reached over and locked the other doors and then gave me a little wave and was gone.

In the back driveway, I walked along the edge of the trees to the place where there was a path worn by the neighborhood kids on knobby-tired bikes. I slid down the litter of oak leaves and snow and fell twice in the dark. I followed the path to the next block and walked down Penobscot Street all the way to downtown.

At the Food Stop, I turned left up the hill and doubled back. In five minutes, I was above the house in the trees that you reached from the next block. Crouched in the dark, I looked at the lights of the living room windows and tried to remember everything I could about Roxanne's last visit.

We'd sat in the living room and had drinks. After a while, we had gone to bed, but I was sure we had pulled the shades in the bedroom. But we hadn't closed the door. I crunched through the brush to my left to see if the bedroom ever came into view. Branches tore at my hair. I slipped and caught myself on a branch, which snapped off. But the bedroom couldn't be seen, not from this side of the house. And the embankment dropped off behind the house. From there, you'd need a helicopter.

Had Roxanne walked through the living room in her underwear? I tried to remember. She had gone to get her wine off the table by the couch. But had she been undressed? I couldn't remember. I did know she had left early Monday morning and had dressed in the dark. That meant it had to have been Sunday night. And without a lens of some kind, there was no way that you could tell the color of anything, much less a pair of moving panties.

So it must have been a vigil. Waiting in the cold for a flicker of movement. Who would go through that for a glimpse of a woman? Arthur. But Arthur was dead that day. The caller had been very much alive.

I turned stiffly and gave the house a last look.

Someone was in the living room window.

I plunged down the hill, sliding and running and falling through the trees, and ran across the lawn and up the driveway. When I got to the door, I slowed and opened it, closing it carefully behind me. Staying close to the wall to keep the stairs from creaking, I crept to the second floor and stood outside the kitchen door. Music was playing; Brubeck. "Pennies from Heaven." I pushed the door open slowly.

No one was in the kitchen. No one was in the hallway.

I picked up a paring knife from the dish rack on the counter and walked slowly toward the living room. "Pennies from Heaven" ended. The tape was between tracks. When the next song started, drums, then piano, I stepped around the corner.

"Hey, Jackson," a voice boomed. "Where you been? I thought the Martians beamed you up or something."

Vern was sitting sideways in the big chair, his legs over one arm and one of my Ballantine Ales in his hand. He was reading the *Newsweek*, folded in half.

I felt nauseated as the adrenaline rush cut off, but I tried to smile and at the same time slide the knife into my back pocket. The point stuck in the seam at the bottom of the pocket and the ivory-colored plastic handle showed at the top.

Vern still looked at the magazine.

"Careful where you sit with that thing," he said.

I took the knife out and tossed it on the table.

"You doing potatoes, or should I wait for a formal invitation next time?" he said. "If you're expecting somebody else, I hope they don't show up."

"No, I was just—"

"Acute paranoia," Vern said. "Tell me: How long ago did you start arming yourself? Do you keep loaded guns in the house? Do you feel like everyone's out to get you?"

"Today, no, and they are," I said.

"I was afraid of that," Vern said, and he smiled.

Vern was a pretty good sports reporter. He was a pretty good writer, and he knew sports inside and out. But what made him better than the usual reporter was his ability to listen. He was big and shapeless and he had a way of smiling and listening at the same time that was disarming. It worked on kids. It worked on coaches. Sometimes it worked on me.

He listened that night. I told him about Roxanne's calls and Martin and his picture and Vigue and the picture of the waitress. He knew which waitress I meant.

"Jesus," Vern said, putting his beer on the floor. "I knew Arthur was strange, but I didn't know he was so ambitious."

"An obsession," I said. "Probably he knew it was wrong, but the more he tried to stop, the more he was driven to it."

"Guy needed help."

"Too late now."

Vern picked up his beer but it was empty. I went and got him another one. He opened it and took a gulp.

"I don't know, Jackson," he said. "You New York agitators. I don't know. I think you've got something with this mill tax crap. I know it seems routine to you, but you're going after the sacred cow here. And you're from away."

"So are you," I said.

"Yeah, but I write about their kids. I say nice things. Like it when they win."

"Cheerleader."

"I know," Vern said. "They're tight skirts, but somebody has to wear them. No, really. Don't get me wrong. I think this mill story should be done. Company's been pushing this place around for too long. Forever. But think about it. Martin's idea of a hard-hitting piece was reporting the actual vote at the council meeting instead of just saying things were approved. You come in with this *Wall Street Journal* stuff and sources and all that, and you've got to expect the manure to hit the fan."

"That's the way I do it," I said. "Either that or I leave."

"And by the sounds of it, there are some people around here who would love to see it."

I got up and looked out the window toward where I'd been standing in the cold, but couldn't see anything. Vern still sat in the chair.

"Another thing," he said, behind me. "You forget sometimes, coming from away. Just because this is a small town, don't think everybody's quaint. Some of these guys would give the scumbags in New York a run for their money."

"I know that."

"I'm not saying you don't. Reminding you, I guess."

"But this sex stuff. That's not tough. That's just weird. And Vigue knowing something about it but not saying? I always liked him. Straight cop, I thought."

"Straight but bitter," Vern said.

"Just because he can't be chief, is he gonna start lying or whatever it is he's doing? Covering up?"

"I doubt it."

"And these calls. Is this place filled with perverts or what?"

"Just Paul, and he's got his hands full," Vern said.

"I'm serious," I said.

"So am I," Vern said. "You've got to watch out—watch out for Roxanne, too."

"I know," I said, suddenly weary.

"And another thing," Vern said. "Get some curtains."

So what am I supposed to do, I thought. Watch television? College football highlights to take my mind off the wacko looking in the windows? Or sit back with a good book, a thriller about somebody being stalked by some nut? Call an old friend from the city and tell him how my life was going?

Right.

That didn't leave much. Clean up the mess a little more, do the dishes, wrap up the trash and take the bag down to the cans in the shed. Sit in the dark and drink until I was in enough of a stupor to go to bed. Add a hangover to the problems that weren't going to go away while I slept. They weren't going anywhere.

I walked into the kitchen and took three pieces of pizza out of the box and wrapped them in foil because there wasn't any Saran Wrap.

I stuffed the box in the trash and threw a dirty knife and fork in the sink. There were two Samuel Smiths left in the six-pack carton on the counter and I started to stick them in the refrigerator, then stuck one back on the counter. I took the opener out of the sink and popped the top on the one and took it out to the living room, turning the kitchen light out on the way. That left the one lamp on in the living room, and I turned it off and dragged my chair over by the window.

I sat in the chair in the dark and looked out toward the blackness that was the trees. When the wind blew there was a faint rustle from the oaks, almost like the sound of waves crashing on a beach. I drank the beer slowly, setting the bottle between my legs and watching the vague darkness. There were things out there but I couldn't quite make them out. Trees. Houses. Lights. People who were doing something—something that was wrong and strange and had more and more to do with me.

But even in daylight, even looking as hard as I could, thinking and thinking, I couldn't see any of it. So, unseeing, I finished the beer and then found myself dozing in the chair. I forced myself up and grabbed the phone and took it with me to bed, which was still a sleeping bag. The phone went on the floor beside the bed, in case Roxanne called, in case I wanted to call her. For a second, I wondered if this meant I was falling in love, but then I closed my eyes and fell asleep.

The room was still blue-black when I woke up. I looked at the ceiling and waited for my eyes to focus. As I waited, I heard something.

A sound in the living room. Someone sitting down in the chair.

She shouldn't have driven all the way back, I thought, groggily. She must be exhausted. She could have had an accident. I dragged the sleeping bag aside and lurched out of bed.

"Hey, hon," I said, shuffling into the living room in my boxer shorts. "You should have just called. You must be—"

I tensed.

There was a figure in the dark. And a smell. Soap. Perfume. The wrong smell. I took a half-step back and patted the wall for the switch. The light was blinding.

It wasn't Roxanne.

"Mrs. Wiggins?" I said.

She was wearing a green parka and a red beret sort of hat. The beret was pulled over her white hair at an angle, like Che Guevara. She was holding a shotgun. Martin's Parker, off the rack on the wall. The butt was under her arm and both barrels were pointing at me.

"What the fu—"

"Sorry to disappoint you," Pauline said. She sounded like it was funny. Something was funny.

"I gather you were expecting your floozy. I don't know why you bother to smuggle her in here at this hour. The whole town knows about her. And you."

"What's going on?" I sputtered. "Put that—"

"We're going to have a talk, Mr. McMorrow. That's the first thing. Sit over there on the couch, please. Sit down. Now."

Her voice was calm but also tense, as if she were in control of the situation, but the situation was serious. Like somebody trying to tell other people not to panic. Her face was dry and white and her lipstick was red and fresh, like a drag queen's. She sat in the big chair with the shotgun pointed at my midsection. The barrel was shiny and long, and the round ends were very black.

I sat slowly on the kitchen chair that I'd brought out when Vern had been in her chair. Martin's killed himself, I thought. He blew his brains out, and she wants to take me with her when she goes after him.

Her long fingers were around the trigger and I could see her wedding band and diamond under the barrel.

"I'm going to tell you something about decency," Pauline said, in the same assured, controlled tone. "It is a subject with which you may not be familiar."

She looked right at me, right at my eyes. I watched the end of the shotgun make small circles in the air.

"My husband is a decent man. A good man, I think. I'm not boring you, am I? Good. Well, Mr. McMorrow, we have had fifty-one years together, pretty good years, and he has been a devoted husband, a good man. A respected man in the community. Oh, yes, people thought a lot of Martin, in ways you would never understand. Not ever."

She shifted her left hand. The barrel dropped. I watched her finger on the trigger. One squeeze. It would take one squeeze.

"A long time ago, my husband slipped. Not badly. Just a momentary fall. There was a woman in town who had designs on him, and in a moment of weakness or vanity or insecurity, or whatever it is that makes men do such things, he accepted. Briefly. I knew; I knew all about it, but I had faith in him. You wouldn't know about that either. It didn't last long and we went on with our lives. You do those things. My husband never knew I knew, and he devoted himself to me after that. He did. He really did. A fine man. He was ready to carry his secret to his grave, and it must have been a burden, just to keep from hurting me."

I shifted my legs, which were cold and bare. The gun went to my face.

"Please listen," Pauline said.

She waited a moment and continued.

"That grave is approaching for both of us, Mr. McMorrow. And let me tell you something else, sir. Life is remembered as it ends. We like to go out on a happy note, as it were. A word to the wise, let's say."

She smiled crazily. A strange serene smile.

"Yesterday, Mr. Wiggins came to me a broken man. He came to me and said he wanted me to hear it from him and not from the gossips on the street. And like a man, he stood there and told me about his indiscretion. He told me about Arthur Bertin and his filthy photographs. There's at least one person in this town who did not mourn his passing, I'll tell you. And that is me."

I was eight feet away from her. The kitchen was to her right. To my right were the living room windows. Fifteen to twenty feet down but storms and window. Too much glass to go through. I'd hang up and get shot.

The butt of the heavy gun had dropped from her armpit to the crook of her arm.

"Another thing you probably don't know much about is pride. You are not half the man he is, for all your big-city background. This picture you gave to the police—it will make him the butt of jokes all over town. Everywhere he goes. He will not be able to get a cup of coffee, to talk to his friends, to walk down the street. A mockery. That's what you've made of his life. After all he's done, after all we've done for this town. We didn't have children, you know. This town was our child."

She hesitated.

"Mrs. Wiggins, I never wanted to hurt Martin. I didn't—"

She stopped me with a wave of the gun.

"That man walked out of our house last night and he was ruined. Ruined. Because of some big-city big shot up here on a lark to laugh at the locals. A vacation for you and your floozy. It makes me so angry. So sick. Oh, God."

Tears welled up in her eyes. She sobbed and her body and the shotgun jerked up and down. From my belly to my face. Up and down.

The phone rang and I flinched. She turned and there was a white flash and a rocking explosion and I was off the chair and had the shotgun and heaved it behind me. It clattered and I stood over Pauline. The phone had only rung once.

Pauline had her eyes closed and her left hand was holding her right upper arm. She rocked slowly back and forth, her knees and feet pressed together.

"You okay?" I said.

She rocked and didn't answer.

15

The butt of the gun had recoiled into her upper arm. The bone, old and brittle, could have been broken or even shattered. I started to go to call an ambulance, but when I got to the door of the bedroom, I could see the phone receiver off the hook and the base upside down.

Thank you, Annie Oakley.

Fortunately, I could hear that irritating beeping sound the phone company uses to tell you your phone has been shot but still is working. I flipped the base over, picked up the pitted receiver, and dialed 911. A woman, probably a county dispatcher, answered. I told her my address and said I needed an ambulance.

"What is the nature of the emergency?" she asked.

"A woman shot a gun off in my living room and I think she broke her arm."

"Does she still have the firearm?" the dispatcher asked. "No. I threw it over the couch," I said.

"Is the firearm in her proximity?"

"I guess, but I don't think she feels like shooting it anymore."

"Where is she now?" the dispatcher said.

"She's in the living room, crying."

And she was. I went in and sat with her for a few minutes. Pauline sobbed silently and I patted her on the shoulder. Her shoulders were very thin and bony, and it was like consoling a skeleton. We waited what seemed like a very long time, sitting there in the quiet, and then there were heavy footsteps and voices in the hallway and the room filled with uniforms.

Vigue and a couple of other Androscoggin cops came in first. Then a bunch of volunteer firemen who came to the ambulance call as much for something to do as to help. A big state trooper who had heard the call on her radio and came in case there was a real shoot-out.

Pauline buried her face in her arms and the cops and firemen stood over her like they were visiting a sick aunt. They brought a stretcher up from the ambulance and lifted her onto it and she didn't look at anybody as they maneuvered her through the kitchen and out the door and down the stairs.

After she'd left, I went in and found the state trooper in the bedroom, looking at the basketball-size hole in the wall. The plaster was blown away, the wooden laths underneath were splintered, and there were dime-size holes going through to the darkness outside.

"Buckshot," the trooper said.

"It's always something," I said.

"Where's this friggin' picture?" Vigue said.

He was behind the wheel of his cruiser with a clipboard balanced in the steering wheel. The radio was coughing up static, the motor was running, and the heat was blasting onto my feet in the passenger seat.

"At the paper," I said.

"What's it of?"

"Martin and Arthur's mother. Meredith something."

"So what's the big deal about it?"

"I don't know. It's of Martin and this woman sitting together. Sort of hugging."

"So?"

"So, I don't know. I guess Martin had some kind of fling with this lady a hundred years ago."

"When he could get it up," Vigue said.

"Whatever. What happened is, I found this picture in Arthur's stuff after he died. Or drowned. He had all these pictures, and this was with them."

"Like the pictures of the girls."

"Yeah. They were in a folder. I was looking for stuff for the paper, and there was all this other stuff. I didn't think anything of it. Sort of funny, I thought. Some high-school date or something. No, it was too old for high school. But anyway, I didn't think much of it. But I said something to him about it. Kidding or whatever. He said he wanted it back, but I said I'd have to give it to the police because it wasn't mine to give away, and the police were handling the investigation of Arthur's death."

"So where is it?" Vigue said.

I shrugged.

"I wasn't sure what to do. I guess I didn't do anything."

He had stopped taking notes and was smoking a cigarette. He hit the power button and whirred the window down to flick out an ash.

"So that's it?" Vigue said.

I looked at him.

"Is that what all this is about? Some old picture? You gotta be shittin' me."

"I told you what she said."

Vigue whirred the window down and flicked the cigarette down again. The ambulance had left and LeMaire, J. and another Andro-scoggin cop were talking with the trooper next to the trooper's cruiser. All of the cars were running.

"A couple days ago, Martin came and asked me for the picture again. He told me Arthur told him about the picture, and told him—Arthur told Martin, I mean—that the picture was some kind of proof that Martin was Arthur's real father."

Vigue looked at me.

"Is this *Guiding Light*, or what?" he said.

"'Hey, don't look at me. That's what he said. Pauline gets there and she's just sitting in the room, and she says Martin told her I had the picture and I was going to give it to you. She said she knew, but he didn't know she knew because she never told him. About this fling."

"Jesus," Vigue said.

"I don't know. I know it sounds crazy, but if he thought the whole town was going to find out this deep, dark secret about his past—"

Martin. The pillar of the community, third row at the Baptist Church, writing nice stories about all his nice friends. Vigue had put the pen back in his pocket. It was a gold Cross that went with his uniform. He took it back out.

"I think he had wanted her to think he could be trusted, but then he figured everyone in town would know because of this picture. That's what it looks like, anyway."

Vigue exhaled the last drag on his cigarette and flicked it out the window onto the driveway.

"Okay," he said. "Forget the picture. You're all nuts. Did she have the firearm aimed at your person?"

"My general direction. Not when she shot it."

"She didn't fire it at you."

"Nope, she was shooting at the phone. It rang. Like I told you. Saved by the bell, I guess."

Vigue scribbled on the pad.

"You would have been splattered all over that wall, my friend," he said, without looking up. "The buckshot in that gun would have cut you in two. They'd be in there for weeks with scrub brushes, trying to get Mr. McMorrow off the walls."

"Funny thought."

"I'm chuckling," Vigue said.

"So what happens to her? They put her in jail or the hospital?"

"No way. She's an old lady. She'll get reckless conduct with a firearm, terrorizing, maybe. Keep her in the rubber room for a while, pump her full of dope, and send her home in a few weeks. I got guys who do the same thing and get sixty days and five hundred bucks. Judge tells them not to play with guns in the house anymore."

"Nice."

"Goddamn great. Junior gets out and we have to go up and see him next time. Round and round. Same scumbags. All related. This one's father, this one's kids. I get these little bastards, I used to arrest their grandfather. Goes on forever. We'll be six feet under and somebody else will be chasing 'em."

"You sound like a man who likes his work," I said.

"Once upon a friggin' time," Vigue said.

The downtown was deserted that afternoon, as if everyone had been invited to a funeral I didn't know about. I parked the Volvo a block over on Front Street and walked to the paper. There was no one around, and I locked the door behind me. The word would be out soon enough. Pauline Wiggins went nuts. Tried to shoot the guy from the paper. Pauline? You're kidding. No, I'm serious. Jimmy Lancaster, he told me. His brother-in-law's an EMT. Married to Wendy. Said she almost killed the guy. No, I'm serious. Pauline Wiggins. Almost killed the guy in this house on . . . well, I'm not sure what street it was on, but it did happen. No, really.

I dreaded it.

Sunday was my day for planning and writing the stories that were hard to do when the office was buzzing, so that's what I pretended to do. I made a pot of coffee at the plastic machine and sat at my desk with a blank legal pad. At the top, I wrote Arthur's name. Then I listed everyone who had anything to do with him. I stared at the names. A loud four-wheel-drive truck went by, five feet off the ground on big tires and red mags. I got a glimpse of it, then listened to the blare of the exhaust until that grew softer and softer and then faded away.

My list was still there.

I had been in the office three minutes, by the clock on the wall. Four minutes and I stared at the names. Arthur. Martin. Pauline and Vigue and Cormier. Me. I had forgotten myself. I put my name on the bottom of the list. I knew him. After my name, I put Cindy and Vern and Marion and Paul. LeMaire, J. Meredith, Arthur's mother. She was dead, but I put her on the list anyway. A list of names. I stared at it and waited for illumination. Seven minutes now. Eight.

I felt hopelessly inadequate, utterly powerless. I knew these names, but little more. Cormier's friend. I added him. The phone caller. I wrote "caller" under Cormier's friend. But the caller could have been some-body already on the list. Not Arthur or Meredith. Or Cormier or his friend. Unless the call was taped, but that was unlikely. Roxanne would have known if it was a tape recording. I put her name on the list, too.

Twelve minutes.

I looked at the names. It looked like an invitation list for a dinner party. I would have them all to dinner at my house and we would discuss it all in a very British way until the suspect, unable to conceal his guilt, or to live with the cancerous knowledge of his crime, would confess, screaming and crying and sobbing until the credits marched over his bowed head.

Fifteen minutes.

Confess to what? A crime that nobody felt had even happened? To an obscene phone call? To shooting a shotgun through my bedroom wall? No confession needed there. To tossing Arthur in the water and leaving him to drown? He would call out. He would claw at the wall of the canal. He would call out in the night until he was too cold, and then? Would he cry to himself in the dark? Would he pray as death took him? Was there anyone on this list of acquaintances who was capable of leaving a man to die so slowly? You'd have to be crazy—to have a crazy streak.

Pauline.

Nineteen minutes.

The horn sounded at the fire station, three blasts. A rescue call, with volunteers needed. As I walked to the window, a police cruiser whined by, blue lights and siren on. A few seconds later, the rescue truck followed, hissing flat out down the empty street.

My camera was in the car. I jogged over and jumped in and floored it out Front Street and west on to Route 2, just in time to see a fire truck heading up the hill past the falls. I followed as fast as the Volvo would go until I got to the top of the hill and saw the back end of the rescue truck and the blue lights stopped a couple of miles up the road. A hundred yards behind the rescue truck, I slowed down. I had seen enough car accidents to know there was no need to race. If there was death and destruction, it would be there when I arrived. I slowed down a little more. The readers of the *Review* would have to forgive me for not racing to the scene of the carnage. I fulfilled this part of our contract without enthusiasm, reporting the tragedy because I had to, not because I liked it.

The two cars had hit head-on. They sat crumpled in the middle of the two-lane highway, bleeding gasoline and radiator fluid onto the pavement. I parked behind the ambulance on the shoulder and shut off the motor. Camera in hand, I walked slowly toward the wrecks.

Police and fire radios crackled everywhere. Volunteers in rubber boots ran from their trucks. Two guys from the rescue unit were leaning into the windows of what had been a little Japanese car, a Nissan or a Toyota. It was blue, and there was glass all around it on the road. When I got closer I could hear a woman's voice. She was sobbing, saying "Oh my God" over and over in a high-pitched unnatural voice. One of the rescue guys leaned farther into the window and she screamed.

The other car was a big Chrysler from the early seventies, a big green boat of a car, an armored troop carrier. On the side of the road beside it, four teenage boys stood watching the rescue operation. They were expressionless, as if they had been sedated. Everyone else was running and they were standing still. I shot their picture with the wrecks in the foreground.

LeMaire, J. had a fifth kid off to the side. The kid had shoulder-length black hair tied with a red bandanna. His dungarees were ripped and his boots were unlaced with his pant legs tucked in, the way I'd seen kids wear them. Country kids, trying to look tough.

This kid did not look tough, though. Next to LeMaire, J., he looked small and skinny. LeMaire, J. had him by the arm with his big paw of a hand and was talking to him in a loud voice that could be heard even over the police radios.

"Have you been drinking?" LeMaire, J. said.

The kid looked at him sullenly.

"I think you've been drinking, and I'm going to have to ask you to put your arms behind your back," LeMaire, J. said, speaking slowly and methodically in his police voice.

"I ain't putting my arms nowhere, get your hands—" the kid said, but then LeMaire, J. whipped the kid's arms behind him, slipping the cuffs on in the same practiced motion. The kid stumbled and LeMaire, J. held him up by the arms and pushed him toward the cruiser. I backed up a few feet and focused the camera.

I got off three quick shots. As I took the last one, the kid lunged toward me and spat, and I felt something wet on my hands.

"You little bastard," LeMaire, J. said between his teeth, and spun the kid around and slammed him into the side of the cruiser hard enough to snap the kid's head back and lift his feet off the ground. In some cities it would have been enough to bring on a brutality suit, but in Androscoggin, some of the quaint old ways survived.

LeMaire, J. stuffed the kid in the backseat of the cruiser and came back to the car, where four rescue workers and firemen were taking the woman out of the car on a spine board. She was strapped down like she was going in for shock treatments and she had blonde hair that was curly and had blood in it. The blood looked dark, almost black.

I took a shot of them lifting her out of the window. It had all the elements, as Arthur used to say. The victim, the rescue workers, both cars, the crowd in the background. In the crowd were familiar faces from town, truckers with their names on their shirt pockets. A man in a green chamois shirt and khaki pants had the prosperous look of a tourist, and sure enough, there was a car on the west side of the wreck with blue license plates. Ohio or Connecticut.

LeMaire, J. walked up behind me, carrying his automatic Canon.

"You're having a busy day," he said, his eye in the viewfinder.

"You, too," I said.

"At least nobody's shooting at me."

"Give it time," I said.

He moved past me. Crouching awkwardly, then backing up, one step and then another. LeMaire, J. did not look like a professional.

"Getting this one in black and white," he said. "We are gonna put this little shit away."

"What for?"

"Third OUI arrest this year. Probation says no alcohol, and he's plastered. No license, no registration. She dies, they ought to hang him by the balls."

"Sounds reasonable," I said.

LeMaire, J. moved away and I got a shot of him taking pictures, elbows out like a tourist.

I had enough. We'd use one, maybe two pics if it was a fatal. And we'd need a good shot of the kid, the villain. I walked back to the cruiser and leaned close to the glass. The kid was pouting in the backseat.

America's future.

When I walked into the police station, the sound of someone vomiting echoed in the concrete corridor. I knocked once and the metal door to the duty room buzzed and I pushed it open. LeMaire, J. was sitting at a wooden desk writing in the arrest log, a big blue ring binder. Vigue was on the phone.

"She'd be arriving about now, sir. In Lewiston. That's right. Now, Mr. Gamache, I know you're upset. If I was you, I'd be climbing the walls, let me tell you. But listen, sir. Please try to understand what I'm saying. It isn't going to help your daughter if you're in an accident, too. After twenty years, I know. I can tell you I've seen it. It can and does happen. So I know you're going to want to see her, and you're going to want to get there as fast as possible. Do that. But if you obey the speed limits, take it easy, you'll get there just as fast, and you'll be able to help your daughter. Yessir. I know you're upset. Yessir. Please think of what I said."

Vigue put the phone down.

"Jesus H. Christ," he said. "For this they pay me twelve bucks an hour. Guy's so friggin' upset, he'll probably kill himself on the way to the hospital. Should have asked him if somebody else could drive him. Probably doing eighty-five down the one-oh-four by now."

LeMaire, J. grunted.

Vigue lit a cigarette and drew a third of it into his lungs. "What a way to make a living. Let me tell you."

He looked at me.

"What can we do you for, Mr. Clark Kent?"

Before I could answer, the patrolman named Plaistow, who looked almost old enough to be in high school, walked in from the booking area, his uniform splattered with vomit.

"Man, Lieutenant," he said.

"Get the hell back in there," Vigue barked. "He'll drown in the toilet, and your ass and mine will be in court."

Plaistow started to say something but stopped, then turned and walked out of the room.

"Don't teach you about puke at the academy," LeMaire, J. said, poring over forms at the desk. "Report's not done. Not much to it, though. Driver of the Toyota, Lori Gamache, east on Route Two. Second car, Toby Tansey, nineteen, Androscoggin, local dirtbag, swerved from the westbound lane, collided with vehicle one, the Toyota. You saw what was left. Girl is headed for Central Maine Medical Center in Lewiston. Multiple injuries. Tansey is fine, of course."

I got out my notebook.

"Charges?" I said.

"Oh, maybe a couple. We've got to talk to the DA's office again, but he's already been charged with criminal OUI. A point-two-three."

"Not bad for a Sunday morning," Vigue said.

"Probably just out of church," I said.

"Our Lady of Jack Daniel's," Vigue said.

LeMaire, J. continued with his report.

"Okay, the OUI. You got that. Operating without a license. Operating an uninspected motor vehicle. Failure to show proof of insurance. Reckless driving. Let's see. What else was there, Lieutenant?"

"Possession."

"Oh, yeah. Illegal possession of and transportation of alcohol."

"And that's if the girl lives," Vigue said.

"It might be a fatal?" I said.

"I don't know," LeMaire, J. said. "They were talking about internal injuries, internal bleeding. Her insides are all stove up. Steering wheel sort of crushed her chest and abdomen."

"How old is she?"

"Twenty-two. Nurse. Lives in Lewiston, works at the hospital down there, I guess. Up here to visit her parents. Good kid. Comes home on weekends. Father, Lionel Gamache, used to work in the mill. Blackie Gamache, they call him. Lives on Penobscot Street, I think. Used to, anyway."

I scribbled. LeMaire, J. got up from the desk and picked up his camera and started rewinding the film. When the winder spun freely, he popped the camera back open and the yellow Kodak canister dropped on the floor and rolled. He grunted when he picked it up.

"Hey, you know, without Bertin around, where are we gonna get this developed? What are you guys doing with your film?"

"Cindy, our receptionist. She did X-rays at the hospital. She can do it, or I could do it myself if we were in a jam. Takes me forever. What are you gonna do with that?"

"I don't know. Take it to LaVerdiere's? I'm not gonna do it, I know that," LeMaire, J. said.

"You process film?"

"Hated it. All those timers and little reel things. Remember that, Lieutenant? When we hired Bertin to teach us a few years ago. What a joke that was. Remember that, Lieutenant? Ten seconds. Twenty seconds. You couldn't see what you were doing. None of us were any good at it, but we got detail pay. Lieutenant here was the only one who got anything on his pictures. Spit in the water, I think."

Vigue growled.

"Trying to teach you numbskulls is like trying to teach a friggin' chimpanzee. Except a chimp can learn something. You guys would screw up a wet dream."

"What was the idea?" I said.

"Save money," Vigue said. "Bozos on the council decided they'd all get reelected by saving money. Had us walking to save gas. Cut the uniform allowance. What a joke. So we go through all this crap and then the guy behind it, Millington or Pillington, skinny freak, goes back to Mass. or wherever the hell he came from, the son of a bitch."

"I like a happy ending," I said.

"The stuff that goes on," Vigue muttered, and got up and hitched his equipment belt.

We stood for a moment or two.

"Your friend Mrs. Wiggins is in Central Maine Med, too," Vigue said. "Held for observation."

I nodded.

"You should come in tomorrow and sign the reports, after they're typed up. Somebody from the DA's office will want to talk to you."

"I don't think I want—"

There was a shout from the cell block. Then a crash.

Vigue and LeMaire, J. bolted through the door and I followed.

The kid from the accident was on his back on the floor. There was blood on his nose and mouth and he was laughing. Plaistow, the patrolman, stood over him, panting.

"Got behind me," he sputtered. "Tried to choke me, the son of a bitch."

The kid was laughing so hard that tears were running from the corners of his eyes. Vigue used his boot to flip him onto his stomach, then stood with his boot pressing the kid's face hard into the concrete floor. The laughing stopped.

Under the boot, the kid whined.

"Fundamentals," Vigue said. "You've got to keep your prisoner secured."

16

Late Sunday afternoon, I saw LeMaire, J. on the street. I was walking up to the Pine Tree to get something to eat and he was sitting in a cruiser outside the Federal Bank, waiting as a clerk from LaVerdiere's made a deposit. The deposit escorts were one of the department's services for local business.

"How'd your pictures come out?" I said.

"Don't know," he said. "Might get lucky."

"You have a darkroom down there?"

"Got a room full of sinks. Supposed to make our own pictures, sell them to insurance companies. Accidents and stuff like that. So we go out and buy all this stuff and then the whole thing is forgotten."

"So much for that."

"Big ideas come and go. The rest of the stuff never changes."

The clerk from LaVerdiere's came back and got in her car, a white Volkswagen Rabbit. She waved at LeMaire, J. as she pulled away and he gave his siren a blip.

Service with a smile.

"How's the girl from the accident?" I said, still standing beside the cruiser.

"Gonna make it, I guess. Broken ribs. Something about her spleen. Ruptured. Possible punctured lung. I gotta call again tonight. Still hope the little bastard hangs."

"Before he kills somebody else," I said.

"It was my daughter, they wouldn't have to worry about that," LeMaire, J. said, and he put the cruiser into gear and pulled away.

I kept walking. Even if she lived, it was still page one. I made a note to call the parents for an interview. If they were both in Lewiston at the hospital, would one of them come home? I hated hospital waiting-room interviews, especially over the phone. Every one I'd ever done had left me feeling dirty.

For this, I made twelve bucks an hour.

I went into the Pine Tree and saw the heads turn as I walked to the counter.

"Rumors of my death have been greatly exaggerated," I murmured to myself, and picked a stool two from the door, four away from the next diner. I turned as I sat down and saw two old women turn in their booth to look me over. I smiled at them and nodded and they turned back, flustered. One came in every week with notes from the Androscoggin Baptist Church Auxiliary. She turned and peeked at me again.

So this was what Pauline and Martin would get. Times a hundred. For the rest of their lives. The lady who took a shot at the fella from the newspaper. What was his name? Almost blew his head off with a shotgun. Martin had an affair—you remember her, Meredith? Well, he did, and the fella wanted to do a story on it and she went over there and tried to kill him. I knew she wasn't right. Sad. You know, I don't think they should have let her out. Put her someplace where they can look after her, poor dear. Get some medication. You know she always was high-strung. Oh, yes. Even when she was at the school. You didn't think so? Oh, I always did. Maybe if I had said something to somebody, it wouldn't have happened. Oh, I know. You mind your own business or you get nothing but trouble. Oh, yes, I've learned my lesson on that score, believe you me.

Jo, the owner, waited on me at the counter. She was fifty and looked sixty, the answer to anybody who thought hard work kept you young.

"What'll it be today?" she said, wiping the counter with a white cloth and dropping a coffee cup in front of me.

"Tuna fish, I guess. Whole wheat and lettuce, and I guess that's it."

"You had some trouble, I hear."

"A little bit."

"Everybody okay?" Jo asked, pouring water in my glass.

"She hurt her arm. Could have been worse. You think I could have that to go? It's later than I thought, and I've got work to do."

"Sure, dear," Jo said. In a minute she came back with a waxed paper bag holding my sandwich on a paper plate.

Heads turned again as I left.

The trials of a celebrity.

I did have work to do, which said something about the relentlessness of this little paper. It didn't stop for my problems. It didn't stop for Arthur's death. It didn't stop for anything. The *Review* was like a train that always left on time and we were the crew, stoking its fire, taking the tickets, cleaning the bathrooms, and trying to keep it on schedule, and on the track. The same was true for any newspaper, but sometimes this one seemed even more demanding, maybe because there was no other crew to take over.

The crew.

Vern would have to write something about the shooting at my house, I guessed. If we didn't report anything, people would say we covered it up. Maybe something straight for the police log, bare bones from the report. Cover ourselves and nothing more. There was no need to exploit Pauline's mental problems—or was that all there was to it? Jack McMorrow, the great rationalizer. The man of a million excuses, the answer to every ethical question. Like most news people, I did not apply the same standards to my coverage and to myself.

So the pragmatist ate his sandwich at his computer terminal, focusing not on larger issues but on the task at hand, which was to get the editorial page done and out of the way by Monday. That was when the pre-deadline chaos would begin. But if this was not chaos, what was? Did chaos plus chaos equal calm? Screw it. I started typing. And when I felt I'd said everything that needed to be said, I stopped and reread it.

> As most of us know, Arthur Bertin drowned last week in a canal near the St. Amand Co. mill.
> Some of us saw Bertin pulled from the water by rescue crews. Some of us may still grieve over the death of someone who was such a familiar face at ball games and Grange meetings and school plays, someone who was such a part of the fabric of life in Androscoggin.
> And many still may wonder what happened.
> This was not a typical drowning, if there is such a thing. Arthur Bertin did not go for a moonlight swim. He did not capsize a canoe in cold waters on a spring fishing trip. Arthur Bertin died in the murky water of a walled canal in a remote and deserted industrial area. The circumstances of his death would lead any sensible person to ask questions. Apparently, the local and state authorities charged with investigating incidents of this type are not sensible people.
> What other explanation could there be?

After examining the body, Chief Medical Examiner Dr. Richard Ritano ruled that Bertin's death was an accidental drowning. When pressed by the *Review*, Ritano himself said there were no discernible signs of foul play. He also said the fact that no one knows why Bertin was in the area isn't enough to rule the death suspicious.

But if these circumstances are not enough to raise the question of foul play, what does it take?

Facts to consider:

As of this writing, the Androscoggin Police Department has not interviewed any of Bertin's acquaintances to determine if the victim was despondent or suffering from any other mental condition that might be relevant to his death.

Police did not search the canal or surrounding area to see if any clues to the death could be found.

The autopsy showed the secondary cause of death was hypothermia, indicating Bertin was in the water for some time before he died.

State and local police are responsible for two things in the event of a violent crime: One, they must uphold the rights of the victim by bringing the perpetrator of the deed to justice. Two, they must protect the public by keeping the criminal from repeating his crime.

In this case, local and state authorities have done neither. They have not upheld Bertin's rights. Nor are they protecting the rest of us. A full investigation should begin immediately. The community deserves more from its police and prosecutors than just a rubber stamp.

It was long, but they'd read it.

I pored over it for a few minutes before closing the screen. As I pushed the chair back from the desk, I hoped I was doing the right thing. New York agitator, Vern had said. Maybe I was. And what about New York? If they had pulled Arthur out of the East River, would the investigation have been any more thorough? Would there have been any investigation at all? Would I have cared?

Maybe not, but Androscoggin was different. The numbness that comes from anonymity had not found its way here. People lived in a town like this because they expected to matter to many people. They gave to the community and the community gave back. That was the deal. And in this case the deal had been broken. Arthur had given to the town and the town was not giving back. It was a double cross—welshing on a debt. It wasn't right, and the newspaper was the only institution in this town that would do anything about it. And the newspaper was me.

I opened the screen, read the top few lines, skipped down to the conclusion, and closed the file. And when I did, when the screen went blank, I felt something else.

Fear.

I was crawling out on a limb on this one, way out, farther out than I'd ever gone at the *Times* or the *Courant* or the *Journal*. I was the paper. I was the whole thing. The entire paper was my opinion column, and this opinion was not going to be well received. The day it came out, I would walk down the street. I would walk into the Pine Tree and sit at the counter. I would sit at my desk and answer the telephone. I would sit at home with my name in the phone book. And things had been nuts already. What would the next Pauline Wiggins do? Who would I find in my living room next week?

In New York, the security guards would catch the crazies in the lobby. I was anonymous, a face in a room that couldn't be reached, a gun in a building where nobody knew anybody else.

This was not like that.

I couldn't avoid it forever, and Monday morning, I got it full force.

When I walked in the door, Cindy, Marion, Paul, and even a woman I didn't know, hopefully a paid-up subscriber, crowded around me. Vern watched from his desk, a phone stuck in his ear, the model of discretion.

They wanted details. How many shots were fired? How close did I come to getting hit? Did I have to wrestle with her to get the gun away? Did I break her arm?

I looked at them, at the woman I didn't know, and held my arms out straight.

"It wasn't like that," I said. "She's got some problems, that's all. That's all there is to it. Really. She got upset and it happened and it's too bad. For everybody. But it worked out the best it could, and that's all I can really tell you. You understand, I'm sure."

We understand one thing, their faces said. It was the most excitement around the *Review* in years, and I was ruining it.

"Well, God, Jack," Cindy said, speaking for the group. "You could have been killed. It's not like this happens every day. You make it sound like, 'Oh, yeah, somebody came over and tried to shoot me. La dee dah dee dum. Pass the potatoes.' I mean, you could've been killed, you know? I mean, it's Pauline. It's not like it's some criminal. So why did she do it? I mean, go over and try to blow you away. It's unreal; I mean, it's just unbelievable."

And wonderful.

Cindy's eyes were glittering. She was energized, as alive as I'd ever seen her. A monotonous life transformed instantly by proximity to near tragedy. Something extraordinary could have happened. It could have happened to this guy she knew. Oh, yeah. She saw him every day. And then bang. Shot dead by somebody else she knew. If this was possible, anything could happen. Cindy could meet some really rich and cute guy and he would think she was great and they would get married with this really ritzy ceremony and move to California or Florida, where the whole town didn't stink like something had spilled in the oven and it was burning. Marion could win the lottery and buy her kids new mobile homes and put in a pool, an in-the-ground pool, none of this above-the-ground junk, and they would get a camper or even a motor home and drive to Alaska. Paul could get into this business where you never have to do anything, once it gets off the ground, but you rake in the dough and you buy a new 'Vette and you never have to kiss ass in this town again. And Vern . . . I didn't know about Vern.

"Maybe we ought to give Jack a break," he said. "You know, 'Stand back, give him some air.' Think so, Cindy? Get the dirt later. Let the guy at least take his coat off."

"God, Vern, I was just worried about him," Cindy shot back. "Something wrong with wanting to know what happened? This is a newspaper, you know."

"That's the rumor," Vern said, leaning against the counter, a toothpick in the corner of his mouth.

"Well, I don't care," Cindy said. "Do what you want. I've got work to do."

Then, as she turned and walked back behind the counter, she said, "I don't know where the hell you get off."

I stood there in the middle of the entryway for a second, then sighed and went to my desk. The phone rang. A college kid named Dirk or Bert or something wanted to spend the month of January working with us as part of a journalism course at the University of Maine at Orono.

Do us both a favor and stay home, I thought.

"Call me in a week," I said.

A middle-aged woman came in to put in a classified, apartment for rent. Something about her daughter and her boyfriend. Paul was on the phone, taking some heat about an ad. Vern drifted over.

"How you doing?" he said quietly, sliding his sandbag body onto the edge of my desk.

"Could be better. Could be worse."

"I guess. Missed you, huh?"

"You did?"

"Pauline did," Vern said.

"Had me all choked up there for a minute."

"Sentimental fool," Vern said, and he smiled.

He had his coffee cup resting on his lap. When he lifted it up, it left a dark damp ring on his pants.

"It boggles the mind," he said. "This old lady. She probably never shot a gun. Never did anything violent at all. In her whole life. Then she goes berserk. Nutzo. You know what it shows?"

"What?"

"That people have sides to them that nobody sees. Nobody. I've always said that. You only see what shows on the outside. The tip of the iceberg."

Vern held his forefinger and thumb an inch apart. "The tip," he said. "What pissed her off?"

I hesitated.

"I'll . . . I'll tell you later. No, I can tell you."

I lowered my voice.

"You know the picture of Martin? Well, I guess he just went to her and told her all about it. A clean breast of things and all that. I guess she decided it was gonna ruin the guy or something."

"Stuck by her man, huh?"

"And then some. It was kind of noble, really. And sad. Jeez, I still can't believe it happened. Think it'll be in the *Sun*? God almighty. That's all I need. God, talk about ruining a guy."

"Hey, it's what we do best," Vern said. "But the Sunday people, not from around here, might not have even heard about it."

"About time I got lucky. Hey, you got a second? I'd like you to give something a read for me."

Standing at my desk while I flipped most of the mail in the trash, Vern read the editorial twice.

"Two things," he said.

He flipped the toothpick from the left side of his mouth to the right.

"I'm glad it's you and not me. And I think you're right. No, I really do. He wasn't canoeing down there."

"Nope."

"He had bad circulation. He'd turn blue in a cool breeze. Remember how I tried to get him to do those ice-fishing pics last spring? First time Arthur, meek, mild-mannered Arthur, told me to take a hike."

"Yeah, I remember that. He said he wasn't going to get frostbite for pictures of dead fish."

I smiled.

"Son of a bitch," Vern said. "Should have fired his ass."

"Always the hard guy," I said.

The phone rang. And then it rang again. And again after that.

A request for a picture of a ninetieth birthday party. Kids from the school, fourth graders, had written letters to pen pals in Kiev, Russia. The teacher, a woman who sounded young and nice, suggested a picture of the kids in front of a mailbox, mailing the letters. If she could take the picture herself, she was hired.

Some guy from the mill, a worker who wouldn't give his name, bent my ear for fifteen minutes about how the town needed St. Amand Paper, and if we didn't accommodate them, somebody else would. And then where would my paper be? And then where would the town be? There would be no town, and this country would be owned by the Japanese, and they wouldn't have to bomb Pearl Harbor because they'd own it.

International Day at the *Androscoggin Review.*

I told him all the facts should be brought out, then the town could decide whatever the hell they wanted to decide. He went back to the beginning, but I lied and said I had another call and he hung up, just in time for Cindy to hand me another stack of mail, spilling half of it on the floor.

She bent and picked up the envelopes, while I threw the bigger stuff in the wastebasket. The recognizable stuff I separated into piles for Rewrite or Sports or Letters. Still kneeling, Cindy handed me a large brown envelope addressed to JACK MCMORROW, personal. I sniffed it and couldn't smell perfume, but I opened it anyway and then shook it. A note came out and landed on the floor, and there was a photograph left inside, which I started to take out.

From the floor, Cindy gasped.

"Oh my God," she said, straightening.

She was looking at the picture in my hand. I turned it over to see.

Roxanne.

17

She was naked. The word WHORE was written across her belly. I couldn't get a breath. I couldn't swallow.

Cindy handed me the note.

It was the same printing that was on the photo.

> Your trash. The girl is a whore. You leave now or she's a dead whore. You're trouble for this town. You've got bigger problems, Mr. Newspaperman. Like dead whores at 192 Brackett St. Portland. Go back to New Jersey, or you will be dead too.

"You all right, Jack?" Cindy whispered.

I nodded, holding the picture by the edges.

It was black-and-white, a five-by-seven print. It showed Roxanne leaning over the table in my apartment, the low coffee table in the living room. It was blurred, but I could see the picture on the wall in the background. An Indian on a horse. *The Scout*. Frederic Remington. Roxanne looked like she was picking something up. Her breasts were in the picture above a blurred triangle of dark hair.

I picked up the phone.

The receptionist at Human Services had a bright metallic voice, like a computer. Roxanne was in an interview. I told her it was urgent, and she said she'd get the message to her. Her tone said there was no need to discuss it further because her position was set in the stone of department policy.

I hung up and still looked. Cindy was standing as if she didn't know whether to stay or go. Roxanne was reaching for something. A plate, maybe, or a glass. Cleaning up, maybe. Vern walked over. I stuck the picture in the envelope.

"Hey, Jack," Vern said. "You may know this, but with this basketball extravaganza that is going to pay all our salaries—don't thank me—without Arthur taking photos, we're screwed. I can't even fill the thing. What do you want? File shots or something?"

I tried to focus.

"Yeah, I guess," I mumbled. "You mean last year's stuff?"

"Some, not all. Arthur covered two games this year before he . . . before he died."

"What about that high-school kid we used for sports pictures?"

"You said his stuff was junk," Vern said.

"I don't know. It's all relative. Call him and see if he can shoot a few for you. If he can't, you can have my camera."

"You want to see junk."

The envelope was in my hand. Cindy had drifted back toward the front counter, but was still looking back at me, watching. Vern went back to his desk but came back. Bug off, I thought.

He had a folder in his hand.

"Some of these guys have graduated," Vern began, thumbing through a stack of photos that showed blue crop marks. "We have to see what we can salvage here. What we need is a cover photo. And I'm not sure Arthur got anything usable in those first two games. Maybe. I'd have to look again. Maybe he got lucky, so to speak."

Dammit, shut up. Shut up for once.

"These three are possibilities," Vern went on.

He held out three photos: one of a curly-haired kid about to release a jumper, another of two guys wrestling for a rebound, the third one of an Androscoggin kid driving to the basket, frozen in midair. Arthur's best stuff, right up there with the Wonder Waitress.

"Jette, this kid here, graduated. Hell of a ballplayer. In the Marines now. This guy's not playing. Screwed-up family. He may flunk out. That's what I heard, anyway. This guy driving is a junior. Now that is a possibility. He's gonna be all-conference. Good ball handler. Real scrapper. Ballsy kid."

"So use him then," I said.

It sounded abrupt and Vern caught it and looked at me like something was wrong. Then he took his folder and pictures and went back to his desk. I sat down with my picture and looked again.

But Vern was back. He tossed a photo on my desk and I almost jumped.

"That's all sized and ready to go. Here's the dummy for the cover. If you want to send it down early to be shot or whatever. It's up to you. Be nice to give them a little more time to foul it up."

"Great," I said, in a voice that said it was anything but.

I took Vern's photo and slid the brown envelope under it. Vern went out front and I walked to the back of the office, where the baskets were set up for material to be sent to North Conway. I walked past the baskets to the hallway and into the bathroom. Behind the closed door, I took Roxanne's picture out again.

The pen had dug deep grooves in the paper, as if the word had been carved into Roxanne's body. I held the picture up to the light and tried to look at it objectively. Analytically. Roxanne. And he knew where she lived. The picture, Jack. Come on now.

It was grainy, barely in focus, with such a narrow depth of field that the rest of the room—the kitchen door, the bookshelves—weren't recognizable. That meant a long lens. A two-hundred at least.

I pictured the house and the table. By the angle of the photo, it had to have been taken from across the driveway. The embankment there. Someone could get high enough up there to be level with or above the window. And they had to use fast film. Four-hundred. From that distance, that meant a tripod.

This was someone who knew something about photography. And it was someone who had the patience to sit in the dark, peering through a lens for hours, waiting for just the right moment.

Arthur.

But Arthur was dead. He'd been dead a week. When had Roxanne been in town? When had she been in my living room naked?

She'd visited twice. We had made love both times, in the bedroom. I remembered that the first time, she had worn my shirt afterwards. She had said the place was freezing. The second time I couldn't seem to remember if she had worn anything after. But Arthur had been dead then. He'd been dead for days.

I looked at the back of the photo. It was Kodak paper. That narrowed it down. I turned it over and looked at the photo again.

Who printed it? Who would or could print it? We had a darkroom. Arthur did. I'd heard Martin talk about printing pictures, but I'd always thought of that as being centuries ago. But Arthur had taught the cops. That didn't narrow it down, either.

The print wasn't great quality. Along with the blurring and the overall graininess, there were tiny marks, lines that might have been dust or scratches on the negative.

I picked up the basketball photo from the edge of the bathroom sink and held it up.

The basketball shot was cleaner. Sharper. The only blemish was a feathered line on the right edge of the print. I looked at the two prints. The basketball player was a vertical. Roxanne was a horizontal. I turned Roxanne on her side so they were both verticals.

I looked again. The same marks.

For months I'd handled Arthur's prints and I'd never noticed it. Now that I knew it was there, it jumped out as if someone had branded the prints with an iron.

I left the bathroom and went out into the back room to where the files and prints and back issues were kept in no particular order. There were boxes of photos, and I grabbed one that was relatively recent and started digging through it.

The mark was everywhere, wherever the photograph was dark. Grass on a football field. A table at the town hall. The black away uniform of the Androscoggin High basketball team.

It was about a half-inch long on a five-by-seven. A little longer on an eight-by-ten. It was always on the edge of the print and it always had the same shape: feathered, with a slight crook at the inner end, the end toward the center of the picture.

I went to my desk with a few of Arthur's prints and tried to go through the photo process in my mind.

There were any number of ways you could end up with an imperfection on a print. The camera lens could be dirty. Or the film could be scratched as it was drawn through the camera. Sometimes spots or hairlines were caused by dust or dirt that got on the negative in the printing process. Some photographers blew the dust off with compressed air, sold in cans like deodorant spray.

But a scratch on a camera lens didn't show as a fine line on a print. If it showed at all, it would cause a little fogging on part of the picture. And dust didn't land in the same place twice, never mind over and over for months.

So where? How?

I went over the process.

In the darkroom, the negative is placed in a negative holder, a metal plate with an opening the size of a single frame. The negative holder is inserted in the enlarger, above a blank sheet of photo paper and below the condenser. The condenser, a lamp with a thick convex lens attached, throws light on the paper through the negative. The image shows on the light-sensitive paper and, after baths in the developer and fixer solutions, the print is ready.

I ran through the process in my mind as I looked at the two prints.

The common denominator had to be the enlarger. And I'd never known Arthur to use any darkroom but his own.

The jump shot. The rebound. Roxanne. All processed at Arthur's studio? By Arthur? If not Arthur, who?

I sat and fiddled with my notes for a minute and then took out the note and Roxanne's picture. After a minute, my brain made the connection that it should have made immediately.

Fishing the key out of the drawer, I unlocked the file cabinet and took a folder out of the drawer. I opened it and slid the picture of the waitress from the Pine Tree onto the desk. She lay there on the stained oak in her underwear. I looked around to see that everyone was busy, then held the photo up to the light.

There it was.

The line was there. The same line, small and light and feathery and jabbing at me like a tiny knife.

But what did that mean? Arthur took them all? Arthur wasn't dead? No, I'd seen him dead. That someone was still using his dark-room? That—

A hand touched my shoulder.

"Jack, it's Roxanne on the phone," Cindy said, whispering. "She says it's important."

She gave me a knowing, sympathetic look. I reached for the receiver and punched the button.

"Hi," I said. "Sorry to pull you out of your meeting, but something's come up."

"Yeah," Roxanne said. "I got your message, but that's not exactly why I'm calling."

Her voice wasn't right.

"Jack," she said, almost in a whisper. "I got something in the mail."

She took a breath.

"A picture."

It was the same. Same photo. Same inscription. Same theme. They didn't need McMorrow the newspaperman and they didn't need his whore. The message had been addressed to "Roxanne Masterson, Social worker, State Department of Human Services, Portland, Maine."

No zip.

"I don't care about the picture," Roxanne said, her voice hesitant and hushed. "It's just the idea that he's out there. The person on the phone. He, or it, is watching me. God, Jack. They know where I live."

She coughed back a sob, this young woman who earned her living fighting with guys who beat their kids with appliance cords. Mothers who forgot to feed their babies because they were drunk and stoned. People who, no matter what their problem, weren't thrilled to see a social worker coming, and were even less thrilled when she came with a deputy sheriff and took their children away.

Roxanne had told me she'd been spit on, threatened, and called all kinds of names, most of which had something to do with her gender and anatomy. But she was tough, a lot tougher than me in a lot of ways. She just said it was worth taking a little abuse if it saved a kid from a worse fate.

But this one had shaken her, and it was my fault. I had brought her into it. It was my responsibility.

"It's okay," I said. "Probably some yokel from up here who has an ax to grind. With me, not you. Really. He probably couldn't even find Portland."

"Jack, what the hell is going on? You're not telling me. You pretend to tell me, but you're not telling me anything. You're really not. Are you? Are you?"

Was I?

"I don't know," I said. "The guy in the bar. Cormier. The one I got in the fight with. I don't know, but he said the word around town is that I'm out to shut the mill down. Try to do a balanced story on the town's biggest employer pushing for a major tax break, and they think you're out to do something. For them or against them. I guess some of them think I'm against them. But it doesn't have anything to do with you. You're just an easy way for them to try to get to me."

"What do you mean, it doesn't have anything to do with me, Jack. Goddamn it! I'm looking at this, oh, this sick picture taken by some god-awful cretin, and it's of me, and he knows where I live, and you say it doesn't have anything to do with me? I get a phone call from somebody who says these awful things, who was looking in the window, and you act like it's some disgruntled subscriber. Goddamn it, Jack. Somebody put a lot of time into this."

"Yes, they did."

"So what are you going to do about it?"

"Roxanne, I don't know. I've got to think. I've just got to think."

She didn't say anything.

"I'll call you this afternoon," I said. "How long will you be there?"

"Here 'til four-thirty or so. Home after that."

"I'll call you."

"I'll be here or there. With the door locked."

"Yup," I said, and I was going to say I was sorry, but she had hung up.

Oh, man, I thought. What a mess. Going from bad to worse to even worse than that. And I couldn't let it ride. Not with all this going on. Pictures—of her, not of me. A phone call—to her, not to me. Somebody was zeroing in on Roxanne. But would they stop there? How could I know? I just couldn't let her get more involved, drag her in any more than she was already. Because it didn't have anything to do with her. Nothing. Just that she let herself get mixed up with a guy she met at a party.

No, she didn't deserve this, but what was I supposed to do? Pack up and leave town? Let myself be chased out by some crackpot? It was a legitimate story, for God's sake. At any newspaper worth anything, and some that weren't, a story like this would be standard procedure. A company wants a tax break, threatens to pull out of town, you see if they're hearing the same stuff in the next place. Big bloody deal. What kind of a whacked-out place was this?

The phone rang before I could come up with any kind of answer.

It was Cooper Wheeler, my buddy from the *Wall Street Journal*, where he was C. Cooper Wheeler, and very good at what he did.

"Hi, Jack," he said. "How's life with the Eskimo people?"

"Except for sharing wives and rubbing noses, couldn't be better. How's things in the city?"

"Caught some jazz last week and got home alive to tell about it," Wheeler said. "Also, the cockroaches in my apartment are getting smaller. I think it's a genetic selection thing. The bigger ones are easier to see so they get caught easier. The little ones get away, so over the years, the gene pool favors little cockroaches."

"Your thesis stinks, and your research methods do, too," I said.

"Hey, that's why I'm a journalist. Never let the facts get in the way of a good story."

"You're at the wrong paper for that."

"So that's why I never get ahead," Wheeler said.

Actually, he did.

Wheeler was the kind of reporter who made it look easy. He was breezy, charming, very good-looking, and relentless when it came to getting information. He was a journalist James Bond, with contacts in the United States, Mexico, and Europe, and a keen mind, cockroaches notwithstanding. Add to all of that the ability to write very well, and you had a guy who could go to any paper, anywhere.

If he could take pictures, I'd consider him.

Wheeler said he had asked around about my questions regarding St. Amand Paper and their parent firm, Quinn-Hillson, Ltd. For me, it would have been a three-day project. For him, it was like looking up a number in the Manhattan White Pages.

He said he had checked in six states, with five different mills owned by Quinn-Hillson. The word was that the company was in a flat period in sales. It was six months into a strike at a mill in Georgia, which was costing it a fortune, millions of dollars each week. The company had also bought a tissue mill in Oregon that was proving to be a bit of a dog.

"So they're feeling the pinch, and they want to pass it on to the towns where they do business," Wheeler said. "If they can whack twenty million a year off a property valuation, that's money in their pocket every year."

"So in Maine, they threaten to move to Georgia."

"And in Georgia," Wheeler said, "they threaten to move to Maine."

"How well can I document that?"

"I got a couple more newspaper articles. Some more union people you can call. Some other stuff. Fax it up to you?"

"Stick it in the mail," I said.

"How primitive. What do they do? Fly in with one of those floatplanes?"

"No, they fly over. Don't bother to land."

"Is it like an Eddie Bauer catalog, or what?" Wheeler said.

"Just like that. I owe you one."

"Don't worry about it. When you get sick of moose meat and come back to civilization, we'll hit Sweet Basil's, take in some jazz. You remember jazz?"

"Saw 'em last week. Lost by two to the Lakers," I said.

So he had some good stuff. Enough for another story—if not for this week, then for next. Show the town that the company was playing it for a sucker. Show these people that the company wasn't the Great White Father.

A good story. More trouble.

I couldn't leave. It was that simple. I couldn't back off on this story, or any other. The editorial on Arthur wasn't going to win me many friends, either, but it was true. I couldn't start telling lies, even if they were lies of omission.

And where did that leave Roxanne?

The solution was to solve the problem myself. Go after it, push until he or she or they showed themselves. Hope that Roxanne wouldn't be hurt in the meantime. And somehow put out a paper at the same time.

That meant doing things like taking pictures of old people, which I had to do in nine minutes, at eleven o'clock at the Androscoggin Manor Nursing Home. A woman was being presented the Boston Post Cane, an honor bestowed on the oldest resident of the town. The canes were a *Boston Post* promotion that had long outlived the *Boston Post*. For as long as anyone could remember, the canes had been given for the oldest person in town to hold. When a cane changed hands, it was a bittersweet occasion, because in order for one person to get the cane, someone else had to give it up. And the cane-holders rarely handed their canes over voluntarily.

In this case, the cane was being transferred from a man who had been ninety-seven to a woman who was ninety-six. I stuck my photos in the folder, put them back in the file cabinet, and locked it. Without looking at or talking to anyone, I left the office, went to the car, and drove the mile to the nursing home. The manager of the place was loud and patronizing, probably from habit. The old woman sat in a chair in her room and smiled for me as I took her picture. When I left, I squeezed her hand. She was a nice person. She had just lived too long.

It troubled me, this mockery of what had probably been a fulfilling life. Driving back downtown, I had half-decided not to use the picture at all when the flash of blue strobe lights in the rearview mirror jerked me back to reality.

I pulled over on Penobscot Street and unrolled the window to the cold. Vigue walked up and leaned toward the window.

"Something I thought you should know, chief," he said, peeking over the top of his aviator sunglasses.

"What's that, Lieutenant?"

"Mrs. Wiggins walked out of the hospital in Lewiston this afternoon."

"Just walked out?"

"Hey, it's not a jail. Happens."

"She mention my name on the way out?"

"I don't believe so. Didn't even stop to pay the bill."

A car drove by and the driver tooted at Vigue. He waved absently.

"No," Vigue said, "I figure somebody will pick her up walking on the side of some road someplace. Old lady hitchhikers are hard to come by."

"You think she's dangerous?" I asked.

"I don't know," he said. "I wasn't looking down the business end of that Parker. What do you think?"

I thought for a second while a pickup went by.

"No," I said. "I don't know. I think it was just one of those things. Something that happened once."

"Once is all it takes," Vigue said, sliding his sunglasses back up. "That's why I carry this."

He put his hand on his holster and turned and walked back to his car and pulled away fast. I sat and watched his car until it turned the corner a block up. When he had disappeared, I sat some more.

That's why I carry this? What the hell was *that* supposed to mean? Was I supposed to go out and buy a gun so I could shoot an old lady? Was Pauline going to pick me off as I walked down Main Street? Put a bomb under my car, crawling under there on her skinny fragile elbows, one of which was now broken? Or was she going to go down to one of the local dives and offer somebody five hundred bucks to off me?

Vigue couldn't possibly think so. She had been irrational, upset, maybe a little senile. But a hysterical old woman was not a killer. If she was not a killer, then what did he mean? Why did I feel more threatened after his warning than before?

And why couldn't I bring myself to tell him about the pictures and Roxanne?

It was the logical thing to do. Roxanne undoubtedly assumed I'd done it as soon as I saw the picture. But I couldn't bring myself to go to the cops. Not these cops. Not now.

If they happened to catch somebody, which was highly unlikely, the charge would be criminal threatening. Maybe terrorizing. I wasn't sure exactly where one began and the other left off. I was sure that Roxanne felt terrorized. Terrorized and terrified. And I was beginning to feel a little terrorized, too.

But the issue wasn't the crime. The issue now was what I was going to do about it, why I wouldn't go to the cops. And that issue was trust. I did not trust Vigue. I trusted LeMaire, J. a little more, but not much more. I didn't trust anybody, and in this town, way up here in the woods, it really was a terrifying feeling. It wasn't a feeling that I was going to be harmed. It was worse than that. It was a feeling that, up here in the woods, on the edge of the cold, black mountains, I was very much alone.

When I went home to eat that afternoon, I got out of the car slowly and stopped and looked up at my bedroom window. It was still closed. I couldn't see anyone. I turned and looked back at the woods, listened to the red squirrels chirring at each other in the oaks. That was the only sound. I waited to make sure.

I stopped on the landing outside the door and listened, hearing only the hum of the refrigerator. I pushed the door open slowly and listened again. Then I walked very slowly through the kitchen, the living room, the bedroom. After I looked in the bedroom, I went back through the kitchen to the bathroom and flipped the shower curtain aside.

There was nothing there but a bottle of shampoo and a bar of white soap with a hair embedded in it.

I felt a little silly, but not a lot.

Standing in the kitchen, I ate a sandwich. Cheddar cheese on wheat with good mustard. I tossed the knife in the sink, brushed the crumbs off the counter into my hand, and went back downstairs and outside. I walked around the front of the house, crunching through the inch of crusty snow, and looked up at my living room windows. Then I walked across the yard, across the driveway and into the trees, and began walking up the hill between the spruces and hemlocks. The snow was sprinkled with hemlock cones dropped by the red squirrels, but there was no sign that anyone had been there. No tracks, no nothing, until I got halfway up the hill.

And then there were tracks. Lots of tracks, in front of a big hemlock.

The footprints were bigger than mine, and rounder, like they were made with rubber boots. Flurries had settled in them, but they had been made after the last light snow, on Thursday. They came down the hill, shuffled around for a while in front of the tree, and then turned back up the hill again. I followed them and about thirty feet up, only fifteen feet from the edge of the street on the next block, found what I was looking for.

Three small round holes in the crust of the snow.

This was the spot. Roxanne had come out of the bedroom, leaned over the table, and the shutter had opened. It had stayed open for a tenth of a second, maybe less. It had been enough to capture the image on film, and the image had been delivered to both of us, with message attached.

The three holes had to be from a tripod. I took a plastic calendar card from my wallet. The card had a three-inch rule on the side and I crouched down and measured the tripod hole. Three-quarters of an inch. I turned the card end over end and measured one of the footprints. Thirteen inches. Big feet—or at least big boots.

18

There were sixteen Cormiers in the phone book and nine in the town of Androscoggin. I called seven before I found a woman who said she knew my Cormier because he was her cousin. She said she didn't know where he lived and hadn't seen him in months. I asked very sweetly if she knew somebody who might know a little more, and she sighed and finally gave me the name of somebody called Chereel.

"What's the first name?" I asked.

"That is her first name," she said.

I called the number she gave me and a kid answered. He sounded nine or ten and he shouted something over the blare of a television that was tuned to a show with a laugh track. Somebody shouted back and I heard the receiver clatter as the kid put it down. Then he was back.

"What do you want?" he said.

"I want to know where Roger Cormier lives," I said.

"He ain't living here."

"I know that. I wondered if you would know where he is living."

The kid didn't answer and then I heard the phone clatter again. It sounded like he was throwing it against a concrete wall.

I waited. He came back.

"My ma says she ain't seen him, but he used to be living with Tammy, but he left there and now he's got a place on Waldo. Waldo Street. You a friend of his?"

"I haven't seen him in a while. Where on Waldo Street?"

"Where on Waldo Street, the guy wants to know," the kid yelled. "He says he's a friend of Roger's. How the hell should I know? . . . Behind Lockhart's store. Ma says behind Lockhart's store."

"Thanks a lot," I said.

"You're a cop, ain'tcha," the kid said.

It turned out that there were a lot of places behind Lockhart's store, which was officially known as West End Variety. The lady behind the counter said she knew Cormier lived back there someplace, but didn't know where, so I bought my Pepsi and left.

Around the corner, I handed it unopened to a little kid, a boy with long hair tied with a bandanna. He looked at me like I had handed him a can of cyanide.

Behind Lockhart's store were four cars, old with mag wheels and Bondo spots here and there like camouflage. One was crammed with parts and junk. Pieces of broken plastic toys were strewn over the hard-packed gravel—the yard for a four-story block of apartments, on which rickety wooden porches hung like scaffolding. Garbage bags, some ripped, some open, were lined up in front of the stairs. When I stepped on the first step a gray cat shot out from the bags and across the yard.

I crossed the porch on punky floorboards and knocked on the window of a wooden door. I knocked again and waited like a Jehovah's Witness until a gray head appeared behind the glass and a short but very wide woman in her sixties opened the door. When she did, the smell of cat urine billowed out into the cool November air.

"Eh?" she said.

"Jack McMorrow," I said, matching her for succinctness. "Looking for a guy named Cormier. Lives out here, but I don't know which apartment."

The woman looked at me like I had asked directions to Zimbabwe. She was wearing a print shift, the kind they used to call a housecoat. In the background a game show announcer was shouting.

"Out back," the woman growled suddenly. "Up the driveway, then left. A couple doors down."

"First floor?"

She nodded yes as the door closed. I thanked the door very much for its time and assistance.

Out back meant another building, another porch. There were trash bags on the steps and more kids, younger this time, but they ran past me. One, a girl about two, fell down on the last step and sprawled in the yard and an older kid came back and helped her up. A flicker of humanity.

There were two doors. I walked past the first one and heard a baby crying inside. It was a manic kind of sobbing, and it hurt to even listen to it. I walked to the next door. Because the glass was held in with duct tape, I knocked very carefully.

I waited and knocked again and the door opened. Cormier looked sleepy. I could smell alcohol.

"Yeah?" he said.

"Need to talk to you," I said.

Recognition came slowly, but when it did, Cormier turned around and walked back into the apartment. I followed him into a small stuffy room with a cloth couch with ripped arms and a wooden cable spool in front of it for a table. There were four opened Budweiser cans on the table and a bottle of Jack Daniel's. The apartment was strangely silent. No music playing. No television on. Just a table with beer and whiskey. An Androscoggin ascetic.

There weren't any chairs. Cormier sat down on the couch and put his arms behind his head. His belly showed in an inch-wide strip where his black T-shirt pulled up. His eye patch was gone.

"We going to court?" he said.

"That's one of the things we have to talk about," I said. I was standing in the middle of the room wishing I had somewhere to lean.

"So talk," Cormier said.

I looked at him for a second and plunged in.

"So what are they saying about me at the mill?"

Cormier closed his eyes, bored already.

"The mill. He wants to talk about the friggin' mill. Why should I talk to you about anything?"

I couldn't think of a good reason so I didn't say anything at all.

"Oh, man, are we going to court or what? I hope not, 'cause I want to get the hell out of here. Okay, the mill. What are they sayin' about you at the mill."

"Yeah, you said you picked me out because I was gonna close down the mill. Trying to, I mean."

"Could be. I'd had a few. I could've said a lot of things."

"I want to hear more about that."

"You do. Well, hell, let's see. They say there's this pussy from the newspaper, if you want to call it that. He's gonna take away their bread and butter, you know what I'm sayin'? That is almost enough to piss them off because they got kids and fat-assed wives."

Cormier hauled his big flabby frame off the couch and walked into an alcove that was the kitchen. I heard a refrigerator door open.

It swung into view. There was a girlie-magazine foldout taped on it. She swung out of sight and the door slammed shut.

He came back with two bottles of Bud. He opened one for himself and handed one to me. I opened it and took a swallow. He drained half of his, his neck muscles undulating like a snake as he swallowed.

"How'd you know who I was that night in the bar? I want to hear it again."

"I knew. Somebody told me. One of the guys I knew from the mill. He said he's seen you around. His buddy's a cop and the cops knew you, or something like that. But we knew who you were."

"Why come over and pick a fight?"

Cormier half-smiled.

"Why not?" he said. "Hey, man, I was pretty buzzed. These guys are talking about this newspaper guy and he walks in. It was, like, meant to be, you know. No big deal. Then you go and stick your finger in my eye. That was unfriendly, man."

"Accident. I was trying to keep from getting pulverized."

Cormier finished his beer and put the bottle on the wire-spool table. Leaning back, he fished a pack of Salems out of his front pocket.

"So we going to court?" he said, puffing a cloud of smoke.

I sipped my beer and looked around the apartment. There was nothing on the walls. A cheap stereo sat on top of a wooden crate. Cassette tapes were scattered all over the floor.

"You trash my place?" I said.

Cormier shook his head no.

"When was this?"

"Last week. My place got busted up pretty good."

"Not by me. You really aren't on my mind that much, I gotta tell you that. No offense."

"You didn't know about my place getting wrecked?"

"News to me," Cormier said, and he got up from the couch and went to get another beer, this time only one, and it wasn't for me.

"You know Arthur Bertin?" I asked.

"The guy who took the pictures."

"Yeah. For the paper."

"Knew who he was, I guess. Skinny guy, right? Wore weird clothes."

"Ever hear anything around that he was sort of a pervert?" I said. "Following high-school girls around and all that?"

"Hey, I do that," Cormier said.

"No, I mean stuff like peeking in people's windows at night. Taking pictures of women as they're getting dressed."

"Sounds great. Where do I sign up?"

He tilted his beer bottle back and drained another six ounces. I'd lose him if I waited much longer.

"You never heard of this Arthur guy doing that kind of thing?"

Cormier rested the bottle between his legs and put his feet, in black leather boots, on the table. The bourbon bottle wobbled.

"How the hell should I know? Some weird old fart. He diddles himself, he calls me up?"

I waited.

"Okay," Cormier said slowly. "There was some story. I don't know. The guy, Artie or whoever he was. This was a long time ago. Years maybe. Well, this guy with the camera had the hots for this high-school bitch, some piece of jailbait, and the cops . . . what did they do? They did something. Like put him on probation or something. I remember being someplace and hearing some guy hassling the camera guy about it. Some bar. No, wait a minute, it was . . . I can't remember. But the cops did something."

"Vigue?"

"Vigue, man. That friggin' guy is on a power trip. Big man with the big gun. I'd like to get him without his badge and that goddamn three-fifty-seven. Stick his head up his—"

He caught himself.

"We going to court?" Cormier said again.

I took a swallow of beer and made him wait. The Budweiser tasted pretty good, considering.

"If I say I don't want to sign a complaint, what happens?" I said. "You get off with disorderly conduct?"

"How the hell should I know? Maybe I pay my hundred bucks over at court and that's it. Hey, I just want to get out of here. Armpit of the Earth."

"That the only thing you remember about Bertin? The photographer?"

"What do you want, the Shell Answer Man?" Cormier said, still leaning back on the couch. "Dirty old man. Wanted to get his rocks off and couldn't. It's going around. Chicks around here are either married, fat, or jailbait. Another reason to hit the road."

I put my empty bottle on the table.

"Another thing," I said. "Somebody called my girlfriend up here and said some nasty things to her. You hear about that?"

He shook his head, no.

"Who's your buddy?" I said. "From the driveway?"

"Jimmy Libby. He's a good shit. Just trying to help me out."

"That's nice of him. Well, listen. I'm probably going to let the thing drop. Probably. You hear anything about the phone call or anything else, if you let me know, it could make a difference."

"But you're not gonna push this thing with the cops?"

"That's the way I'm leaning," I said.

Cormier smiled.

"There's some people around here who'll be glad to hear it," he said.

Roxanne called a little before five that afternoon. I was standing in the window of the office watching a family pile out of their car, a big, black clunker. It looked like foreign dignitaries arriving at the White House. Roxanne asked if there was anything new. She sounded better. Regrouped and shored up. I said there wasn't anything big, but I told her about the enlarger.

"So you go around looking for the right enlarger thing," she asked.

"I think I know where it is," I said. "Right in Arthur's studio."

"What'd the police say?"

"Not much. Not yet. I'll know more tonight. What are you doing?"

"I'm not going home and hiding under the bed. Even though that's what I really feel like doing. There's a new woman in the office. Sort of new. She's from Philadelphia. Her husband is an engineer or something. I think it's an engineer. She asked me if I'd like to go with her up to Freeport. Her husband has meetings or something. Something where he has to go to present plans to town selectmen. We might get something to eat in the Old Port on the way home."

"Sounds good."

"I can't hide away, Jack," Roxanne said. "I've got to live my life. I really do. But I'm not going to live it in Androscoggin. Not for a while. Do you understand?"

"Sure. The Welcome Wagon hasn't been all that great up here."

"It doesn't have anything to do with you."

"Sure it does."

"No, our relationship, I mean," Roxanne said.

"You mean the way we can't keep our hands off each other?"

"Yeah. That's the same. But that place and everything that happened. I can't."

"I know. I'll call you. After ten."

"I'd like that."

"Next best thing to being there," I said.

"Not what I would call a close second," Roxanne said.

"Nope."

"Jack, be careful. Really. For my sake. I want you all in one piece. Don't do anything foolish. Let the police take care of it. They get paid for doing that."

"Underpaid, they say."

"I'm serious. You remember."

"I will," I said.

And I did remember.

I was careful when I pulled into the vacant lot diagonally across the street from Arthur's studio. It was eight-thirty by the digital clock, three bucks at Kmart, glued to the dash. I forced myself to wait until nine. Nobody came or went. A few cars drove by, but nobody seemed to pay any attention to the old black car parked with the rest of the wrecks.

The building was owned by a guy who had run a paint and wallpaper store in the space next to Arthur's. I remembered that Arthur had told me the guy lived in Zephyrhills, Florida, that he had a mobile home in a park. Arthur had been worried about sending his rent money that far.

At two minutes after nine, I got out of the car and walked to the studio door. I looked both ways, like all kids are taught, then took out a screwdriver and removed the screws on the padlock hasp. I left the padlock hanging and slipped inside.

The same musty odor hit me before I flicked on my flashlight and moved the pale beam over the cardboard cartons and piles of newspapers. I crossed the room and swung the blanket aside. The air was close in the darkroom and there was an odor of mildew. I stood for a minute and listened. The faucet dripped slowly but steadily.

Sinks were on the left and the counter was on the right. The room was ten feet deep and about seven feet wide. There were two enlargers on the counter. One was partly dismantled.

I looked at it closely.

It stood about three feet high, with a print holder at the bottom and a black paper bellows for moving the light above the negative tray. The lamp and condenser had been removed and sat at the back of the counter with some empty coffee cans. The enlarger, the parts, and the cans were covered with a fine layer of dust.

The second enlarger was about the same vintage but intact. It wasn't covered with dust. How much dust would accumulate in the week since Arthur had died?

A car passed outside. I switched off the flashlight and listened. When the sound faded, I looked for wall switches until a chain brushed my face. I pulled it and the safe light came on with an amber glow.

I needed photo paper. In most darkrooms, the paper would be within easy reach of the enlarger. I scanned the counter, then opened a cupboard below. There was a box of eight-by-ten paper. Where the box had been slid onto the shelf, there was a dark patch cleared in the dust.

The box was half-full. The wastebasket was empty. It was possible that Arthur had emptied it before he died, but unlikely.

I put a sheet of paper in the tray at the bottom of the enlarger and slid an empty negative holder under the condenser. When the condenser, a black cylinder, was pressed against the negative holder, I set the timer for fifteen seconds and pulled the cord to shut off the light. Then I hit the switch.

The light from the enlarger lamp showed pale in the darkness; the photo paper glowed white and blank. I turned the focusing wheel and bent closer to the rectangle of light as the lamp moved down and up in its carriage.

And there it was.

It was in the lower right corner of the paper. The same feathery line. White in the photo of Roxanne and the other pictures, it showed gray on the undeveloped blank sheet of paper.

I moved it in and out of focus. There were dust particles and what looked like tiny hairs. The line was darker and thicker. I moved the paper left and right and the line moved across the paper, one way and the other, as permanent and recognizable as a fingerprint. I put my hand under the light. It showed faintly on the skin of my palm.

The light went out, plunging the room into darkness. My fifteen seconds was up.

It took a few minutes to find the scratch that was leaving the line, the enlarger's signature. I unscrewed the condenser cowling and took out the lens. The lens was about four inches across. Near the center was a barely visible scratch, about a sixteenth of an inch long. It looked like the lens might have been put down on a piece of sand or metal.

"It was here," I said, startling myself with the sound of my own voice.

I put the enlarger back together, putting the piece of photo paper in my pocket. On the way out, I checked the sinks. There were four trays for processing film, three plastic and one aluminum for the acetic-acid stop bath. The faucet was dripping into the last tray, which was overflowing into the sink. I turned the cold-water handle and the drip stopped.

In the outer room, I picked my way with the flashlight. I looked behind the counter in the rubble and opened a metal cabinet along the wall. Beside the cabinet stood an aluminum tripod. It was dusty, with Arthur's name written on a piece of adhesive tape on one leg. The legs on this tripod were square. The holes in the snow had been round.

On the drive back, I decided it was time to go to somebody. Not the locals. Not Vigue. Maybe the DA's office. Maybe the AG. Neither prospect thrilled me, but if not them, who? There was no one else.

The lights were on in the office when I drove down Main Street. Vern's station wagon was out front, which meant that at least I would have a sounding board. I was afraid I had lost Roxanne for the duration.

I parked behind Vern. A car drove by and the driver beeped. I waved but didn't recognize the guy. It didn't really matter; this was a town of wavers and beepers. I wondered how that would work in Manhattan. A *New Yorker* cartoon in the making.

The door was open and I could hear Vern typing on the terminal out back. He typed like it was a typewriter, pounding on the keyboard in a way that probably voided the warranty.

I started toward the back of the office, but something caught my eye to my left.

"Hello, Mr. McMorrow," a voice said.

I turned.

Pauline Wiggins had found her way home.

19

She was wearing a bright green ski parka over the same blue dress she'd had on when she came to visit me before. Her hands were on her lap and she was sitting in a wooden straight-backed chair. Her face was white as a mime's.

It was one of those awkward moments. Out back, Vern was typing furiously. I considered yelling. Maybe running out to get to a phone. Or even just walking calmly up to Pauline and telling her she'd have to go back to the hospital.

As usual, I did none of the above.

"How you feeling?" I said.

She pulled at her sleeve.

"I was hospitalized briefly for stress," she said. "The treatment was of limited value, and I chose to leave and spare Mr. Wiggins the expense. I'll have to return this coat to the hospital as soon as I get home. I'll mail it. Or maybe UPS would be faster. What do you think?"

Again, no decision.

"This isn't easy for me," Pauline said. "I've come to personally request that you not file homicide charges against me. I do not want to spend the few years I have left in some squalid women's penitentiary. I don't think I could make that adjustment at my age."

Her voice was strangely detached. Calm and almost childlike.

"Don't worry about it," I said. She didn't seem to have heard me.

"It was not my intention to do you any harm. I am almost positive I did not fire the gun intentionally. I think I was startled and the gun went off accidentally. I must also say I have not come to apologize. Oh, no. I meant what I said. I did. Our relationship may normalize over time, but I will never have the respect I had for you before this unpleasant incident."

Likewise, I'm sure, I thought. I took my parka off and sat on the edge of the table.

"Jack," Vern called. "That you?"

"Yeah, it's me," I called back.

"Keep it down, will ya, buddy? I'm trying to put out a newspaper back here."

I looked at Pauline.

"Been home yet?" I asked.

"I'm on my way. Mr. Wiggins will be worried. He's a man of regular habits. Even in his years in the newspaper business, he managed to maintain a normal home life."

She smiled weakly and I wondered if she was on medication.

"Arthur Bertin was a very hardworking man," Pauline said. "But like many people, he had a flaw. He was weak. If life did not meet his expectations, he would alter it in his mind."

"Like when he said he thought Martin was his father?"

"A fantasy. Another of his fantasies. Of course, he had no father. Martin was a father figure to him. It was natural for him to want him to be more."

"Were there other fantasies?" I asked.

I sat very still on the table. She sat very still in the chair.

"Police, I think. Arthur wanted to be a policeman. One time, it was years ago, he came to Martin and said he had been made a reserve officer. He seemed so thrilled that Martin put the story in as a news item. To please him, really. Of course, the police chief, Brennan was his name then, called to say it wasn't true at all. Martin had to run a correction, which was something he always prided himself on not having to do. He prided himself on his accuracy. Arthur tried to explain his way out of it, but I think most people knew."

Vern was on the phone now.

"Hey, Coach," he shouted. "Heard your boys are ready to play some basketball at Lake Region next week."

"So did Arthur get in trouble doing this stuff, Mrs. Wiggins?" I asked.

Pauline nodded and smiled. Her hair had fallen onto one side of her face. She didn't appear to notice.

"Especially when they involved romantic interests, I guess you would call them."

"Dates?"

"No, not dates. Crushes. I suppose that's the word. Infatuations. And indecent photographs. One time one of these women—I knew who she was because I had her mother in school, the Holbrooks— used to have a big dairy farm out where the River Road is now, but she received one of these photographs and the police were notified. This is your character witness, Mr. McMorrow. This is the man who is condemning Mr. Wiggins. Remember that. How credible is your source for a story? Isn't that what you're supposed to ask? You'd know better than I."

Suddenly she stood up.

"I'll call Martin," I said.

"Oh, no. I can get along quite well without your help," Pauline said. She was suddenly cool, as if she'd just remembered that we were supposed to be enemies. With her head held high, she walked slowly to the door, opened it, and went out, turning up Main Street.

I grabbed the phone and dialed Martin's number. He answered.

"Pauline was here, Martin," I said. "Just now. She's going up the street toward Woolworths. No, she's fine. Just talking a little funny. She's wearing a bright green jacket. I can see her right now."

I waited in the window. In five minutes, Martin's old Chevy went by. It pulled up near the fire station and the interior light went on. I saw one figure get out and two figures get in. When the car had pulled away, I called the police. As I waited for somebody to answer, I remembered what Vigue had said.

That they're all nuts. Just the right push and they go over the edge.

I didn't sleep well that night. When I called Roxanne after ten, there was no answer. I dreamed that she was murdered and I saw it on the six o'clock news. Vern was the anchorman because the regular guy was out sick, and I was allowed to sit on the set but not to speak.

It was beginning to get light when I finally fell into a deep sleep. When I woke up, it was after eight. It had snowed four or five inches and the rooftops looked like a Currier & Ives print. Snow-covered town with mushroom cloud hovering paternally overhead.

I parked a block down from the paper, on Court Street again, but hadn't gone ten feet from the car when I was waylaid by a man named Park who was shoveling snow in front of his insurance office.

"What is this I hear about you and Martin Wiggins's wife?" Park said, leaning on his shovel. "You had some kind of trouble?"

"A misunderstanding," I said. "Just a misunderstanding. It was unfortunate."

He wanted more but I smiled and moved on, and kept my head down until I got to the office. I was a moving target, and the Main Street gossips let me slip through, but Cindy did not.

She was made up like a geisha and she met me inside the front door, standing so close I could see the flecks of mascara on her eyelashes. The top two buttons of her blouse were unbuttoned and a pearl pendant hung in the shadow of her cleavage.

"I have to talk to you," she said, confidentially motioning me over from the door to the front window. "I heard Pauline Wiggins is back. She escaped from the hospital. She's home, and I guess nobody is doing anything about it."

"Somebody must be doing something," I said.

"No, Jack," Cindy insisted. "I mean the cops. I heard they aren't going to send her back or anything."

"Where'd you hear that?"

"At the Pine Tree. Jo told me. Martin called the police himself, and they told him not to do anything."

I thanked Cindy and told her not to worry. She said she was worried, and I told her she had no need to be. I did not tell her that I wasn't worried about a nut with a shotgun. I was worried about somebody much more calculating, more rational, more dangerous.

There were messages on my desk but no plain brown envelopes. No express mail from New York. I saw that Wheeler had called, along with a couple of names I didn't recognize. Taking a deep breath, I tried to begin the process of getting organized.

Paul had gone out on the road selling, but he'd left me a memo. It said he'd sold three hundred inches of ads and had commitments for another hundred and sixty. The Christmas rush was on, and Paul predicted a record week. I planned to go twenty-four pages, and if Paul was on the mark, we'd have as good an ad line as we'd had since I'd been at the paper.

I asked Cindy about classifieds and she said they were light. People were shopping, not selling used cars, Marion said without looking up from her keyboard. Vern was on the phone, but when I asked him how many pages he'd need, he held up five fingers, indicating five wide-open pages. I made a note to call North Conway to see when they'd need the stuff for the basketball section.

With the plan taking shape, I took a look at the dummies, then sat down to write the story about the Route 2 accident. I had to check with the hospital to get a condition report on Lori Gamache, and I had to see if the driver, El Scumbag, had bailed. Wouldn't want him to miss Christmas because of a little fender bender.

I tried Roxanne at the office and they said she was out on an evaluation. I left a message, relieved that she was safe in the company of an alleged child molester, somewhere in the wilds of Cumberland County.

With a few minutes to spare, I decided to run down and check the cop log and find out about the accident charges. I pulled my parka back on and was on my way out the door when the phone rang.

Cindy called that it was for me and I grabbed the phone.

"Jack McMorrow," I said.

"Mr. McMorrow," a youngish-sounding guy said. "Yeah. Hey, I don't know if you're interested, but I thought I'd call you. My buddy and I figured, you know, that you might want a picture in the paper and everything. We didn't know, but we thought you might want it."

"Want what?"

"A coyote. Big son of a whore, too. Must go forty, fifty pounds, easy. I'm not shittin' ya. Big male. We thought you might want to come and take a picture, maybe put a write-up in the paper."

Great. Another dead animal photo. News, features, and taxidermy.

"Oh, I don't know," I said. "We're kind of on deadline right now, and I don't really have anybody I can break free to send out there. Could you bring it in and we could see what we could do here?"

He snorted.

"Sure. I mean, shit, it's up to you, but I gotta warn you. He ain't too fond of people."

"He's alive?"

"Shit yes. Alive as you and me."

"What did you do, trap him?"

"Live-trapped him. Bacon grease, sheep guts, some hamburger. I think there was something wrong with him. He was hanging around near my uncle's farm, you know, on the tree line, never went away. Got so hungry he screwed up."

"I thought they were smarter than that," I said.

"I did, too," he said. "Like I said, I think there's something wrong with this guy. But I ain't gettin' close enough to look him over."

"The game warden there yet?"

"He's coming, but they said it would be a while."

A live coyote. Now that was worth a picture. Dead ones we saw once a month. Live and snarling was something else.

"Okay," I said. "Where is it?"

"You gonna come yourself?" he asked.

"Yeah, there's nobody else. How do I get there?"

"You know how to get to Roxbury Pond?"

"Yup."

"Go past the pond. You go up one-twenty, right? Take a right on the Roxbury Road and go past the pond and then you'll come to the Andover Road. You go on that and after maybe four, five miles you'll see a blue trailer. Another half-mile, you come to this tote road on your right. There's pulp piled right before it. Come in there, about a quarter of a mile. You'll see a four-wheel-drive. Black one. That's mine."

"What's your name?"

"Blaine Cole," he said.

"I thought you said it was up by your uncle's farm."

"It was," he said. "But these critters travel. We tracked him with a dog, found where he was laying up near this deer yard, you know? Trapped him in this friggin' wire pen. You gotta see it. Worked slick as shit."

Route 120 snakes its way north of Androscoggin along the Swift River up to Andover. I'd swing off before that, going maybe ten or twelve miles all told before I came to the stretch of road Cole was talking about. I'd driven it a few times, usually on my rest and recreation jaunts. There was a camp road off it that led down to Garland Pond, but I'd never been down in there. I thought that might be the road he was talking about, and I hoped it wouldn't be too rough for the Volvo, with its low-slung suspension. Cole had said he'd gotten in with a four-wheel-drive.

I drove as fast as the road would allow, slowing for ice patches as the road snaked between ridges of spruce and granite ledges. A couple of loaded pulp trucks passed me coming the other way, and I swung way over onto the shoulder as they careened around the bends, bound for the mill and a paycheck. Far be it from me to slow them down on the road to prosperity.

The snow had turned the landscape from rugged to beautiful, and, for the first time in days, I felt a surge of rejuvenation, then a slow-spreading feeling of relaxation. It was beautiful and still up here, and the stillness was contagious. I passed Roxbury Pond, which was white with a dark stain at the center, where it looked like a spring had kept the water open. They weren't ice-fishing yet, but in two months the pond would look like a refugee camp, dotted with ice shacks and crisscrossed by tire tracks.

I watched the odometer and after four miles, I slowed down. I counted six-tenths of a mile and the trailer came up on the left, abandoned, and more rust than blue. Then came the tote road, a brown gash in the wall of spruce. I turned in.

There was a single set of fresh tire tracks in the road, which was really more like a wide path, a pickup truck wide, with deep ruts. I eased along in first gear, trying to keep to the left of the ruts. The road veered to the right after about fifty feet, then wound downhill past the tangles of uprooted birches and spruce, tipped back by the skidder that cut the road. I drove another seventy yards and came to a turnaround. The other tracks made a circle and left the way they had come.

So where were they? Was there another road after this one? Maybe they didn't even consider this a road, and I'd come in on this skidder trail for nothing.

I got out and looked around and spotted footprints that led farther in. Grabbing my camera and notebook, I followed them through the woods, listening to the twittering siskins in the hemlocks and the *dee-dee* of chickadees in the brush. The tracks went fifty yards or so and then the tote road hit a better road, a camp road, maybe, with more tire tracks. It led down toward where I thought the pond would be, where I probably was supposed to go in the first place. I followed the tracks, thinking in the back of my mind that it would be a nuisance if this turned out to be a wild-goose chase.

Just what I needed with all I had to get done in the next—

The sound was to my left and behind me. A *thump* sort of sound. I started to turn. Was hit and falling, the camera swinging, then grinding into my belly.

I was on my stomach in the snow. I tried to roll to my right. Knees slammed into my back. I gasped. An arm—blue sleeve and glove—wrapped around my neck and jerked against my windpipe. I whipped my neck straight back to get some slack but the arm stayed with me.

I couldn't breathe. I was choking.

My legs kicked up over my back and hit something hard. I kicked again. Again. The grip loosened on my neck and I swung my left elbow back as hard as I could. I hit air.

I bellowed and swung again. Something snapped. Feet pounded in the snow, and mud and hands and knees and chests pressed my face into the ground.

"What the goddamn hell were you waiting for?" a voice sputtered.

"For you."

"If my friggin' nose is broke, I'm gonna kick your ass."

I tried to move but I couldn't. I tried to yell and it was like screaming underwater. Something hard and metal, like a gun, jabbed me in the base of the neck.

"Shut your mouth or you're dead," a voice said.

20

Idiot. Sucker. Dummy. A coyote in a cage. God almighty!

I strained to see through the knit material of the bag or hat or whatever it was that they had jammed over my head, but could only pick out shadowy figures and the outline of a door or a window. The bag was dusty, and I sneezed and felt saliva on my chin.

They'd tied a rag around my head and through my mouth and then put the bag over my head, terrorist-style. The bag was fastened with something tied around my neck. I'd been dumped in the back of a van and driven more than three minutes, because I had counted very carefully, "One thousand one, one thousand two, one thousand three . . ." Now I was propped up against a wall, my hands tied behind me.

I counted the shadows. Three of them. Two stood near the window or door and watched. The third was doing something with canvas. Maybe a window shade. The room was cold.

One of the shadows came close and untied the ropes on my wrists. I smelled body odor, cigarettes, and something sweet. Gum or candy. When my left hand came loose, I jerked it straight up, catching a face with the bony part of my wrist.

"You friggin' son of a bitch," the face said.

A hand gripped my left wrist. I braced and waited. The blow was low and forced the breath from my lungs. I waited but the next blow didn't come.

Cold metal brushed my wrists. Something clattered on the floor. A tool. The metal, a cable maybe, looped twice around my wrists. Hands worked behind me and a tool hit my arm. Once, twice, three times.

The cable tightened. A wrench. They were using a wrench to tighten the cable. That meant nuts and bolts. A clamp.

A shadow passed in front of me, very close, from left to right. I kicked out as far as I could and hit bone.

"Ow!" the shadow yelled. I waited.

This time it was the head. The top. White hot pain. Sickening pain. I bit down on the gag to keep from screaming.

"Jesus," someone said. "He didn't say to kill him."

I felt a wrench turn, tightening the cable on my right wrist, and a draft of air brushed by me as someone stood up. A door opened and then shut. There were steps outside. Inside a floorboard creaked.

I wasn't alone.

I slid my legs up and down to ease the stiffness behind my knees. Nothing moved. I worked my arms and found that they weren't bound together. I could stretch my arms out behind me, but the cable was too short to get my arms out in front.

"You can flap your wings there, but you can't fly," a voice said.

I gave him the finger. He laughed, and I could hear him coming closer. He was at my left. I tried to get to my feet and he pushed me back down by the top of my head.

"Pussy," he said. "What a little pussy."

The voice was familiar. Strong Maine accent. High-pitched and young. I wanted to keep him talking. I wanted to know who he was. Why they were doing this.

I kicked to my left. He shuffled and cackled. His shadow passed in front of me, but I didn't let on that I could see him.

He tapped my right cheek. Then my left temple, harder but not hard enough to hurt. The voice came from my left.

"I'm over here, tough guy. Over here. No here. What's the matter? Why don't you run to the cops now, dink? Or do you like it? I think he likes it. I think he's one of those pussies."

The patter continued. The taps became slaps and light punches. Back of the head. Belly. Upper arms.

As he talked, I listened intently and tried to place his voice. Young. A punk. Maybe I'd seen him in court or the police station. The drunk driver? No, he wouldn't be out, would he? And how would he know me? How would he have had the time to set up the trap that I'd walked right into?

A live coyote trapped with bacon grease.

Back of the head. Right shin. A kick to the thigh. I winced.

Feet shuffled, like a boxer in a workout. I sat and took it, lashing out with my feet when he seemed to be tiring of the game. Keep him talking, I told myself. Keep him talking.

He was breathing hard from jumping around. Probably some skinny-assed guy who hadn't had any exercise since he got kicked off the basketball team in junior high. He stopped and I gave him the finger.

And I heard it.

He coughed and cleared the phlegm from his throat with a guttural, gargling sound and spat.

The driveway. Cormier's friend. That bastard Cormier.

234 • GERRY BOYLE

When I had told him I wasn't going to press my complaint, he had said that there were people in town who would be glad to hear it. And then he hadn't passed the word. Or he had and this was pure recreation.

Vigue had said to come back and sign a complaint. I hadn't, but maybe it had gone forward anyway. Maybe a court date was coming up. Maybe they had decided it would be better if the complainant wasn't around and their buddy was safely whisked off to some lumber camp north of Spokane. Of course, they might call him back if there was a kidnapping investigation, but these guys weren't big on foresight.

You don't want him to go to court? We'll take care of that. We'll tie him up until you're gone. We'll tell him we caught a live coyote.

If that was the plan, I could feel a snag coming on, at least for me. The cold was already seeping into my limbs. If I sat here even one night, I could get frostbite. Hypothermia. And I had a paper to put out.

I hadn't even told anyone where I was going. All they knew was that I had picked up my camera and walked out the door. The panic began to well up inside me, and I forced it back down, biting hard on the gag.

The buddy was still coughing, and finally I heard him open the door and go outside. I crossed my hands and felt the cable. It felt about an eighth of an inch thick, fed through U-shaped clamps. There were nuts on the ends of the clamps that tightened and clinched the two strands of cable together. I tried to undo them with my fingers. They wouldn't budge.

I reached behind me and found that the cable was looped around a pipe. A water pipe? A heat pipe? Was it copper or steel? It felt smooth but I couldn't tell.

Sitting still, I listened. I couldn't hear Cormier's buddy. Maybe he'd chickened out. I listened another ten seconds and then decided to move.

If I turned around, I'd get leverage. I pulled my feet up under me until I was in crouch. Inched my feet backwards underneath me and then pitched forward onto my knees, leaving my arms spread-eagled behind me. I knelt there for a moment and then lifted my legs back and over the right end of the cable, between my arm and wall. One leg went over and then the other and I squirmed and kicked until I was on my side, both arms and the cable out in front of me like a steel jump rope. I turned to face the wall, my arms and legs out in front of me. I kicked at the pipe, hard. Nothing.

I sat and rested. Cutting pipes. Who cuts pipes? Plumbers, with hacksaws. And those blades that they turn and tighten until the pipe snaps off. I didn't have a blade and I didn't have a saw. I had four feet of cable.

"Think, McMorrow," I muttered. "Think."

Maybe I could rub the pipe with the cable, weaken it. If it was copper it might work. If it wasn't copper, at least I'd stay warm.

I listened for Cormier's friend. Nothing. Maybe that was the idea from the beginning. Tie me up and leave me for hours, or even days. I'd like to see Vigue call this one an accidental death.

My left wrist was cut worse than my right. I dug in my pocket and got out a handkerchief and tried to cram it under the cable on the underside of my wrist. It wouldn't fit, so I let it drop to the floor. And then I began.

The motion was like the arm swing in running, except more compact. I counted fifty strokes and was encouraged by the sound of the cable on the pipe, a sound like sawing. Too bad the cable was sawing through my wrists faster than through the pipe.

I couldn't think of the pain. I counted more strokes, up to a hundred. I told myself I was like a swimmer, working to keep up the pace. I concentrated on the rhythm until sweat ran down my face in rivulets and dripped down my neck. My shoulder muscles cramped, and finally, I couldn't stand the pain in my wrists anymore.

But the motion had grooved the pipe. I could feel it. It was a definite groove. I looped the cable around the palm of my hand and started again.

Would they come back and tie me tighter, tie my hands together? I didn't want this to be for nothing, not for them.

I bit the gag so hard that my teeth ached and picked up my speed. Two hundred strokes, then three hundred and four hundred. The blood ran warm and sticky on my palms and between my fingers.

The cable broke through to the hollow core of the pipe at eleven hundred, sixty-one. I could feel myself beginning to cry and fought it off. I thought of slave labor, captives on galleys. If they could do it for years, I could do it for an hour. I thought of strokes of oars, of guys paying thousands of dollars to do something like this in New York health clubs. I thought of Roxanne and the stories I had to write, next week, the week after. I thought about Arthur and Ritano, that smug son of a bitch. He was on my list, that bastard.

When the pipe began to bend, I had long since stopped counting. My shoulders cramped unbearably, like one giant muscle spasm had gripped the upper half of my body.

But it was coming.

Another five hundred, I told myself. Twenty-three, twenty-four, twenty-five . . .

It broke at seven forty-eight, throwing me on my back on the floor, a glorious feeling. As I pulled myself up from the floor, I heard a truck coming. The van. I clutched at the bag over my head. The knot was at the back of my neck and my bloody fingers couldn't loosen it. Finally, I got a grip on the fabric on top of my head and pulled and pulled as hard as I could until it tore and I ripped it in two pieces off my neck.

The room was empty. A summer camp. The pipe was copper, a water pipe bent away from the wall. I slammed through the door, dove to my left, and crashed through the brambles and woods with the cable held in front of me.

It was a race against time as much as flight from Cormier's friends. I had no hat, no gloves, and was wearing cotton corduroy pants that were fine for the office but no protection at all in the woods at night.

Hypothermia would kill me, and I'd be just as dead as if that guy back there had smashed my skull.

I moved in a zigzag trot toward the brightest light. That would be the west, where the sun had already set. I felt like they had stayed on the same side of Route 120, which would put the road between me and the sun. If I was wrong, I was running deeper and deeper into the woods.

The light faded by the minute. I took a winding route around the worst brambles but kept the light ahead of me. Every few minutes, I glanced behind me to make sure it was darker in that direction. In a half-hour it would all be the same. Very dark and very cold.

I tried to pull the cable off but my hands were numb and sore and I couldn't turn the nuts. The loop kept springing out of my hands, snagging around branches and my legs and feet. I fell. Got up. Stopped to pull the cable from a snarl of branches that felt like blackberry brambles. It got darker.

The ride had been three or four minutes. I tried to remember if he got the van out of second gear. It didn't seem like he had, but I couldn't be sure. If he hadn't, that meant he had stayed on logging roads, and we couldn't have gone more than two or three miles. Did we go south or north? North, I thought. It had felt like we had taken a lot of right turns.

A bramble raked my face. I reached out to grab it and the cable slapped me in the face. I flung it aside and started to run, flat out, plunging through small spruce and birches. Panic. I forced myself to slow down and conserve energy. Counted to ten. Took a deep breath. Gathered up the cable and trotted on.

And then stopped.

It was faint, but it was not my imagination. There, it shifted. Then again. A diesel motor. A truck that had to be on Route 120, on the highway.

I'd gambled and won.

I broke into a lope again, but the road was farther away than I'd hoped. When I pushed through a spruce thicket, there was always another. I couldn't hear the truck, but I kept going in that direction, running, walking, then running again. Then the last wall of spruce broke open and I fell into the ditch beside the road. I scrambled up the embankment and came on to the pavement on my hands and knees. On my feet, I ran along the pavement, my boots pounding. South was to the left, and I wanted to see if I could spot the tote road before it was completely dark.

Headlights appeared up ahead. I slid down into the ditch and lay with my face against the sand and ice until the car passed. A small car. Not a van. But I wasn't taking any chances.

I hit the turnoff in what felt like about ten minutes. It was the tire tracks that I remembered. The truck tracks, wide and deep, and the print of my Michelins in between. The truck had come out, but it didn't look like it had gone back in.

The woods were black. Every few steps I stopped and listened. I could hear the wind. Branches snapping from the cold. Nothing else. When my car came in sight, I felt in my pocket for my keys and clenched them in my fist in relief. With the car fifty feet away, I took out the keys and sprinted. Clattering up to the car, I found the driver's window smashed but the door open. I got in and jammed the key in the ignition and floored it, hitting the lights and second gear at the same time. The car slammed over the ruts all the way back to the highway, and then I raced all the way back to town, the cold air blasting me in the face and the cable coiled in my lap.

My first stop was Waldo Street.

There was a car parked in front of Cormier's building and the lights were on in his apartment. I took the stairs two at a time and saw him with two women on the couch as I flung open the storm door.

The inside door was locked. I took a step back and swung the cable. Glass shattered and there were screams. I yanked the cable back and swung again, taking out more glass. The women ran into the kitchen. I reached a bloody hand through the window and opened the door from the inside. Cormier was standing in front of the table with a beer bottle in his hand.

"You son of a bitch," I shouted. "You. Your goddamn friends did this. And now you're gonna pay for it. We're going to court big-time. Son of a bitch."

"Call the cops," a woman's voice shrieked. "Call the cops."

"Hey, you're crazy, man," Cormier said, backing up a step. "I didn't do nothing to you. I swear. I swear it, man. I don't know what you're talking about."

"From the driveway. Your little friend. Libby or whatever the hell his name was. He was there."

"I don't know—"

"Hey, I don't care. You're buddies. Gonna keep me out of court. So they smash up my car and put a goddamn bag over my head and tie me to a pipe and that's kidnapping, and that's a Class A felony, and you do time for that. Real time. And you'll go down with them. You think you got problems now, oh, baby, they're just starting."

I was shouting but I could feel the anger draining from me. A woman, young and blonde with black eye makeup, peeked out from the kitchen. She had a butcher knife in her hand.

"Get a wrench. Pliers," I told Cormier. "Get 'em now."

He stood there for a second, weaving on his feet with his bottle in his hand.

"You got it all wrong. I don't know what happened to you, but it didn't have nothing to do—"

"Get 'em."

He backed into the kitchen and I followed. I held the cable by both hands, down by my side.

"You friggin' nuts?" the blonde snarled.

"Could be," I said. "Fit right in around here."

Cormier dug in a toolbox on the floor and came up with a pair of pliers. I took them from him and worked on my left hand first, one eye on the woman with the knife. The other woman was crouched behind the table. I could see dark hair and black sneakers.

The pliers slipped with each turn but the nut finally dropped off. I pulled the clamp off and slid my hand out. The wrist was raw and black with dirt.

I did the other hand and when it came free, I kept the cable ready, doubled once. They watched me.

"The guy in the driveway. Spits a lot," I said.

"He's just a guy I know," Cormier said.

"He's just a guy you know who just got you in big trouble."

"I didn't tell Libby to do nothing. I didn't."

"We're going for a ride," I said. "You and me."

"Like hell."

"Or I go to the cops right now," I said.

Cormier looked too big for the Volvo. His knees were drawn up as he told me he hadn't told anybody to do anything to me, that they wouldn't have done anything like this anyway because it wasn't worth going to jail over. He kept saying it, but I told him what had happened, I told him what had been said, I told him about how his pal had enjoyed harassing me, and after a while he stopped saying it wasn't true.

We drove out Route 2 to the west, past McDonald's and the Andro-scoggin Shopping Center and a couple of tourist motels. I turned around in the parking lot of one of them, and came back toward town. By the time we went over the metal bridge, I had decided I believed him.

Cormier had no reason to rough me up. He had thought he was home-free, until now.

"'Don't suppose there's any way you'd forget it," he said. "I'll get your car fixed. Just tell me how much. I'll give you the money tonight."

I kept driving. He looked out the window. The trucks were lined up to unload at the pulp mill which was across the canal. Arthur's canal.

"I want the window fixed," I said. "But that's not all I want. I want information. And I want you to get it. You do that for me, maybe you'll stay out of this."

"What do I look like, friggin' Sherlock Holmes?"

"That's your problem. You don't want to do it, we can go right over to the police station and I'll file a complaint all right. I'll get some nice color pictures taken of my hands all bloody. See what a jury thinks about that."

Cormier looked at me, then looked out the window.

"Somebody is sending my girlfriend nasty pictures with nasty letters. They called her on the phone. I don't know who; do you?"

He was looking at me now. I watched his face. It was relaxed and blank, as if he didn't know what I was talking about. I relaxed, too, 95 percent sure that he didn't know anything about any of it.

"It could be somebody from the mill," I said. "You see if you can find out."

"How the hell am I gonna do that?"

"You know a lot of people. Ask around. Make it a joke. I don't know. Do whatever you want."

He looked at me as if I'd asked him to find a cure for cancer.

"Your buddies were told to do this tonight. You say it wasn't you. I want to know who it was, and I want to know who's hassling my girlfriend. You can find out."

"You want all this by tomorrow morning or what?" Cormier said.

"You want to do five years in prison?"

"You're pushing your friggin' luck, you know that?" Cormier said.

"That's just what I was gonna say about you."

I went past the pulp mill and turned around under the glare of the mill-yard lights.

"That's not all," I said, driving back toward town. "This guy Arthur Bertin. The guy who died. See what you hear on the street about it. The cops haven't done a thing on it. Like they don't want to get involved. It's weird. See what you hear."

"How the hell am I gonna do that?"

"You and your buddy, Libby. In the driveway, you acted like you had an in with the cops."

We crossed the downtown bridge, turned on to Front Street.

"So does he have an in with cops or what?" I asked.

"I don't know what you call an in. His sister is married to a cop, is all."

"What cop is that?"

"LeMaire. Jimmy LeMaire."

It all hit me after I dropped Cormier off at a variety store on Waldo Street. I felt sick to my stomach and broke out in a sweat. It was all I could do to shift the car and get home, and when I did, I stood in front of the toilet, head down, feeling like I was going to vomit. I didn't, and finally I ran hot water from the tap and washed my face and hands.

Using a soft wet towel, I dabbed at my wrists until most of the black came off and they were red, stinging raw. My face was chafed on one side and there was a lump on the top of my head that was tender to touch.

Great shape to put out the paper.

I wiped my face and brushed my teeth and dabbed at my hair with a hairbrush. With all that, I still looked like hell.

I went into the kitchen and thought about eating. Instead, I opened a can of beer and took two long swallows. Just like in the movies: Take this. It will calm your nerves.

Numb them was more like it. I stood against the counter and ate a few crackers as I finished the beer. I was numb. My mind was shut down. The only thing I really wanted to do was crawl in bed and go to sleep. Instead, I had to go down and deal with the real world and real problems and turn a pile of junk into a newspaper that people would buy and read. Oh, the bed was inviting, but I didn't accept. After a last cracker, I put on my now-dirty parka and went back to work.

Yes. I was true to my profession and true to the *Androscoggin Review*, and, when it came down to it, true to Cormier. I didn't go to the cops. But they came to me.

The cruiser was parked in front of the paper. I cursed and drove by and swung around the block, parking on Front Street, way down, so that they wouldn't see the car. Then I realized that would make them wonder more, me walking up on foot, all cut to hell, so I circled around onto Main Street again, but parked just around the corner from the office, away from the lights. When I walked up to the front door, Vigue was coming out. When Cindy and Marion saw me, they bustled out onto the sidewalk.

"What happened?" Cindy Melodrama said. "Are you all right? My God, we didn't know what happened. You didn't tell anybody where you were going, and when you were gone so long, on deadline day, I mean, we didn't know what to think."

What to think, I thought. Try *how* to think. But I fought off the urge to say it, too.

"I'm fine," I said slowly, even coming up with a little smile. "I went off the road, up near Roxbury Pond. Hit some ice and off she went. I cut my hands up a little, but nothing serious. Just took me a while to get the car out. No big deal. I'm fine. I would have called, but the nearest phone was right here."

Cindy looked at me, disappointed that I wasn't more severely maimed.

"Well, you don't look fine," she said.

"A little worse for wear," Vigue put in, eyeing me with that practiced cop's eye, listening with that cop's ear, that ear that can detect a lie intuitively.

Vern came out of the door and asked what happened, and I had to stand on the cold sidewalk, in the light showing from the front office, and give an abridged version of my already-abridged story.

"How's the car?" Vern said.

"Not too bad. Mostly the glass. I cut my hands on the window trying to get the damn door open. That's gonna be fun to replace. A driver's-side window for a sixty-four Volvo. How are you guys doing? Hope you didn't let my absence affect your production schedule. We've got a paper to get out."

It fell flat. They all looked at me like I was either crazy or, in Vigue's case, lying, and I got the feeling that I'd better not make these mishaps a habit, or I'd start to lose their respect. But everyone is entitled to one kidnapping and near-death from thugs and frostbite. Hell, in this town, maybe everybody was entitled to two.

A couple of people stopped—the guy from the florist's across the street, a retired guy who used to drive a truck for the town, and now had something to do with kids' football—so we started to go inside before we drew a real crowd. I was at the door when Vigue nodded toward the street.

"Got a sec?" he said.

I did, so we stood at the curb by his cruiser until the florist and the football guy moved on. Vigue touched his mike and said he'd be back on patrol, then lit a cigarette.

"Must have been a hell of a crash," he said. "What'd you do? Cut yourself out with your wrists?"

I rubbed my wrists and stuck my hands in my pockets. "Ah, not as bad as it looks. I just slid off the road. I said turn and the car said no. Road curved and I went straight. Going a little fast for the conditions, as they say. Car's fine, really."

Vigue looked at me, then looked away again.

"I know when somebody's bullshitting me, and you're bull-shitting me," he said. "A car accident don't cut your wrists like that. Unless you get real depressed about the whole thing and decide to do yourself in. You got anything to tell me, you can tell me now. Or you can keep it. I'm not gonna drag it out of you."

I shrugged my shoulders.

"Shoot yourself," Vigue said.

He tossed the cigarette butt onto the street, where it scattered red sparks and then died.

"I think you're full of shit," he said.

"Isn't that state police territory up there?"

"Unless there's some connection to Androscoggin, chappie. And something tells me you weren't tangling with a bunch of upcountry hillbillies. Am I right?"

I looked down the street.

"I'm not too popular in town right now," I said. "People at St. Amand think I'm out to get the mill. And I think somebody ought to do something about Arthur getting killed, to be honest. People are calling my girlfriend. She's getting threatening letters. Then I was supposed to come in and file a complaint against Cormier, but I didn't. Stuff still happened."

"Change your mind?"

"He's leaving town anyway," I said. "Let him go."

The radio in the cruiser bleated something unintelligible, like a message from a space alien.

"You can report all these things, you know," Vigue said. "There's laws. Criminal threatening. Intimidating a witness. Assault. That's why they have laws."

"Yeah, and one of them says you can't kill mild-mannered photographers. I'm going to write something about that one. Nothing personal. Directed at the state people more than you."

"Ballsy bastard, aren't ya," Vigue said.

"Not particularly."

"No," Vigue said. "Not at all. Well, let me tell you a couple of things, chief. I may not be the smartest guy in the world, but I've been doing this job a hell of a long time, and I've learned a few things. The hard way sometimes. Like I know when somebody says 'Nothin' personal,' it's time to bend over, 'cause they're gonna stick it to you good. And you're gonna say I'm not doing my job on this Bertin thing. Well, look at yourself. You write your little stories, but when it's time to come forward and testify, it's 'Oh, he's gonna leave town anyway.' Well, mister, don't tell me I ain't doing my job, because I can't do it alone. Nobody's coming in to tell me about what happened to Bertin. I got nothing. I can't make it up, like you. I got to have something to go on, and right now I've got a guy in a canal. That's it. And the guy was a fruitcake. You know it and I know it, so let's not kid ourselves. He was a few cards short of a deck, and he turned up dead, and if you've got any suggestion as to why, I'd be glad to listen."

"What do I know about it?" I said. "Go out and talk to people. Talk to cab drivers. See if somebody dropped him off. See if the people in those pictures might have wanted him dead. Talk to Mrs. Wiggins, for God's sake. She hated the guy's guts. And she almost killed me without even trying. I don't know. Don't you think somebody ought to be doing something?"

"Yeah, and if I did all those things you're coming up with, I'd be right back where I started. Nowhere. Because Pauline Wiggins don't know nothing about nothing. You try ID'ing the people in those pictures. And I go up and I say, 'Hey, this guy is dead, and he took your picture, even though you might not know it. So did you kill him or what?' Only place that works is in the movies."

"Nothing works if you don't try it at all," I said.

"Jesus," Vigue said.

He opened the cruiser door and the heat rushed out.

"Hey, that's the way I feel," I said. "It really isn't anything personal."

"Hell, it isn't. Make me look bad, make the department look bad. Run our asses all day and night, trying to keep people happy, and then we get this crap in the paper."

"But a guy died," I said. "This is serious."

"He was friggin' nuts," Vigue snapped. "He could have been down there taking pictures of the moon. He could have been barking at the moon. Maybe he was looking at waitresses and he had to go jerk off. Maybe he got sick of jerking off and jumped. What I'm telling you is, sometimes you don't know. You can ask all the questions in the world and you still won't know, because nobody does. Except the deceased, and they ain't talkin'."

Vigue got in the cruiser. The radio was squawking and snapping.

"The reason I was here was to tell you we need that complaint right away if the case isn't gonna get tossed out. But you don't need to know that now, right? No, you just have to write your stories. Must be nice."

Well, not really.

No. It wasn't nice—not when you had to take all this insane stuff, and then you had to come back and write some news stories. Not when you spent half the day being kicked around and screamed at and beaten up, and then you had to come back and fill the paper. Then it was not nice at all. Then it was so far from nice that I didn't want to think about it.

With two days left, I'd written an editorial and Arthur's obituary. The rest of the news pages would be blank unless I filled them. I stood on the sidewalk in the cold, with my raw hands in my pockets, and watched until Vigue's taillights swung left at the end of the street. It must be nice, I thought, and then turned and walked into the office, emotionally drained and physically exhausted, and ready to write about a girl who had been nearly killed by a drunk driver.

A nice change of pace.

Actually, it was pretty mechanical. I called the hospital and got transferred from one person to another until a nursing supervisor grudgingly told me that Lori Gamache was out of intensive care and in stable condition. I called the police station and asked for LeMaire, J., and they said he was off until Wednesday. I asked if they knew what Tansey had been charged with and they said I'd have to talk to LeMaire, J. or Vigue. I said I'd call back.

At six-thirty I started calling Roxanne, at the office and at home. No one answered at either number. I called every half-hour until nine o'clock, and in between, I called LeMaire, J. at home, where he said nothing had changed. I also called the girl's father at the hospital, asking for him by name and then waiting while they dragged him from some grim waiting room, or worse yet, from beside his daughter's hospital bed.

"Yeah," he said.

The voice was lifeless, like it was a flower and the hope had been pressed out of it.

"Mr. Gamache, this is Jack McMorrow. From the *Androscoggin Review*. I'm sorry about your daughter, and I'm sorry to bother you. I just wanted to see how your daughter was doing. I was at the accident and—"

"You writin' a story?" he said.

"Yes, I am."

"What do you want from me?"

"I want to know how your daughter is," I said.

"You wanna know? I'll tell you. My daughter is hooked up to machines. A whole wall of machines. She got tubes up her nose and in her arms and coming out of her belly. They say she's doin' okay considering her insides were crushed. I got no way of knowing. But I do know one thing. What'd you say your name is?"

"Jack McMorrow."

"Well, Mr. McMorrow, this I know. That son of a bitch better pray for twenty years, because if he gets out, I'm gonna kill him. Put that in your goddamn story. He gets out, he's dead. He should have been dead a long time ago, 'cause he wouldn't stop until he hurt somebody, and now he's hurt my girl, and he isn't worth shit. If I could get my hands on him, I'd kill him right now. 'Cause my little girl never hurt nobody. She comes up to visit me and her mother. I don't dare to bring her mother in here 'cause she'd have a heart attack and die. I told her she could come tomorrow and she might die then. So put that in the story. I got nothin' more to say."

I started to say I was sorry, but he had already hung up. I hung up, too, then went through my notes line by line, filling in the missing words, going over the words that were in shorthand. A relatively routine accident story had just become the lead of the paper. Right across the top of page one, a quote broken out next to the photo. The "tubes in her nose" quote? Or could I get away with the threats? Probably in the body of the story, but not in the head or in a break-out. The guy hadn't been convicted, after all. But I'd move it up high, get Gamache in the lead, and then use the quotes by the third or fourth graf. The human side of a drunk-driving accident. The raw agony of seeing a loved one injured. The senseless waste of drunk driving.

Next time I wanted to go for a drive with a beer, maybe I should think of Mr. Gamache.

But the story was good stuff, and I could feel my heart pounding, that eager bit-champing feeling that reminded me why I was in the business. New York. Boston. Androscoggin, Maine. It didn't matter where you were. A good story, a gut-kicking, hard-driving, knock-their-socks-off story, was the same no matter where you wrote it. The readers would not put this one down. They would not turn the page.

They would read every word and still want more. They would feel for the father, feel for the girl. They would hate the kid and call for his head. And the newspaper would be the catalyst for all of it, rubbing their noses in reality, forcing them to confront this tragedy.

That was our job. That was the true power of the press, and it felt good to be a part of it—so good, in fact, that for a moment, I forgot about my own troubles. I almost forgot about Roxanne.

With a twinge of guilt, I called her at the apartment. No answer. I called her at the office and got the answering service. I called her at home again. Still nothing. With the Gamache notes still in front of me, worry began to push aside euphoria. Would she go out alone? Maybe I should drive down . . . but how could I? Getting the paper out already was going to take a miracle. And I just couldn't. Physically, emotionally, I just couldn't. I should, but I couldn't.

I grabbed my parka and left, telling the room that I'd be back. It was cold on the ride home with the wind rushing through the broken window. I trudged up the stairs, exhausted and sore and numb. All I wanted was sleep. A hot shower and then into the sleeping bag. I opened the door and closed it behind me as I groped for the light switch, found it, and flicked it on.

And stopped.

I tried to speak but I couldn't. I walked to the living room. Touched her back. Her hair. I pulled the hair from her face.

"Baby," I said. "Baby."

21

Roxanne was wearing a black slip. Her dress was on the floor. One leg was bent.

"Oh, my God," I said.

"What's the matter?" she said sleepily. "Is everything okay?"

I sagged.

"Yeah, everything's . . . Oh, God."

She had fallen asleep. She had been waiting for me and she'd fallen asleep.

"I thought—I don't know, I thought something had happened," I said, still standing over her chair.

"Jack," she said. "Jack, take it easy. It's okay, baby, it's okay."

Roxanne reached out and took my wrist. I flinched.

"What the—," she said.

"I think we've got to talk," I said. "I think we really should."

It took a while. Three beers just for the briefing. Roxanne put on my bathrobe and we sat on the couch. She sat close to me, nestled against my side with her legs drawn up underneath her. As I talked, telling her about the coyote, Cormier's buddy, Cormier and his girls, she stroked my hand. When I finished, she took my hand in hers and squeezed.

"Jack, this isn't right," she said softly. "It really isn't. I know police in Portland and South Portland. From work, I mean. And I never hear of anything like this."

"They don't want to worry you," I said.

"I'm serious," Roxanne said, leaning toward me. "This is crazy. I'm afraid of what's going to happen. My God, Jack. Think about it."

"I'm trying not to."

"Well, you have to. People beating you up. Taking pictures of me. My God!"

"I think you're taking his name in vain," I said.

"Jack, come on. It's not something to joke about. Those guys could have killed you today. Or left you to freeze to death or lose your fingers and toes, even. Is a story worth that?"

"Could be my Pulitzer," I said.

I grinned but Roxanne didn't. She didn't answer, either, and I watched her for a minute, saw her eyelashes go up and down as she blinked. She was a very good person for such a good-looking person.

"What are you thinking?" I said, finally.

She blinked a couple of times before answering.

"That you should come and live with me," Roxanne said. "Write to the owner guy in Florida and tell him you're done. Give him two weeks' notice and come to live with me. You could work in Portland. They have a newspaper. You could get a job there. The *Press Herald*. Get a job as an editor or something. God, Jack, wouldn't it be nice? We could make love every night and go places. Out to dinner. Skiing."

"I fall down a lot," I said.

"Jack, come on. We would never have to see this awful place again. Oh, this damned place."

She blinked but it was to blink back tears.

"Jack, I hate it. I hate it, I hate it, I hate it, I hate it."

I put my arm around her and she seemed very small.

"I know," I said. "I know. And you don't have to be here. I'm the one who got you into this."

"Then get me out," Roxanne said. "And get yourself out, too."

I sighed.

"It isn't that easy, Rox," I said. "The paper has to come out and—"

"The paper! Damn the paper; Jack, you aren't the only one who can put out a paper. It isn't worth it. Getting beat up and spied on and who knows what else, just to put out this paper in this hick town? Oh, God, I'm sick of even talking about it. I'm going to bed."

And she did. I sat on the couch with a warm beer and listened to her turn the pages of a magazine for a few minutes. After a few more minutes, the light clicked off. I sat and wondered if she wasn't right.

A paper in a small town. A paper read by high-school sports nuts and little old ladies. Was it worth risking your life for? But then, what kind of a threat could it be? Could anything I wrote be enough to get somebody to kidnap me and beat me up? The mill story? I just couldn't believe that would happen, not millworkers. Not even a bunch of drunk rednecks who didn't like my looks. This wasn't bar-fight stuff. This was the real thing. What could the *Androscoggin Review* do to make somebody take these kinds of chances?

I wouldn't tie somebody up in a cabin over a story about a paper mill. I would if I'd killed somebody and didn't want any more said about it. If the guy at that paper wouldn't let it die, I might do a lot of things to make him change his mind. But had I pushed enough to get somebody's back against the wall? Only if whatever, whoever it was, was close to being exposed. If that was the case, I could be in danger of more than being hauled off to a camp for the evening. And so could Roxanne.

That night I slept with my arm around Roxanne's waist. When I woke up, it was still dark and I could feel her breasts moving up and down as she breathed. She was warm and soft, and my knees fit into the backs of her knees. Her thighs rested against mine.

I lay there and held her for a few minutes and then hoisted myself out of bed. From the closet, I grabbed a warm shirt, holding the hanger to keep it from jangling. I grabbed my pants, boots, and socks off the floor and carried them to the kitchen. The clock on the stove said three thirty-five. I wrote Roxanne a note by the stove light and hoped she wouldn't wake up before I got back.

The heat began to seep into the car as I drove out Route 2 and I took my gloves off and held my hands over the warmth of the defroster vent. Three miles out, I veered to the right and drove slowly past Arthur's studio. It was dark. I pulled into the service station lot between two snow-covered cars and shut off the motor.

Silence.

I could see the front of the studio building and the driveway behind the pool supply store. The street was dark except for the street-lights. No cars. No lights in the houses. I thought of all those people snug in their beds as I burrowed my hands deeper into my pockets, then stuck them under my arms. The chill was setting in.

I was here, sitting in the brutal cold in the middle of the night, because the studio was the only place where anything actually had happened. The pictures of Roxanne had been taken after Arthur had died; the prints had been made here. The studio was being used. And if I didn't budge, didn't move to Portland to sit in hip little bars and write about rich people, then the photographer had to do something more. Maybe more pictures. Sent to more people.

After fifteen minutes, I turned the radio on. The one station I could find was doing a late-night country-western music call-in show. The callers all had southern accents. I wondered what they were doing up so early. Nothing moved until quarter to five when a pickup truck drove by. The driver looked straight ahead as he went past. I felt the lump on my head and picked at the scabs on my wrists.

At five-twelve, a light went on in a small house a couple of hundred yards up the road. After a couple of minutes, it went out. I flexed my frozen toes inside my boots and began to wonder if I was cracking up.

If the photographer had a stack of prints already made, I was freezing for nothing. But that wasn't the way I pictured it. What I pictured was him, or her, slipping in and out as fast as possible. Two or three prints and get out. One for Roxanne and one for the newspaperman. Knock them off and clear out. Take as few chances as possible.

It seemed like this would be the best time to do it. It was early enough that most people would be asleep, but not so early that there weren't a few other cars moving. Driving around at three a.m. left the chance that you'd be pulled over by a cop with nothing to do. By five, the day had begun.

As I rubbed my wrists, I thought of the cabin. What if they had a few beers and decided to pay me a visit; what if Cormier hadn't talked to them? What if he had and told them to try again? If they found Roxanne in bed, alone in the house. . . .

I turned the key in the ignition and the oil-pressure light glowed red. I hesitated. Hesitated some more. Then turned the key off.

A car passed, headed toward town. A woman driving. She was smoking a cigarette. The studio looked like it had been vacant for ten years. My toes were going numb as my brain sucked the blood back from my extremities. That was the way they explained hypothermia.

The body protects its core by sacrificing the extremities. Toes and fingers first. Next, the feet and hands. For Arthur, the extremities had probably gone all at once.

Numb. Frozen solid. Blue and bloodless.

I untied my boots and moved my toes some more. Every few minutes. I took the plastic windshield scraper and shaved the frozen film of condensation from the inside of the windshield. The shavings fell in a white pile on the inside of the dashboard. They looked like fake snow.

At five-thirty, I turned the radio on again. A woman from Georgia was telling the announcer about the time she saw the inside of Tammy Wynette's tour bus. The woman said it was "beeyootiful," and said she understood that Tammy was a regular person, too. I turned the radio off and scraped some more.

Ten more minutes, I told myself. Ten more minutes and home. I checked my watch, looking down for just a second.

And I almost missed it.

The figure came out of the darkness at the far side of the building, walked quickly to Arthur's door, and disappeared inside.

I had been right.

Without taking my eyes off the door, I bent and tied my boots, first the left, then the right. I took the flashlight from the passenger seat and stuck it in my right pocket, then popped the door latch. I slid out from behind the steering wheel and closed the door but didn't latch it. Then I squatted by the front left wheel and watched.

The figure had moved quickly, as if he had done this many times and had every move down. If he was as efficient inside the building, I might not have a lot of time.

There was a lug wrench in the trunk, the kind with a single-size head. I rose from my crouch and then eased back down.

After another minute, I crept to the back of the car and opened the trunk slowly and carefully. I felt for the wrench and found it half under the spare tire. I took a glove off and slid it out, then went back to the front of the car and waited. For what? When should I move? I didn't want to lose him. Maybe I should go and stand by the door. When he came out, get a look at the face. If he tried anything, use the wrench. Could I actually hit somebody with it? I didn't know. If he swung first, maybe I could.

I got up and crouched back down. Twice. Three times. I had to move. Couldn't move. The sky was turning from black to navy blue. Now, I thought. Go. I stood up and he slipped from the door. He was going around the far corner. He was gone.

Still crouching, I ran across the street, the wrench down close to my leg. At the corner of the building, I stopped. Listened. Stepped out. Nothing.

I ran around to the back, past trash cans. He was halfway down the side street, walking on the edge of the pavement. I followed. He was walking quickly. At the end of the street, he went left, out of sight. I broke into a trot, picking my way around pieces of ice and snow that crunched underfoot.

There were streetlights on and I tried to see a face. I made out a dark jacket, dark pants. A black hat, maybe knit. No face. Not big, not small.

We passed one street, then another. I needed a car. At least a car and a license number. I closed to forty yards. Trotted. Backed off. He took the next left and headed back to the main road. I turned the corner. He went between two houses and disappeared.

I sprinted. My boots clumped on the pavement. The houses were dark, with cars in the driveways. I slowed as I got to the backyards.

There was a garage, a shed. I banged into a lawn mower, or something like a lawn mower. There was a space in a hedge and I moved through it and ran down another driveway to the next street.

Nothing.

He wasn't in sight. I stood in the middle of the street with the lug wrench in my hand and listened. A truck whined in the distance. Then downshifted. And then I heard it.

A starter grinding. A motor starting. Tires crunching on pavement.

It was another street over. I ran up a driveway but there was a six-foot fence. A dog started barking.

He was gone.

"Damn it all to hell," I said.

I stood there for a minute, forced myself to wait instead of succumbing to the adrenaline-fed urge to get the hell out of there. The dog was still barking, woofing in that rhythmic way dogs bark when they realize that they've got nothing else to do. I walked down the driveway away from the barking and went back to the studio the way I had come, still holding the wrench.

When I got there, everything was still and quiet, as if I had dreamt the whole thing. I looked around once, then went to the door where the person had come in and out. The door was padlocked but the person hadn't unlocked anything. I gave the knob a pull and the hasp came away from the frame. The screws had been stripped or the holes drilled out. The door opened.

Inside, I flipped on my flashlight and walked slowly to the darkroom. It was empty. I checked the sinks. They were wet. I bent and smelled the drain. It smelled of fixer. Whoever it was that made the prints had dumped the chemicals down the drain. I looked at the enlarger. It was clean. The negative holder was still in place.

I walked to the bedroom and flashed the light over the junk. It looked different. The cartons that had been piled everywhere were stacked along the wall. I peered into them. The contents were just stuffed in. Papers and magazines, plastic knives and forks, junk. Someone had emptied the boxes and gone through the stuff and then dumped everything back in. The shelves were the same. Books were in stacks. The toy animals were piled on the floor, like bodies in a mass grave.

What I needed was records. Arthur's records of assignments. The little notebooks he pulled out whenever he thought his pay was wrong. They wouldn't be in the cartons; everything I saw there was old. Arthur the packrat. The notebook he kept with him, like a pen. His wallet. Get out of bed and stuff them in his pockets. First thing. First thing out of bed. The carton that had been beside the bed was gone, probably shoved in with all the others. I flashed the light over them again. They all looked the same.

I got down on the floor and lifted the blankets. The light showed dust and dirt and a newspaper. I pulled it out. The *Review*, before my time. Front page had a picture of kids holding posters they had drawn. A keeper.

Standing up, I picked up a pillow and shook it. Nothing fell out. I ripped the blankets and sheets off the bed and shook them, too.

Nothing.

The mattress was stained at the center. I patted it reluctantly, then lifted it up and looked underneath. The bottom was stained, too. I pulled it off the bed. Something fell to the floor, next to the wall. I bent down and reached under the bed, through the dust and grime, and pulled it out.

A white reporter's notebook.

22

The note was still on the table when I got home. I went in and touched Roxanne on the shoulder and she opened her eyes and grabbed the alarm clock.

"I'm late," she said, and bounded out of the bedroom, still in her slip. I heard the shower curtain rustle and the water hiss on. I went into the kitchen and put on water for coffee and got two mugs out of the cupboard. Black for me. Milk and sugar for her. Roxanne trotted from the bathroom to the bedroom, a blue towel held loosely in front of her. It occurred to me that we hadn't made love lately. For good reason, I supposed, but damn, she was sexy.

I made the coffee and put the toast in the toaster as Roxanne came out of the bedroom, zipping a tweed skirt and trying to slide on a pair of black pumps at the same time. She scuffed across the floor and I put a spoonful of sugar in her mug.

"Take it easy," I said. "You'll get there."

"I know, but this is a first meeting with this family, and they're not going to be too glad to see me in the first place. Never mind being an hour late."

"Where is it?"

"Cumberland."

A good hour and a half away.

"What time?" I asked.

"Family at eight. Support team at seven-fifteen."

"So you'll be a few minutes late."

"So I will," Roxanne said, putting more sugar in her coffee. "Where were you? Did you go out?"

"For a while. I was awake so I went for a ride. I saw somebody come out of Arthur's place. Come out of the studio."

Roxanne stopped in mid-sip.

"At six in the morning?" she said.

"Five-thirty-three."

"Who?"

"Couldn't see."

"Did you call the police?" Roxanne asked.

I looked at her. She put her mug down.

"Jack. What the hell is this? Some kind of game? You act like it is. You act like it's some kind of a game, you against somebody or something or whatever the hell it is. Well, I hope you're having fun playing detective, but I'm not. I feel like I'm in danger. I do, Jack. I feel like I'm in danger and you don't care. You're thinking of yourself or your paper or something, but you're not thinking of me."

"But I am," I said.

"No, you're not. If you were, you'd go to the cops; you'd do something to put an end to this foolishness. Like leave. Oh, God, I don't have time to talk about it now."

Roxanne put her mug in the sink and went into the living room for her coat, which was long and gray. She came back with it on and I stood and went to the door. Her face was hard and grim.

"I'll tell you right out, Jack," she said. "I don't understand this. I don't feel like you're telling me everything—not at all. Maybe you're protecting me or something, but I just can't live like this. I want to be with you. I think maybe I'm falling in love with you. Maybe it's not even maybe. But I don't want to be here with you. Not here. Not with all this . . . this shit going on, Jack; I just can't."

I waited.

"My offer still stands from last night. Effective immediately. Today. Tomorrow. Follow me home. Come to Portland. We could, I don't know—you know what I mean."

"It would be great," I said, "but I can't do it now."

"When? Two weeks? Two months? Two years?"

"I don't know. I can't just run away whenever a problem comes up."

"A problem comes up?" Roxanne said. "Do you have these problems all the time? Getting kidnapped? Getting beat up. Having your girlfriends threatened? What is this? James Bond or something? No, I don't think this is your problem. This stuff with the mill, that's the town's problem. Arthur's dead. I'm sorry it happened, but you didn't do it. Can't you see? You don't have to do all this yourself. Let somebody else worry about something."

I opened my mouth to say something but changed my mind. Roxanne leaned over and kissed me coldly on the cheek, her lips like dry fingers on my skin.

"I've got to go," she said, and opened the door.

"I'll call you," I said, and she walked down the stairs, her pumps snapping on the steps. As her car swung out of the driveway, I pulled out the notebook.

It was white. Spiral-bound. Arthur had doodled long cylindrical shapes on the back cover. Inside the front cover he had written

SEPTEM and an arrow pointing to the right. I riffled the pages; the notebook was three-quarters full.

I started at the back. The last entry said SNO MO BANQ. DIX. THURS. 11 O'CLOCK. I remembered that one. It was a promo for a snowmobile club kick-off dinner. I'd asked Arthur to do it the last Thursday we went to the printers. Three days before he died. I flipped the pages toward the front.

A Christmas fair at the Catholic Church in Mexico. A quilt raffle at the Baptist Church in Androscoggin Center. Boy, we used a lot of this stuff. But the people wanted it. What the hell.

That same day, Arthur had noted going to a car accident on Route 17. Next to it, he had written NU. Not used. I remembered that one, too. Nobody had been hurt and the photo was flat. Blah. Under our agreement, Arthur got paid ten bucks for going to something like that, fifteen if we used it. If I didn't pay him for enterprise stuff, the paper would be wall-to-wall fair pictures.

The rest of the stuff looked routine. BBALL AHS. 3 P.M. 11/14. Something Vern had assigned. It had been taken two weeks before Arthur had died. There was an entry for supplies purchased: $48.80 for a case of Tri-X film. More promos. Then back to football, another accident, a fire in a chimney, not used. Another ten bucks.

And there it ended. Thursday to Sunday, the day Arthur's body was found, was a blank. I turned the notebook over and flipped through the reverse side of pages. Nothing.

So what next? Wait for something to happen? Get grabbed again and hope for everybody to break and confess.

I stood leaning against the counter and let the pages of Arthur's notebook flutter. Promo . . . basketball . . . 90th birthday . . . Arthur's existence. The chapter headings of his life, a series of—

The entry was toward the back, on a single page, on the reverse side. It was scrawled in big letters, at an angle—written in a hurry.

s/o w/v.

I looked at it. Nothing came to me.

s/o w/v.

Sheriff's office. Wide-vision. Studio office. Sports offering. Sandy Ogden. It wasn't one of the abbreviations Arthur used. I couldn't remember him using it at all. And how would I check? I didn't have any other notebooks, though I was sure Arthur kept them someplace. Looking for them would mean another visit to the studio. They had to be there because Arthur was always digging them out, looking for some piece of trivia, an answer to an offhand question nobody really cared about, or if his pay was short, which it was sometimes, usually because of something I did—

His pay.

That's what I did have. Payroll records. We had to keep them for taxes and the feds, and Arthur used the same kind of abbreviations on his pay vouchers. BBALL. PROMO. NU. I had them for the six months I'd been at the paper, anyway. There were more records in the basement someplace. If he had used that one, that s/o w/v, maybe I could find it. Then I could check with the back issues to see what assignment he was talking about. It might work. If it didn't, I wasn't any worse off.

It was snowing lightly again and the streets were greasy and slick. I eased the Volvo down the hill, trying not to ram the Jeep in front of me at the stop sign. It had fat tires and was raised up high, a macho vehicle for a guy with feelings of inadequacy, I figured. The roar from his exhaust when he pulled away confirmed it.

I headed into town, stopping at the light on the downtown side of the bridge and staring idly at the people going into LaVerdiere's.

"Hey," somebody shouted, and I turned, startled. The light changed to green and an old blue pickup, a sixties GMC with a green passenger door, pulled alongside.

It was Cormier. He waved for me to follow and I did, as he made a U-turn in the LaVerdiere's lot and headed back over the bridge and up Penobscot Street, out of town. He drove over the hill to the White Mountain Road and took a right. I followed him a couple of miles before he pulled off onto a dirt side road. He wouldn't try the same thing again, would he? I was about to turn around and blast out of there when he pulled over, with nothing in sight but birch and poplar woods. Cormier got out and started to walk back. I got out and walked toward him.

"Hey," he said.

"How's it going?" I said back.

"Hey, okay," Cormier said.

We were standing beside the truck, which was rusted, with big gaping holes in the bed. Where there weren't holes, there was a gas can and a Jonsered chain saw and a few dozen beer cans, Bud talls. Maybe he just drove around until they all fell out.

Cormier was wearing a faded denim jacket, jeans, and boots. His hat was green camouflage and advertised Winchester ammunition.

"Hey, listen," he said. "How much will that window run you? I can give you the money, but I'm not gonna be around to, like, get it fixed."

"You got off?"

"Filed. Fifty bucks. Lawyer got it done this morning."

"Not a bad deal."

"What the hell," Cormier said. "About what it was worth."

I shrugged. He looked away again. Nobody had told him about Dale Carnegie.

"Hey, so sorry about that, or whatever," he said.

I nodded. He picked at a piece of Bondo that was hanging like loose skin on the side of the truck.

"What you wanted to know about."

"What?" I said.

"The picture guy. I talked to some people."

He looked uneasy and looked even farther away from me.

"Bad news on that one, man," Cormier said.

"What do you mean, bad news?"

"Like, leave it alone."

"Who's saying that?"

Cormier looked at me, then away. Sniffed. Reached out and broke a twig off a birch branch that hung over the road.

"LeMaire," I said.

He didn't say anything.

"I'm just telling you what the word is. And the word is that it's hands off. Stay the hell away. That's from up above. Coming down to the peons. Like it never happened."

"Why would anybody say that?"

Cormier pulled at his hat and smiled.

"That's not my problem. Word is, don't touch it. Back right the hell off. In my position, that's what I did."

He walked back to the cab of his truck and got in. I walked behind him and leaned toward the window, saw him stick an open

Bud between his legs. He turned the key and the solenoid clicked a couple of times before the starter caught and the motor roared.

He put the truck in gear and sat with his foot on the clutch.

"Listen, I mean it," Cormier said. "Our little ruckus was fun and games, you know what I'm saying? This other stuff is serious business. You're smart, you'll forget it. Back off. Go back where you come from and take your babe with you. You don't want to end up iced, you know what I'm saying? I don't know how to tell you any more direct than that."

"You're serious?"

"Listen, I've lived here my whole life. And there are people you just don't mess with. Make me look like a friggin' Boy Scout. You know who they are and you stay away from 'em, you know? And there are times to mess and times to walk away. You know the difference, you stay out of trouble. I'll tell you friggin' straight out. If I were you, I'd walk away. Leave it the hell alone."

He revved the motor and pulled up the road, turning around and coming back by me with a small wave of his hand, still on the steering wheel. I stood beside the car for a minute and when Cormier had disappeared around the bend in the road, I got in the car and considered what he had said. I considered it for a millisecond before coming to the conclusion that I had been right.

The word had come down from the top. Vigue.

As I sat there, the implications of it swept over me. From the top down to the peons, Cormier had put it. The patrolmen. Orders to leave it alone. Not talk about it. To act like Arthur had died in his bed, with a history of heart problems. He had swallowed a bottle of pills, ending a losing battle with depression.

Nor would it have taken actual orders. A word or a shake of the head would have done it. The message would have trickled down that this one was off limits. And the staties? A few words would have worked there, too. Crackpot. Flake. A few bricks short of a load. The rubber stamp would have come out much more easily then. No reason to delve into the mysteries of the human mind if you didn't absolutely have to.

And all along I had been going to Vigue, asking him why there was no investigation. I pushed and prodded and Vigue had already put out the word to lay off. But why? Because he had killed Arthur? What other reason could there be? Because he was protecting somebody who had killed Arthur? Why would he do that? He knew about Arthur's peeping pictures. What else did he know?

The longer I sat there, the worse it got.

If Vigue had arranged for me to be jumped and brought to the cabin, he also knew I hadn't reported it. In fact, I had gone to some lengths to cover it up. I didn't run to him because I didn't trust him. Maybe now he knew that, too.

How long would he let me keep digging? How long could he afford to? If he killed Arthur, or knew who did it, how well had he covered his tracks? How close could I get before he panicked?

I sat in the car on the deserted road and felt sick. The wind was blowing through the bare trees, rustling the grass and burdocks beside the car. A scattering of starlings streaked across the sky, like a cluster of dark shooting stars. It should have seemed beautiful, but instead the place seemed dead and grim. I put the car in gear and turned around in Cormier's tracks, following them back to town in much worse spirits than I had been in when I left.

When I got to the paper, everyone was in motion. They told me where everything stood—news copy, ad line, sports, classified—but I barely heard them. My mind was racing, jumping from one problem to another. God, the editorial was running. Stay away from it, Cormier had said, but I was issuing a public challenge. I was about to tell the town that the head of their police department had been derelict in his duty. The cops in his own department had been gagged, and I was going to dare Vigue not to investigate Arthur's death. Back off, Cormier had said, and I was going head to head, probably beyond what even Vigue could have imagined. He thought I was nosing around too much. I was going to splash the thing like he had never seen before.

To make matters worse, I had other things to do. Four stories to write, one relatively major one on the mill issue. It was Tuesday, two days from press day, and I had to keep the operation moving. It all had to get done, and there was no one else to do it.

And then there was s/o w/v.

People were hurrying around like it was a metro newsroom at eleven p.m. Vern was pounding on his terminal like a teletype, his hat on backwards, a toothpick in his mouth. Marion was setting type out front and Cindy was on the phone, and it actually sounded like business. Paul slammed through the door and walked directly to my desk, slapping a contract down in front of me.

"Check that baby out, Jack," he said, proudly. "Dick's Foodliner in Dixfield. Eight-hundred-inch contract. I've been trying to get him back for six months, the tight son of a bitch."

"Great, Paul," I said. "Now we know who buys the beer."

"Beer," Vern said, still typing. "The drink that has fueled armies, nourished civilizations, opiated the masses."

No one responded, so he raised the volume a notch.

"Feel the pulse of the newsroom," Vern shouted. "We are humming, yes, humming at news control. And now, back to you, Jack."

"Can it, Vern," Cindy called.

I even managed a smile.

A weak one.

The envelope from Wheeler at the *Wall Street Journal* came mid-morning by express mail. I opened it and flipped through the stacks of clips and abstracts and took a deep breath. Good stuff, but it was going to take some work. It was a major project, and I already had several going, both at the paper and elsewhere.

Vern came over and stood, big and wise and comforting.

"How's Roxanne?" he said.

"Okay," I said. "But I don't think I'll be seeing much of her up here for a while. She's decided to stay away until things settle down."

"When will that be?" Vern said quietly.

"Maybe soon," I said. "But they'll get worse before they get better."

"You know, Jack, I don't mean to tell you what to do, but I guess that's exactly what I'm gonna do. Hope you take it in the spirit in which it's offered, but even if you don't, if I were you, I'd put all this down on paper. Arthur. The pictures. The threats and everything. The stuff with Martin and Pauline. I'd go to the AG with it. They'd keep it confidential. Just tell them it's such a small town, you aren't comfortable sticking with the local law enforcement."

"I'm not."

"So they could look into it. Hey, it's a crime using the mails. Maybe the feds could get involved. I don't know."

I ran my hand over the bump on my head.

"You're probably right. But, I don't know; It's such a big step. Christ, once you turn that stuff over, it's out of your hands. They take it and off they go."

"Yeah, but isn't that what you want?"

I thought for a second.

"I don't know. I'm not sure what I want."

Vern went back to his desk and I got out the Maine Directory and looked over the list of assistant AGs. I knew a couple of them, but only superficially. If I went to them with what I knew, it would be like putting my life in their hands. And Roxanne's. Maybe that was the answer. I could call the AP bureau in Portland and ask who they trusted in the AG's office. The number was in my card file. I got it out. I didn't make the call.

I got out my payroll files for the past six months, took out Arthur's folder, and began flipping through his vouchers, one by one.

They ran to two and three pages every two weeks. I went back six months without seeing an s/o or w/v, but I did find something.

Arthur used the letter "w" on several occasions to mean the word *with*. He wrote PIX W/CONTACT when he supplied photos with a contact or proof sheet. When I'd taken him with me on a couple out-of-town assignments, he'd written FEAT. W/JM on the voucher. Who else would he go with?

That was all the six months of vouchers yielded. I stuffed them in the folder and went down in the cellar and searched in the old file cabinets for payroll records. After five minutes, I gave up and came back to ask Cindy where they would be. She strode off and came back upstairs with a thick bundle of files, wrapped in rubber bands.

"That's five years," she said proudly.

"Beautiful," I said.

I didn't have to go back five years. After eighteen months, thirty-six vouchers, I found it.

23

—◊—

It was Sunday, July 29, the year before I came to the paper. I'd heard the story fifty times since.

That night, Arthur had worked four hours without taking a picture. The cops had gotten a tip that the QuikStop was going to be robbed and Arthur had gotten wind of it. He'd been tighter with the police before I came on board and began pushing them. They'd allowed him to go on the stakeout, and he'd sat in the back of an unmarked car. The robbers never showed, but Arthur had figured he still ought to get paid.

He'd put in for the time: S/O W/APD, 4 HOURS."

Androscoggin Police Department. There was only one cop whose name started with a "V," and that was Vigue. But a stakeout? I hadn't heard of anything going on that weekend. And Arthur would have told me—if he'd had a chance.

I took out the notebook and looked at the scrawled letters. They'd been written in a hurry. As if somebody was waiting at the door with the motor running.

It would have been just like the old days. Years ago, Arthur had ridden with the cops in the cruisers. He'd been their confidant because they knew they could trust him. He didn't serve the readers, but he could keep a secret.

I'd changed all that within three months. When I came on board, the cops weren't always right. We reported it when the department budget came under fire. When a patrolman was busted for drunk driving in another county, we ran a story. Arthur's cruises with the cops came to a screeching halt.

But would he refuse if they offered? No way. Arthur had been a lonely person. He liked nothing better than being one of the boys.

It's time, I thought. It's time to gather up the evidence.

The Pine Tree was filled with smoke. Most of the lunch crowd had left, and the few that remained sat at their booths and drank endless cups of coffee and smoked cigarette after cigarette.

I sat at the counter. The counter waitress, a thin, fiftyish woman with dyed black hair, banged a water glass down beside a paper place-mat with word games printed on it. The knife, fork, and spoon were rolled up in a paper napkin.

"Hi," she said. "What can I do you for?"

I smiled.

"Feed me. A tuna-salad sandwich with lettuce and tomato on whole wheat. And coffee."

"That's it?"

"For now."

She turned, still scribbling on her pad, and walked to the end of the counter. Ripping the page off the pad, she impaled it on a hook.

Her name was Marlene. I wasn't looking for her. I was looking for Joy.

Joy probably knew me as the guy from the paper. The guy from out of town. I knew her by sight from eating in the restaurant; I'd heard she was divorced and living with a guy who used to play football for Androscoggin and now drove a truck for St. Amand. I'd only heard that because Paul thought she was hot and lamented the fact that she wasn't single.

The sandwich came. Marlene asked if I wanted anything to drink other than coffee, and I said no. I had taken a couple of bites when Joy came out of the kitchen. She dumped a pile of clean dishes in a rack behind the counter and went back through the swinging doors. I got a glimpse of her face. Flushed cheeks. High cheekbones and blonde hair. She wore white slacks and she was lean, with an athletic swing in her walk.

Paul was right. But she looked like she took nothin' from nobody. So to speak.

I watched for her as I ate but she didn't come back. I finished my sandwich and drank two cups of coffee. Marlene had just poured a third when Joy swung back through the door.

"I'm outta here," she called back to the kitchen. "Things get busy, put a dress on Frank."

She stripped off her apron as she headed through the tables to a door on the opposite wall. I put a five-dollar bill on the counter and followed, carrying my parka and a manila folder.

Joy went in the door and turned right. When I rounded the corner, she was standing in front of a metal locker, hurriedly running a brush through her hair.

"The john's on the other side," she said.

"I'm not looking for it. I was hoping to talk to you."

She turned and looked at me, weary of come-ons.

"Oh, yeah?" she asked.

"About a picture. I work for the paper. The *Review*. And I came across some pictures."

I paused.

"Well, these pictures are of women. One of them is of you."

Her eyes narrowed and the brush fell to her side.

"Listen, you goddamn weirdo. You've got five seconds to get the hell out of here or I'm gonna call Frank and he's gonna kick your head in. I don't need any—"

"I know, I know . . . Easy."

"Easy nothing. You get the hell out."

"One minute. I need to talk to you for one minute. I'm Jack McMorrow. The editor of the paper. The guy who had these pictures worked for me. He's dead."

She looked at me. Her mouth gaped.

"That little weasely guy who took the pictures at the basketball games? Oh, my God."

"You knew him?"

"Who he was. He was a creep. I can't believe—that little creep."

"You never knew?"

"Hell, no. Buddy would have killed him."

She caught herself.

"I don't mean that. I mean, he might have beaten him up. Maybe not."

I waited.

"Well, there's a question about what he did with these pictures. His name was Arthur Bertin. It's sort of part of the investigation."

"But you're not a cop?"

I shook my head.

"We do our own sometimes. Investigative reporting and all that."

"You gonna put this in the paper?"

"No way. Nothing about it. I just want to ask a couple questions."
She looked at me.

"Ask," she said quickly, as if she wanted to get it over with before someone else came.

The photo came in the mail to her apartment on Alden Street, she said. I knew the neighborhood. Neat two-family houses with porches on the front. She said she remembered the mail came at noon, and she had to shove the envelope in a drawer before her daughter came in from kindergarten. She showed it to Buddy when he came home that night.

"He was ripped," she said. "He would have . . . he wanted to have the paper traced or something and find the guy himself. I told him, 'Buddy, just call the cops.' He didn't want to. He's had some run-ins with the cops. He sued 'em a couple times 'cause they took his license illegally. He is not a popular guy down there, let's say."

"Anybody in particular?"

"All of 'em. Vigue on down. Especially Vigue. That's what made it hard."

She realized she was still holding the hairbrush and put it in the locker.

"Was there a note? Or just the picture?"

"A note. A bunch of crap. 'Slut.' Stuff like that. I didn't mind that as much as I minded the picture being taken at my house. Through the window. This guy was out there. And now he's dead."

She pulled a big leather pocketbook out of the locker and dug for cigarettes and a lighter.

"So what else can I tell you?" she said, ripping open a new pack. "I ended up going to the cops. Buddy burned the picture. I talked to Vigue and he asked me a few questions. Then he said something about having a feeling about who it was. You know, they'd gotten other reports. That kind of stuff. Buddy was pissed that they didn't arrest the guy. Figured it was some rich guy's kid or something. But I was just glad to have it stop. Where the hell did you find this picture?"

"With Bertin's stuff after he died. He drowned last week."

"I heard about it. So where is it?"

"It's locked up. It's part of the investigation. Nobody is going to see it, if that's what you're worried about."

She blew out smoke hard.

"Yeah, well, I am worried. I'm very goddamn worried. What'd you say your name is?"

"Jack McMorrow."

"I'll talk to Buddy when he gets back. He may want to talk to you about that."

"Fine," I lied.

She pulled a pink ski jacket out of the locker.

"So your husband doesn't care much for Vigue?"

"He's my boyfriend," Joy said, pulling the jacket on. "And he hates Vigue's guts. They met a long time ago and didn't hit it off."

Out on the street, it was snowing and the wind was blowing, cold and damp. I put my head down and walked back to the paper. As I walked, I tried to look at everything methodically. What would I tell the AG's office? That Vigue knew about Arthur's questionable activities months ago and never arrested him? That he pretended to be surprised when I showed him the photos I found. That Joy never got another photo after she went to Vigue and told her story.

I could also say that it may have been a cop who had arranged to have me beaten up and taken to a cabin. Would it be enough? I wasn't sure.

The Christmas lights were on early because it was so overcast. Bulbs were already burned out and the lights looked ragged, with Christmas three weeks away.

I nodded to people I knew, but didn't stop to talk. Pauline was still the hot gossip on the street, and I didn't feel like getting into it. I didn't feel like it at all.

When I got back, I went to the news files and pulled two yellowed folders, stuffed full of ragged clippings. One was labeled ANDROSCOGGIN POLICE DEPT. The other was labeled LT. JOHN V. VIGUE. I took them to my desk.

The Vigue file had a story on his promotion to lieutenant five years before. It was really more of a press release, all turgid prose and law enforcement jargon. Vigue looked stern in the head-and-shoulders shot. From there, the clips got yellower and Vigue got younger.

He was hired right out of the Marines, nineteen years back. He was a graduate of Androscoggin High, where he played varsity basketball. His wife was the former Susan Lake of Androscoggin. From what I could tell, they had no children.

Vigue was cited for bravery back when he was a rookie. The story said he pulled a man out of a burning trailer. When he was promoted to sergeant, he told the *Review* that he saw police work as more than just a job. "It's a duty to uphold," he was quoted as saying. "It's a responsibility to the good citizens of this community."

He looked good. Sounded good. And he seemed to do a good job. But there was a flaw there. Something had gone wrong. Very wrong.

"Jack," Cindy said, suddenly standing beside me. "I didn't know you were in. You got two calls from the same guy. I don't know who. He wouldn't leave his name. He said he needed to see you and I said you'd be right back."

"When was this?"

"Half-hour, forty-five minutes ago."

"Sound normal or nuts?"

"Hard to say. He didn't sound mad or anything. Maybe a little like he wasn't used to calling a newspaper. But I'm sure he'll call back if he really needs to talk to you. I told him you're in and out all day."

I forced myself to stay in for a couple of hours. It took me an hour to go through the St. Amand package, and when I was through reading, I got on the phone to people in some of the towns that were burned. I called Ohio and Louisiana and Oregon. Ohio was supposed to call back. Louisiana and Oregon were hits, with town officials saying they felt St. Amand had extorted tax breaks with the threat of moving out. Nice and bitter. Good stuff.

My mind wandered. I picked up the Vigue file and looked at the head shots. His "duty to the citizens of this community." *Obligation* was a better word, but people knew what he meant. And I was sure most of them believed him. If they believed him, they wouldn't believe me. Unless I had facts.

My best source was packing when I knocked on the door. The window had been replaced by a piece of cardboard. I wasn't sorry.

Cormier had piled tapes, sheets and blankets, towels, canned goods into cardboard cartons. He was drinking a beer.

"Hey," he said, stuffing clothes in a duffel bag.

He didn't offer a beer. I guessed he figured his debt had been repaid in full.

"Got a question," I said.

He zipped the duffel bag and threw it near the door, beside me.

"Is Vigue pretty straight that you know of? No kinks? Sex stuff, I mean."

Cormier paused and looked at me, bent over a suitcase.

"You aren't interested in living, are you?" he said.

"I am. That's why I'm asking."

He stuffed shirts into the suitcase.

"You're friggin' nuts. I'll tell you that."

I waited.

"No, he's a great guy. Love him like a goddamn brother. Trust him with my sister."

"You serious?"

"Nope. I don't know. How the hell do I know what he does? Maybe he's into sheep. Who cares?"

"I do."

"Maybe you're into sheep."

"Maybe."

I waited some more. He filled a paper bag with socks and underwear.

"Can't help you. Would if I could. I just don't know much about him. Just that he's a dink who would arrest his mother if he thought it would make him look good. He's a hard-ass, you know?"

"Nothing kinky. No going with girls or anything?"

Cormier shook his head. I'd struck out.

I let myself out, closing the cardboard door behind me. On the way down the stairs, I glanced in a window and saw a woman pulling on a brassiere. I looked away and hurried down the steps and didn't see the movement at the corner of the building until it was too late.

24

The shadow moved to my right and I got my hands up. Something crashed into my ear and I fell.

Feet shuffled. A kick hit my side and I rolled. Another kick. The arm. Side. Thighs.

No pain. Burning. Grunts that weren't mine and boots and dungarees moving fast.

I got myself to a crouch and lurched toward the car. Somebody grabbed me and I fell back and rolled again, coming up to knit masks, three of them.

One dark and two orange.

The orange mask lunged in for a kick and I took it in the chest and grabbed boot and denim. I dug fingernails through the cloth and kicks were hitting my back and my knees. I fell with the leg still in my hands and bit as hard as I could near the knee.

He yelled. Fingers dug into my neck. I swung my hands blindly until I felt a mask and pulled down.

The face turned away but I saw enough. Dark. Mustache. I didn't know him.

Two stayed on me and I took a punch on the forearm. One grabbed my arms and the other pulled at me from behind. I lunged, inching down the driveway toward the street. He climbed on my back and I threw myself straight back. I hit the pavement with him underneath me. Something cracked. Not me.

I rolled off the curb into the street and two went by me, running to the edge of the building and turning the corner. One guy was struggling to his feet, his arms crossed, bent over. I lurched over and kicked him hard in the abdomen. It felt soft and he gasped and fell to his knees.

He knelt. I stood in front of him.

"Can't breathe," he moaned.

I didn't want to hit him anymore. My knees trembled; I felt sick. I reached out and pulled the mask up and off his head.

His eyes were closed.

Cormier's buddy.

Libby.

"Why?" I said, panting.

He groaned and bent over again. His nose was bleeding into his mouth.

"Tell me, you son of a bitch," I said. "You do this for Cormier? For him?"

He shook his head.

"He wimped out," he said. "Everybody. Everybody wants you out."

"LeMaire? Vigue?"

He closed his eyes. Too fast, it seemed.

"Did you bother Roxanne?"

"Didn't touch the bitch."

"I'm telling you. You go near her and you're gone. State cops. Kidnapping. You'll like it in prison. They like little boys down there."

He was standing with his hands on his knees. I thought of kicking him in the groin. But I didn't. I walked up the driveway to the Volvo and when I drove out onto the street, he was gone.

When I got home, I started a hot tub. As it ran, I went in the kitchen and called the AP in Portland. Woodbury, the bureau chief, answered. For once something had gone right.

"I've got a problem and I'm hoping you can help me with it," I said.

"You all right, Jack? You don't sound too good."

It hurt to breathe too deeply. It hurt to breathe at all.

"This problem is serious. I need somebody in the AG's office. Somebody I can trust."

"Most of them are all right," he said. "Some are jerks, but I wouldn't call them untrustworthy."

"No. I mean somebody completely straight. Somebody who will take my word against a cop's. Somebody who will listen."

"God, Jack. What'd you get yourself into?"

"Can't tell you now. Maybe later you can have an exclusive. But I need a name. Tonight."

He thought for a moment.

"There's a couple guys I have a lot of respect for. But one, Dave Olin—I'd go to him with just about anything. Is there anything I can do, Jack? Anything to help you on this end?"

"Not now," I said. "But thanks. I'll let you know. Where's Olin live?"

"Cape Elizabeth. Scarborough. Somewhere down there. Got a Portland book?"

"All set," I said.

I went and turned off the water and took off my dirty clothes. My legs were bruised and my neck was covered with scratches. My ear was swollen and throbbing. I took two aspirin from the bottle in the medicine cabinet and went to the kitchen for a glass of water. When I came back to the bathroom, I brought two butcher knives. I put them on the floor beside the tub and covered them with a towel.

The hot water helped. I stretched out and looked at the ceiling. As my muscles relaxed, I wondered if I was overreacting. These punks would get tired of this game. And the St. Amand story would blow over. I wouldn't make any friends, but over time, I'd survive. The paper would continue and the rest of it—

"Who are you kidding, Jack?" I said aloud. "It's not going away."

I couldn't sit on what I knew. They wouldn't let me keep pushing without pushing back.

It was almost seven. I stood up and picked up the towel, uncovering the knives. When I was dry, I took one knife and put it on the counter. The other I took with me to the bedroom.

When I was dressed, I looked up Olin's number in the phone book and dialed it on the phone with the shotgun pellet marks in it. A woman answered and I asked for Mr. Olin. She said he wasn't home and could she take a message. I left my name and number, at home and at the paper. I asked her to have him call me at any hour.

"May I tell him what this is about?" she asked politely.

"It's a long story," I said. "But it is important."

I called Roxanne's apartment and she didn't answer. Working late? Out for a drink? Out with someone else? Someone who didn't work in a town like this, this damn vicious place. I slammed the receiver down and went to find something to eat. There wasn't anything. Wobbly celery. Bread and cheese. Beer. I considered the beer and changed my mind. There would be no time for that now.

On the way back to the office, I stopped at a store downtown and bought some plastic and duct tape. Standing in the parking lot, I sealed the broken window. I didn't need frostbite on top of everything else.

Paul and Marion were gone, but Cindy and Vern were still at the paper. Vern would be there most of the night, and Cindy said she had to finish her accounts for the week and dummy a couple of display ads she'd taken over the counter.

She looked at me closer.

"What happened to you?" she said. "My God, Jack. Have you been in another fight?"

Vern looked up.

"Not really," I said vaguely. "I just got bumped up a little."

It wasn't much of an answer and Cindy knew it.

"Is it the same people with the, you know, the picture?" she whispered.

I shrugged and walked to my desk.

The St. Amand / Quinn-Hillson file was right where I had left it. I moved it aside and slid the typewriter out from under my desk. I plugged it in and grabbed a stack of copy paper. Vern came over and stood over me.

"What's up?" he said solemnly.

"Same old crap," I said.

"You need some help?"

"Not right now. What you can do is give me an hour and then read something for me. It's important."

Vern nodded and walked slowly back to his desk. I put the date on the top of the first page and started typing.

It took five single-spaced pages, but I got it all down, or at least most of it. I started at the beginning, with Arthur's drowning. I listed all the things I'd found at the studio, the threats and photos Roxanne and I had received. Cormier's tips went in, without his name. So did Pauline's visit and subsequent visit, the bar fight, the abduction and Arthur's notebook. I ended with the fight outside Cormier's. I named Jimmy Libby and LeMaire, J. and Vigue. I didn't name Joy the waitress, but I would if I was asked.

A week in the life of a country editor.

When it was done, I went to the copier and made three copies. I put one in a folder and put one on Vern's desk. He picked it up and started reading. I heard him whistle softly.

"Quite a little story when you see it in writing."

The phone rang. Cindy said it was for me.

"Jack McMorrow," I said.

"It's me," Roxanne said weakly.

"What's happened?"

She hesitated. My stomach did a roll.

"Another picture," she said. "A picture in the mail. To my home."

I took a deep breath. "What is it? The same?"

"No. Not the same."

It was her turn to breathe.

"Take it easy," I said. "Just take it easy."

"Oh, Jack. It's me. Walking down the street in Androscoggin. I look like I'm going to get something at the store."

She paused and I waited for the punch line.

"Jack," she cried. "They cut my hair off and stuck holes in me with scissors. It says . . . It says 'Too late' in big letters. That's all it says."

"The bastards," I muttered.

25

Cindy left at six, teetering down the sidewalk in her tight jeans and high-heeled boots. I stood in the office window and watched her. When she'd driven away in her father's pickup, I watched the street. It had started to snow again and everything looked serene, even idyllic. *Main Street Scene* by Norman Rockwell. Don't mind the psychos and crazies waiting in the dark.

Vern banged out and banged back in. He got on the phone and said "Hey, big guy" to somebody and started talking basketball. I went back to my desk and sat. Put another piece of paper in the typewriter. Typed an addendum to my notes.

Roxanne. Clothed but defaced. More obscene than the first.

I looked at my watch. Call Roxanne. No, don't. Let her get settled. Let her have a glass of wine. Calm down.

The minutes passed. I didn't want to go home. I couldn't work. Vern was taking notes, grunting into his phone. I grabbed my parka and left to get the *Globe*. The street was deserted and the store was closed. God forbid that you would want to buy a paper in this burg after six o'clock.

I decided I'd given Roxanne enough time and turned back, snow like flies against my face. Vern was still there. Just sitting at his desk, holding the phone.

"For you," he said. "Guy says he has information."

I took it at my desk. A man's voice. Raspy like a smoker.

"You don't need my name," the caller said. "I used to drive cab and this might be nothin', but I don't know, I thought I'd just call over there in case you might be interested in finding out more about Arthur Bertin, the guy who died."

I had a pad out. I wrote down every word, his and mine. Every sound.

"Sure, I'm interested."

"Hey, I mean, this might be nothin'."

"Try me anyway."

"You could check it. That's what I thought. You can check stuff. And it might not check out to be anything. But I just thought—"

"I'll check it out. Don't worry."

"Well, hey, it's not that big a deal. I don't know. It's just that I knew the guy 'cause he took the cab quite a lot. You get to know people driving them, you know? You talk. They talk. They tell you lots of things. All the old ladies. Hey, I know their life stories."

"So what'd Arthur talk about?"

"Like I said, I don't know if this is that big a deal, you know? But a month ago, maybe more, maybe less. No, it was a month anyway."

"Yeah."

"He's in the cab and he rides in the front—he used to ride in the front. Regulars like to sit up where they can talk, and I don't mind, 'cause it keeps you from stretching your neck around, you know? So whatever, he's sitting up front and he's got something eatin' him. I don't know. Not saying much, not that he chewed your ear or anything."

"But he's quiet."

"Right. Something's not right."

"Yeah."

"So I said to him, 'You sick or something?' These are not exact words, but it was something like this. He looks over and says, 'I got a question for you.' I said, 'Yeah?' He says, 'You ever hear of a guy named Reggie Lockman?' Lockman. I said, 'Nope, why should I?' Arthur says, I think it was something like this, 'Yeah, well I wish I never heard of him either. 'Cause this is the worst mess I ever got myself into.' Maybe it wasn't *mess*. Maybe it was *problem*. But something like that, you know?"

"Reggie Lockman?"

"Yeah. Just like that. I look at him, we're pulling up to his place, and I say, like, 'Anything I can do to help you?' Hey, I liked the guy. If some punk was giving him a hard time, I'd straighten the guy out for him. Some dink bothering the guy or something. He was kind of a wimpy little guy, but he'd do anything for you."

"Is that what it was?"

"I don't know. It's like, I told you it might not be anything. That's all he said. Reggie Lockman. Like the guy had him by the short hairs. He didn't say that, but that's the way it sounded. You just get a feeling, you know? I do, anyway. So when I hear he's dead, drownded down there, I say, 'Hey. Maybe this Lockman did it.' I don't know that but, hey, it could be, right? I don't know."

"Did you tell the police this?"

"Oh, yeah. I told Vigue down there. He knows me. They all know me."

"What'd he say?"

"I don't know. Not much. Said he'd check it out. I figured, hey, I've done my civic duty or whatever. It might not be anything, like I said. Could amount to nothing."

"But you never know. Maybe it's something. What'd you say your name was?"

"Hey, I didn't. I just thought you might want to check this out. If you're doing a write-up on this."

"You have a number where I can reach you?"

He gave me a number. Androscoggin exchange.

"Ask for Earl," he said.

I said I would and hung up. I took a paper clip and fastened the sheaf of yellow pages together.

"So?" Vern said.

He looked at me as I went through the notes, filling in gaps, correcting the scrawled shorthand.

"Anything?"

"Could be," I said. "Ever hear of somebody named Reggie Lockman? Guy says he might have been bothering Arthur."

Vern shook his head.

"This guy, Earl something. A cab driver. He said Arthur told him this Reggie Lockman had him in the worst mess he'd ever been in. Or something like that."

Vern thought.

"Doesn't ring a bell. There was a Barry Lockman, used to play for Androscoggin. Must be six years ago now. Quick little guard. He moved to Massachusetts before graduation. I don't know. I can't think of any others."

I looked at my scribbled notes.

"Another piece for the AG. If I can't get ahold of somebody tonight, I'll get them first thing in the morning. What I should do is go down there to Augusta. Walk right in and drop all this stuff on somebody's desk. 'Listen. Do something, and do it now.' "

"Could save you a few hours on hold," Vern said, heading for the coffee machine.

"I don't know, though," he said, his back to me. "AG's office. State cops. These cops. These guys are so tight. It's like they don't want to touch something if another department has dropped it."

"Or never picked it up."

"Right. It's like some guy gets booted from baseball for bad attitude. Guy's blackballed. You know what I mean. These guys stick together."

"Screw them," I said. "I'll go to the goddamn governor. Hey, this is enough. Who the hell is Reggie Lockman? Jesus, that guy didn't make that up. All they have to do is punch it into the computer. No DOB, but it's a start. I can show them the pictures of Roxanne. Say, 'Look at this and tell me nothing is going on in this goddamn town.' "

Vern looked at me.

"Anything I can do to help . . ."

"I know that. Thanks."

I was hungry. Vern said he wasn't. He'd have his coffee and a few cookies from the bag in his file cabinet. Ginger snaps.

It was snowing a little harder, wetter flakes that packed like mud on your boots. I kicked thick cakes off on the side of the car and drove a block to the store. The guy behind the counter was reading *Midnight Star*. A story about a movie star's wife who was sex-crazed. I read the story upside down.

I sat in the parking lot and ate the sandwich and drank a carton of orange juice that should have been a beer. Every few bites I flipped the wipers on and cut a new swath through the snow. I switched the radio on and off, once and then twice. The sandwich wrapper went on the floor in the backseat. I felt worse, and knew there would be no real relief until it was over.

The AG. Tomorrow.

When I pulled up in front of the office, Vern was standing in the window. He saw the car and came out and when I got to the sidewalk, the snow had made dark spots on his light-blue shirt.

"Jack, some guy just called and said he wants to meet you down at St. Amand, where—"

"The canal?"

"'Yeah. He said he had to talk to you about Arthur. 'Mc-Morrow,' he said. 'Where's McMorrow?' I said you went out to get something to eat and he said, 'You tell him I've got to talk to him about this. I've got something to show him, and he'll want to see it if he wants somebody to go down for drowning the photographer.' I took notes, Jack. I'm pretty sure that's exactly what he said."

We moved inside. Vern went to his desk and picked up a notebook.

"Was it this cab driver guy? Earl, or whatever the hell his name was?"

"I don't know. He wouldn't give me his name. I don't know. Voices are hard."

Vern showed me the notes. I couldn't read his handwriting, but I saw the number eight.

"Eight?"

"He said eight o'clock."

"What'd you tell him?"

"I said I'd give you the message as soon as I found you. You going down there?"

I thought for a minute. "I can't not go."

"We're both going then."

We left at 7:30. Vern asked me to swing by his car, around the corner on Mill Street. He got out and opened the trunk and I could hear things banging and clanking. The lid slammed down and he came back, flakes of fake-looking snow on his hair. He opened the passenger door of the Volvo and tipped the seat back to throw in a long rusty lug wrench and a silver-colored aluminum baseball bat.

"No guns?" I said.

"Short notice."

He slammed his door shut.

We drove in silence, the headlights picking up black ribbons of tire tracks in the snow-covered road. When I swung off Route 108 onto the mill road, there was only one set of tracks in front of us. When I pulled off and headed for the canal, the pavement was white, the area deserted.

"What time do you have?"

Vern held his watch to the window. "Twenty of."

"We should be able to see him coming, then."

"And he can just follow our tracks," Vern said.

I pulled up to the canal, right where they'd pulled Arthur out under the searchlights that night, and turned the car around to face back toward the road. I killed the lights and the motor. The snow fell heavily in the dark.

We sat for a minute. I turned the key to hit the wipers but the windshield was fogging up on the inside. We both wiped with our hands.

"Is this overtime or what?" Vern said.

We wiped some more. There was no sign of lights. No sound.

"Let's get out of the car and go stand in the dark," Vern said. "I feel like a sitting duck in here."

"You have your bat, don't you?"

"Well, let's get out so I can take a few practice swings. It's tough coming off the bench."

We climbed out and Vern left the bat in the backseat but brought the lug wrench. He held it close to his leg.

When we got to the edge of the canal we stood beside the wall and waited. The ice was white but there was a patch of open water in the middle. I thought of Arthur and stepped away from the edge.

Vern stood with his back to the canal and looked toward the darkness that stretched all the way to the streetlights on the mill road.

"Think it was a joke?" I said.

Vern didn't say anything.

"I can think of a few people around here who would like to give me a hard time, but this doesn't seem hard enough. Not so far."

I turned back toward the water.

"We've got better things to do than play these kinds of games."

"It's no game, Jack."

Vern's voice came from behind me, to my left. Different.

I turned. Tensed.

The wrench fell to the ground by his feet. The gun was in his right hand, pointed at my chest.

Vern grinned sheepishly. The gun aimed higher. I couldn't think of anything to say.

"Yeah, I know, Jackson. Low blow. Especially from a drinking buddy."

"Not you?"

"Hey, don't look so blown away. Life's full of surprises. I didn't want you to be on the receiving end of this one, but what can I say, buddy? No choice. No choice at all."

He looked at me. I blinked snow from my eyes.

"Arthur?"

"Yeah, I suppose. Jackson, you must think I'm a real psycho. Loony. Now I don't think so, but I'd be the last to know, wouldn't I. No, I just got backed into a corner and I had to consider all my options. With old Arthur, I didn't have any. I was trying to make some with you, but Jesus, you're such a tough old big-city newsman, you wouldn't take any of the outs I gave you."

"And now there aren't any more?"

Vern shrugged. The gun, a revolver with a six-inch barrel, pointed at my chest.

"The whole thing with Roxanne? All of that? The pictures?"

"Yeah, I know. Pretty sleazy. But it was for you, Jack. I like you. Hey, why do I feel like I'm in a bad movie? No, I do like you. All you had to do was take Roxanne and pack up that old car of yours and go. Anywhere. Just go and leave us here to our own devices. That's what I wanted you to do. Just go."

"I'll be glad to."

Vern shook his head, no.

"You say that, Jackson, but I know you better than that You can't do it, and I'll tell you why. Hey, I even considered it. I did. Right up until tonight, when this guy calls with the cab story."

"Reggie Lockman. You know him."

"Yeah, you could say that. I am him."

I felt sick. Weak. Short of breath.

"It's a long story. Gist of it is that Reggie Lockman did three years in a real nice place called Marietta Correctional Facility in the beautiful city of Marietta, Ohio. Three years. Problem was, he was supposed to do eight, minimum."

"For what?"

"For what? For something I don't even remember. Not at all. Funny, huh? No, I drove a car into this little VW Rabbit and killed a woman and put her kid in the hospital for about six months. Yeah. Nice guy. Stupid. And no way to make it better, you know what I mean? Had a few beers and went out and killed a perfect stranger. Lady was on her way to the grocery store or something. To get a gallon of milk. I went from being a respectable sportswriter to the worst scum on earth. Just like that. Everybody hated me. Oh, walking into that courtroom and feeling those eyes on you. All those people wishing you'd die some horrible slow death. Her husband really did want to kill me, which is understandable. Cops had to threaten him with a conspiracy-to-commit-murder charge to get him to back off. Wanted to hire somebody in prison to cut my throat. Some of 'em would have done it for a pack of cigarettes."

I was getting stiff.

"How'd you get out?"

"Oh, getting out is the easy part. It's staying out that's tough, boy. Hey, when I was inside I was a good boy. Didn't fight unless I had to. Let people spit in my food. Try to kiss me. Oh, yeah. A fun place. When they put me in this minimum-security yard for being a good boy, I threw my shirt up on the razor wire and went over. Never looked back, as they say. When I got here I had a nice résumé. Turned out all I needed to get hired was a pulse."

I watched the gun. The gun and his eyes.

"Six years now and it's getting so sometimes, not all the time or anything, I can really forget Reggie Lockman. Hey, he's from somewhere else. Another time. An earlier life. I'm just the mild-mannered sports reporter. Chronicling the trials and tribulations of high-school athletes. Even spell the names right."

"What's with the gun?"

"Residual paranoia," Vern said. "The great equalizer. Best part is, I can even use it on myself, if the need arises."

"Vern, this is crazy. We can—"

"We can't anything, Jack. Because I'm not running anymore. I don't have it in me to run anymore, and you know they'd chase me down. God, I'd be on the dashboard of every cop car within five hundred miles. Killer. Escaped convict. Armed and dangerous. Use caution if approached. I'd have no chance."

I shifted on my feet and the gun jerked up at my face. I swallowed. Wet my lips with a sticky tongue.

"So Arthur knew?"

"Goddamn Arthur. He knew a lot of stuff, the little weasel. He found out stuff because he was always there. You'd look up and there he'd be. Just listening. You know—I don't know why I'm telling you this. I just want you to know that I'm not doing this because I want to. I've got no choice."

"Sure you do."

"Nope. Really. See, I had this arrangement. I'll tell you this because I like you."

"That helps a lot."

"Really. See, I had this arrangement. It was back when I first got here, and I'd had a few beers—yeah, I know. Never learn. Powerful stuff, that demon rum—and I'm driving home and Vigue stops me. I knew him some. He talked basketball a little and made me walk the line. Touch my nose. I'm borderline, maybe. A judgment call. So he puts me in his cruiser and starts asking me about drinking and stuff, and if I've been arrested before and all this, and Jesus, I'm half in the bag, trying to keep everything straight, and the son of a bitch knows something's not kosher. Cops, good ones, just know. They've been lied to so many times they can smell it. So anyway, he has me in the car in the front seat and I'm still not sure how he did it, but he got a print. A good one. The bastard. He gives me a ride home, lecture and all that, and a couple weeks later he comes knocking."

"You came back a hit?"

"NCIC computer. Name and everything. The whole schmear."

"So why didn't he arrest you?"

"I don't know. He put me on what you might call probation. He says he'll think about it. Leaves me turning in the goddamn wind. I didn't sleep for a week. So a month goes by and I don't hear anything, so I send him a couple hundred bucks. Cash. I don't hear anything, so the next month, I send him a couple of hundred more. I've been doing it ever since. It's like a car payment, except the coupon book never gets any thinner. I don't know what he does with it. Maybe he gives it to Mother Teresa, for all I know. But for me it's an investment. The more he's in, the safer I am."

The snow fell. The gun moved slightly. My neck. My chest. Back to my neck.

"How did Arthur find out?"

"Little weasel. Vigue comes in one night. Looking for somebody and nobody is there but me, I think. So he says, just standing there by my desk, 'You know, we could both go down for this, and it's worse for me 'cause I'm a cop.' So I say, 'You want more money or what?' He says he'll get back to me. I told him he couldn't get more blood out of this stone, and he says I might have to squeeze harder, 'cause who are they gonna believe, him or Reggie Lockman, escaped killer. Something like that. He names the name. Lets it sink in. So he leaves and I'm standing there and I hear this little noise out front, and there's Arthur, scrunched down in a chair behind the counter. Sitting there the whole time. Said he came in to wait for a cab. Not a goddamn word, I said. I told Vigue and he made sure. He'd bagged him for the dirty pictures and let him off."

"He held that over him to keep him quiet?"

"You got it. A triumvirate, sort of. Separation of powers. If one talked, we all took a fall."

"So what happened?"

"Who knows. Arthur got jittery. Too much on his little pea brain. He calls me and says he has to see me. I picked him up and we went for a ride and ended up down here. Turns out the little weasel wants to take off. He's got some relative in New York State. Albany or some-place. Says he can't live like this anymore, it's destroying his nerves and all this crap. His stomach is bothering him."

"So you killed him?"

"Jack. That sounds so cold-blooded. We were standing here, not too far from the edge, and it was like my arm decided it wanted to go home. Had enough of this talk. Like it wasn't attached to me, it just reached out and gave him a shove. Then another shove and—"

"It's too late, Vern."

He looked at me, startled.

"When I went home to eat I called Roxanne. I told her about Lockman. I told her and she was gonna call the staties she knows down there. Right then. Detectives. She was gonna have them run the name right then. As a favor. She gives them a smile and a wiggle and those guys are like puppy dogs. So it's too late for all this. Don't you understand? You're just making it worse. Two murders? One set up like this? It's just—"

I broke to my left.

The shot didn't come, didn't come. Zigged once and crouched, running toward a chain-link fence thirty yards away along the canal.

Twenty . . . ten . . . I jumped.

The top of the fence hit my chin. Neck. Legs. There was a shot. I flipped and the sky spun. My back hit and I was up, running along the wall. I heard another shot and my leg hit something hard and I was sailing and my head hit and there was darkness and cold and my arms churned, clawed at the burning cold water.

26

The scream caught in my throat. Teeth clenched. Don't exhale. Don't exhale. No! Arms flailed against something.

Ice.

Each blow shoved me deeper. I had to breathe . . . had to breathe . . . face against ice . . . feet coming up . . . don't let it out . . . don't let it out!

Would the hole be light? Dark? It was darker behind me. Light from the mill. I went past it. It had to be to the right.

Air started to slip between my teeth. I clenched them. Two kicks. My head grazed the ice and the air started to come faster.

I kicked. Broke through.

Ice slashed my neck and air shrieked from my lungs.

I sucked in a breath, started to go under. I kicked. The air was hot. Snowflakes that burned.

The strobe lights were blipping on the mill tower. I turned in the water. When I'd fallen through the ice, I'd made an oval-shaped hole, maybe five feet across. I'd come up on the far side of the hole and broken through with my head. Now the canal wall was about ten feet away, separated from my hole by six feet of unbroken ice, maybe an inch thick.

And God, it was cold.

I tried to pull myself up onto the ice, like a seal out of a breathing hole, but the ice cracked away underneath me and I was back under. I came back up, boots pulling me down. Hoisted myself and broke through. Again.

The water numbed my face. Three times I went through until the ice near the wall held my chest and my hands scraped the granite wall.

Yell, I thought. I tried. My voice came weakly.

"Help me. Help."

My hands burned. I inched along on my chest, one hand on granite, one on the jagged edge of the ice where it had broken on my last heave.

Vern, I thought. Up there.

I moved ten feet along the wall. The ice shattered, and I slid down into the blackness, my arms flailing. I hit something solid. Something down there, two feet under the water.

My feet hit, deeper. I kept paddling, and my hands and feet bumped it until my boot caught and I was thrown forward. I set my foot again and stood up. Slipped. Stood. Up to my knees in the searing water. I groaned at the pain in my hands. My hands were bloody.

I slipped and fell to a crouch, back in the water. Something jabbed my chest and I grabbed it. A metal rod. I was standing on something. A submerged car. The rod was a radio antenna.

My face shook. My limbs were someone else's. The pain was all mine. I put my hands between my legs but there was no warmth there. I rocked in the dark.

I tried to scream. It came out an unearthly, shivering sound.

Something hit the ice.

Close.

Vern. He didn't have to shoot. Just wait.

I looked up. Saw the sky bright at the top of the wall. I measured the distance and let myself fall toward the granite.

My hands hit and I stood, feet on the car in the water, arms outstretched to the wall. I eased myself along. For what? Delay death five minutes. My teeth rattled. I wanted to see Roxanne. I did. We couldn't end on that note. Not fighting.

I felt something above me and looked up.

"Should have let me shoot you. Save you all this trouble."

I looked up. Vern was looking down, a black figure against the sky. I tried to talk, concentrating on each word, but nothing came out.

"You really call Roxanne, or you bullshitting me?" he said. "Really, Jack. 'Cause if you didn't, hey, maybe there's something we can do. Work something out. Come on, buddy. No crap this time, okay?"

I tried to figure it out. I was too cold. Too cold to think.

If I said I did call, it's too late for him. Word was out. If I didn't call her, I was the only one who knew, except for Vigue. The cab driver. But he doesn't know what he knows. If I didn't call, more reason to kill me? No reason?

My teeth were pounding. I put my hand to my face to stop them and my fingers were blue-gray.

"I called," I said. "I did. I . . . I didn't know it was you. God. God, Vern. We're friends. I could help . . . help you."

"Could nothing. What? Give me an hour head start?"

"Don't. Don't go after her. Get me out . . . out of here."

I could see the gun hanging at his side.

"Go after Roxanne? Jackson, you must think I'm some kind of animal or something. I tried to tell you about this so you wouldn't think that. Too late. Right. I think you're right about too late. Too late for me. Too late for you. Too late to stop this friggin' roller coaster."

The gun cracked. I jerked. Waited to feel pain. Blood.

There was a thud on the wall. A clatter. Vern's boots came over the edge. Then his legs, his belly, fell and crashed and ice and water showered over my head.

He floated, the back of his jacket puffed with air.

"Thanks," I said. "Thanks a lot."

I stood in the water and watched him and felt very tired.

Hypothermia. I was, quite simply, freezing to death.

I couldn't feel my feet. My hands were blue. I took one hand off the wall and tried to flex my fingers. They moved. Barely.

Vern was sinking as the air leaked from his jacket. Air pockets, I thought. Guns in his pockets.

The gun.

It had hit the wall but hadn't come down. If I could fire the gun, somebody might hear. Somebody might come. They might come in time. I slid my hands together on the wall and tried to pull my sleeve off. My fingers wouldn't close on the parka. I clasped one hand with the other and squeezed the right hand shut on the left sleeve. The hand slid up and I shook the coat off, one arm and then the other, and let it fall into the water at my feet. It was wet and heavy and I wondered if I could lift it. I pulled it to my waist and water streamed down my legs. I spread them and swung the parka over my shoulder. Then, like a hook shot in basketball, I swung it toward the top of the wall.

It hit a foot short.

Once.

Twice.

Three times. Each time gathering it up from the water became harder.

I was freezing.

I couldn't feel cold. I couldn't feel much of anything.

Time was running out. I needed something longer but there wasn't anything. No branches. No boards floating. Just Vern.

I crouched and reached for his legs, just below the surface. Pieces of ice bobbed around him and his hair moved under the water. I pulled him by the jacket and turned him over, and his eyes stared upward. There was a dark hole in his temple. I grabbed hold of his hand.

The hand was cold and still. The jacket was sodden and it was hard to work the end of the sleeve over his fingers. I alternately tugged and stuffed the fingers up the sleeve until I could pull the arm of the jacket off him. Then I went to work on the other arm, my fingers like little pieces of wood. Finally, the other sleeve slid off, and Vern turned once and sank out of sight.

The jacket was longer than mine. Not waist-length, but heavier. I gathered up the cloth and felt something in the pocket. I dug the folds. My fingers felt something as if it were miles away.

A box of shells.

I pulled them out and heard one plop into the water. The cardboard box came apart and I quickly rammed the whole mess down the front of my pants.

The coat was heavy as lead. I dropped the sleeves into the water and grabbed the end of the hem and swung it around behind me. Water streamed down my back and I could feel the cold.

Freezing.

The spot I picked was about three feet to the left of where Vern had fallen. If he shot himself with the gun in his right hand, the gun should go to his right. My left. I picked it up with both hands.

It was heavy to lift, all sodden wool. I swung over my right shoulder and it reached the top, the spray draining back down the granite. Again. It slid back.

Nothing.

The sound. I'd hear the metal scraping and I'd trap it against the wall as it came down. I hoped. I had to hope.

I swung again, a foot farther to the right. Something fell and I lunged. Missed it.

It floated. A piece of board a foot long.

Again, I told myself. I screamed. The sound was lost. I swung the jacket.

Something clattered. I fell against the granite, pinning the fabric against the rock. Frisked it.

Nothing.

My feet had disappeared underneath me, somewhere beyond the point where feeling was lost. I was going. Slowly, it was working its way up.

When I couldn't stand, I'd fall. Like Arthur.

I looked up for another try. I'd heard it. Up there, five feet away. Just five feet.

The jacket came up slowly. I swung. It slapped the rock and something scraped and I nearly fell as I pinned the jacket as it fell toward me.

This time I felt it. I put my hands underneath it, two lumps of flesh. I let the jacket fall toward me until a black butt showed against the granite.

I reached one hand up slowly and gripped the gun above the butt. I drew it toward me.

I was armed.

The snow would muffle the sound. If someone heard it, they would listen, hear nothing, and dismiss it. I raised the gun to the sky and pulled the trigger with both hands. My fingers moved by millimeters and the gun banged and kicked.

I screamed.

Shoot and shriek.

I did it four times. The fifth time the revolver clicked. I lowered it and dug in my pants for the other shells.

It took me precious minutes to fish out a shell. Several more minutes to break open the cylinder. Trying to aim the shell into one of the chambers, I dropped it into the water.

The cold.

Methodically, with no other hope, I shoved my hands inside my pants.

I got six in the gun, one at a time. Shrieking hoarsely, I fired into the sky. Once. Twice. Until the gun was empty again.

I was tired. I felt like sitting down.

"Fight it," I screamed. "Fight it."

I had six shells left. After that I had screams. Screams until I ran out of those too.

"Fight it!"

I dug in my pants again.

Stopped.

Something. Something up there. I'd heard it.

I shrieked and fumbled for the shells. Dropped one. Got one in. Another.

Two more made five.

I heard it again. Someone was up there.

Shrieking, I raised the revolver and fired. I shouted.

"Help me! Help me! Help me!"

I heard a voice and stopped.

"Put the gun down and put both hands up."

"Over here!" I screamed. "Over here!"

It was over. There'd be cops. Ambulance. A hospital. They'd get me out. Out of this and into warm.

I shouted again. No words. Just joy.

Standing in the water, I looked up. There was someone standing above me.

Vigue.

27

⎯〰⎯

He looked down, his boots on the edge of the wall.

"My God, get me out," I said, my teeth rattling uncontrollably.

"Put down the weapon," he barked.

"It's . . . it's me. I've got to get out . . . fast."

"Fine. Just put the gun down before you hurt somebody. What's that there?"

I looked down.

"Vern's. Vern's jacket. He's gone. Shot himself. I've got to get out now. Out of here. Get me out of here."

I leaned against the wall, my right hand holding the gun, finger frozen to the trigger. Vigue bent to one knee.

"What'd he tell you?"

I didn't understand.

"Get me out!"

"They're coming. Soon. What happened? With Vern."

I tried to follow the questions.

"He's gone. Killed . . . killed himself. Tried to kill me. Arthur wanted out. He killed him."

"What'd he say about me?"

"Nothing. I don't know. You knew him. About him. Where are they? Where are they?"

"Coming. Just take it easy. Take it easy."

"Out. Out. Get me out!"

He was kneeling on the edge of the wall. His hand came down.

"Toss the gun up here," he said. "Just throw it up here."

I listened. I heard my teeth chattering.

No sirens.

I pushed off the wall. Took the gun in both hands. Pointed it at Vigue's face.

He smiled.

"Jack. I'm here to help you. You've got to get to a hospital. Now drop the gun."

With a frozen thumb, I pulled at the hammer. It started to slip and I caught it. Vigue's smile disappeared.

"You shoot me, we're both dead. We've got one dead. Let's not make it three."

"Call them." My jaw clenched. "Slow. Get out the radio and call. Talk loud. I want . . . I want to hear them answer."

He reached for the portable on his belt. The radio came into view. He raised it slowly to his mouth. He licked his lips.

"Call."

"Twelve-one to comm center. We've got a man in the canal. Off the access road."

The dispatcher answered. He hadn't read the location.

"Tell 'em. Tell 'em it's where Arthur died."

My fingers were frozen. I couldn't pull the trigger.

"I'll kill you. I will."

Vigue looked down at me.

"Twelve-one, comm," he said slowly. "That's the access road. Same place where we had Arthur Bertin."

28

They said the rescue crew had to pry the gun from my hands. I didn't remember it. I didn't remember much, just glimpses of lights and shouting, and a doctor slitting my clothes with giant shears as big as hedge clippers.

It was five o'clock Wednesday afternoon when I woke up, groggy from Demerol. My hands were wrapped in bandages. I thought I had all my fingers; I wasn't sure.

A doctor came in that night. He was very distinguished-looking, with gray at the temples. He said I was very lucky. I said I knew that. He said he thought I'd keep all but the toe he'd removed the night before. The little toe on the right foot.

"So much for playing the violin," I said.

The cops came after supper. A state police detective named Reed whom I'd run into before. An assistant AG named Merritt. I asked her if she knew Olin, and she said she'd heard I'd tried to call him Tuesday.

"Probably should have tried earlier," I said.

"Probably," she said.

A detective sergeant arrived with a tape recorder and we all sat and talked. They had found the notes I had given to Vern and we took it paragraph by paragraph. They were very thorough. Merritt was very professional, very intelligent, very understanding. After two hours, I was very tired.

Merritt told me Vigue had been suspended pending the outcome of the investigation. Vern was in Augusta for an autopsy.

She wrote something on her legal pad.

"We haven't investigated your allegations of kidnapping. But I heard—is that right, Sergeant?—that we have a James Libby in custody, and he's agreed to cooperate in the investigation. We're looking for Cormier."

They looked at me and looked at each other. The detective wrapped a cord around the tape recorder.

"Do I get a guard or anything?" I asked.

"Oh, yeah," Merritt said. "There's a trooper outside. Don't worry. We aren't going to let any bad guys in."

"Good."

After they left, there was a knock at the door.

"Who's minding the store?" I said.

They smiled and stood around the bed, looking concerned. Roxanne started to take my hand, saw the bandages, and patted me on the shoulder.

"How you feeling?" Cindy said.

"Okay, considering."

Roxanne patted. Paul kept his hands in his jacket pockets.

"It's unbelievable," he said quietly. "Is it true? About Vern? An escaped murderer, and he killed Arthur? Tried to kill you?"

I hesitated.

"Not murderer. Manslaughter. That's what he said, anyway. Cops have to check it out."

"My God," Cindy said. "He was such a nice guy. I mean, always joking. I just can't—"

"I liked him," I said. "He said he liked me. Right up until the end." I shook my head.

"I don't know."

We looked at each other. Paul looked like he could use a cigarette. Roxanne looked like it pained her to be there. I knew the feeling.

"So who writes it?"

They looked alarmed.

"I'll have to get somebody," I said. "Any volunteers?"

"Who's going to do sports?" Paul asked.

"Posthumous bylines. It gets a little sticky, doesn't it?"

A nurse padded in with her white shoes and said I was supposed to get medication. Cindy and Paul said good-bye and left. Roxanne moved closer.

"I almost lost you," she said.

"Only counts in horseshoes."

She leaned over and kissed my forehead. I smiled but I knew.

It wasn't the same. As long as I stayed in town, it wouldn't be the same. And I didn't feel like leaving. Not yet.

Jack, you've lost another one, I said to myself.

"I love you," Roxanne said.

It didn't ring true.

I moved my bandaged hand out from under the sheet and patted her wrist.

ABOUT THE AUTHOR

Gerry Boyle is the author of a dozen mystery novels, including the acclaimed Jack McMorrow series, and the Brandon Blake series. A former newspaper reporter and columnist, Boyle lives with his wife, Mary, in a historic home in a small village on a lake. He also is working with his daughter, Emily Westbrooks, on a crime series set in her hometown, Dublin, Ireland. Whether it is Maine or Ireland, Boyle remains true to his pledge to send his characters only to places where he has gone before.